In **James Reasoner**'s "Woollies," a railroad detective must escort a train full of sheep past hostile cattle farms in Wyoming—and track down the locals who like dynamite . . .

A black stock detective finds himself battling prejudice and treachery when he's hired by a young widow to stop a gang of cattle rustlers in **Deborah Morgan**'s "Law West of Lonetree" . . .

In **Wendi Lee**'s "Stanley and the Devil," an Easterner, new to the Secret Service, is sent to Santa Fe to stop counterfeiters—but he's got a lot to learn about the West . . .

. . . and nine more amazing stories of Western law in . . .

TIN STAR

TIN STAR

Edited by
Robert J. Randisi

BERKLEY BOOKS, NEW YORK

Grateful acknowledgment is made to Bob's Old Badges, Bob and Donnie Sue Johnson, 1621 120th Avenue, Hersey, MI 49639; and Star Packer Badges, Eric Swendsboe, P.O. Box 342, Nashua, NH 03061, for kind permission to reprint the badges that appear with each story.

This is a work of fiction. Names, characters, places, and incidents are either the product of the author's imagination or are used fictitiously, and any resemblance to actual persons, living or dead, business establishments, events, or locales is entirely coincidental.

TIN STAR

A Berkley Book / published by arrangement with the editor

PRINTING HISTORY
Berkley edition / April 2000

The Penguin Putnam Inc. World Wide Web site address is
http://www.penguinputnam.com

ISBN: 0-425-17405-0

BERKLEY®
Berkley Books are published by The Berkley Publishing Group, a division of Penguin Putnam Inc., 375 Hudson Street, New York, New York 10014. BERKLEY and the "B" logo are trademarks belonging to Penguin Putnam Inc.

PRINTED IN THE UNITED STATES OF AMERICA

10 9 8 7 6 5 4 3 2 1

CONTENTS

VI CONTENTS

TIN
STAR

INTRODUCTION

King Arthur's Knights of the Round Table had full suits of armor to protect them as they went forth to battle evil and search for the Holy Grail. Well, the lawmen of the Old West certainly weren't searching for the Grail, but they were fighting evil, and the only armor they had for protection was a little tin star they wore over their hearts. (The first badges were actually cut from the tops and bottoms of old tin cans, hence the phrase "tin star.")

The tin star came in various sizes and shapes—actual stars and "shields" were the most prevelant—and they were worn by men of various sizes and shapes, as well. In this collection we have attempted to show you a dozen of the different stars these brave men wore, and the different breed of man who wore them. Not all were so pure of heart; some had their own agenda, and not all were even men. But for the most part they were special, and they held that piece of tin in high regard.

* * *

Among the authors in this book are four past winners of the Western Writers of America Golden Spur Award—Elmer Kelton, Loren D. Estleman, Ed Gorman and Frank Roderus. The other eight men and women who appear here, however, are no less talented. Doug Hirt, Tim Champlin, L. J. Washburn and Wendi Lee have written many western novels over the years. Perhaps the two most prolific authors of westerns in this book—and perhaps in the genre—are James Reasoner and Robert J. Randisi, who have toiled for many years under various pseudonyms and have only recently begun to publish in the genre under their own names. Deborah Morgan appears here with her third western short story—each of her stories in itself a small piece of art—and while Marthayn Pelegrimas has produced more than forty short stories under her own name and some dozen or so more under a pseudonym, she appears here with her first western story.

All these authors have put their own stamp on the tin star they are writing about, and we feel you will come away from this collection with a new understanding of the badges and the people who wore them—or maybe you'll just come away well entertained.

Either one would be fine with us.

—Robert J. Randisi,
St. Louis, MO
July 1999

THE FUGITIVE BOOK

by Elmer Kelton

If Loren Estleman is becoming legendary, then Elmer Kelton already is. Considered the finest living writer of the West, his novels have won awards and been adapted to films. The Good Ol' Boys *was filmed for TNT with Tommy Lee Jones, and the sequel,* The Smiling Country, *is available in stores now. He has also written a novel of the Texas Rangers,* Captain's Rangers, *and so his choice of a Tin Star story for this collection was easy. He was recently voted the "greatest western writer of all time," by the Western Writers of America.*

Fitzhugh Battles realized there were many things in the world he did not know for certain, but of one thing he was sure: outlaws were no damned good and ought to be ridden down like rabid coyotes. One item always with him, besides his Texas Ranger badge, Bowie knife and six-shooter, was a handwritten notebook listing names and descriptions of wanted men. The fugitive book was part of every Ranger's equipment, to be consulted frequently and added to as necessary.

Few things gave him more inner satisfaction than to scratch through a name and write either *apprehended* or *executed*. It did not matter whether he or some other Ranger had done the apprehending or killing. What mattered was that one more miscreant had been locked away or buried, out of everyone's misery. The world would be better off when the last member of that lawless breed had been marked off the list. He did not expect to see it happen during his lifetime, unless that life was much longer than he felt he had any right to expect.

Now Battles was on his way to find and arrest—or if the situation warranted, kill—one Giles Pritchard, wanted in Waco for robbery and murder. The authorities had determined that Pritchard owned a ranch in Comanche County. It seemed plausible he had fled in that direction.

Battles had taken on this job with pleasure. He looked forward to working with the county sheriff, John Durham. They had served together as Rangers a couple of years until Durham had tired of the long horseback trips the Ranger service often required. He was a stay-close-to-home type. He also hated the frequent confrontations with fugitives, sometimes necessitating that they be made to bleed a little, and occasionally a lot. He had decided to run for local office, where such confrontations were likely to be less frequent.

Battles, by contrast, enjoyed the traveling, seeing different country, never remaining in one place long enough to become bored with it. The more he saw of horse thieves and robbers and murderers, the more his contempt grew, the more he was gratified when he saw them brought to ground. If that required spilling blood, well . . . they should have invested their efforts in whatever honest occupation the Lord had fitted them for.

He rode past several sandy-land farms. Most of them appeared to have yielded up good summer crops. He thought if he ever wearied of Ranger life he might enjoy settling down on such a place. Even more, he might enjoy ranching, raising cattle on the rolling grasslands which still dominated this part of the state a hundred miles beyond Fort Worth. But that was a long time in the future, if it was to be at all. In Battles's chosen line of work, he had no assurance that there would *be* a future.

The courthouse was no challenge to find; it was the tallest building in town, though that was hardly enough to brag about. Battles had been there before. He tied his horse and rifled through his saddlebags, sorting out the papers he would need.

Sheriff John Durham met him in the hallway, his hand outstretched, a broad grin lighting the place like sunshine. "Fitz Battles! Saw you through the window. I've been afraid some sneakin' hog thief killed you and it never made the newspapers this far out."

Durham was about thirty. At forty, Battles had had an extra ten years of sun, wind and strife to carve the lines deeper into his face. Durham's strong hand gripped like a vise. Battles tried to squeeze even harder and see if he could make Durham wince. "It'll take somebody with a lot more ambition than a hog thief has got. Glad to see the voters haven't kicked you out of office yet."

"I'd invite you down the street for a drink, but it wouldn't do for the public to see two officers of the law drinkin' whiskey in the light of the day. Come on in. I've got a bottle of contraband in my desk. It ain't prime, but it's cheap."

Battles was impatient to get at the task he had been sent for, but he enjoyed visiting with an old friend, reliving shared experiences, hot trails and cold camps. At length, when they had momentarily run out of talk, Battles laid the papers in front of the sheriff. "Do you know a man named Giles Pritchard?"

Durham looked surprised. "Sure. Got him a little ranch over west of town. Buys and sells horses, peddles them all over the country. Him and me punched cattle together once down on the Pecan Bayou. You got business with him?"

Battles pointed to the arrest warrant. "Seems like he created himself some trouble over in Waco. Best anybody could figure, he and a kid helper took a little string of horses over on the Bosque River and sold them to a trader. Must not have got as much as he wanted, because he stopped off at a bank in Waco that was flush with fresh cotton-crop money. He made a six-shooter withdrawal. Shot a teller dead. Him and his helper got away in a high lope."

"How do you know it was him?"

"Pritchard had a stroke of bad luck. The trader who bought the horses happened to be in the bank too. Ducked down where Pritchard wouldn't see him. Pritchard may not know he's been identified."

Durham frowned. "Shootin' a banker could be considered a service. The country would be better off without so many of them high-interest highbinders."

"Same as it could do without so many lawyers, but the law calls for due process. Pritchard's method was *un*due process."

Reluctance was strong in Durham's eyes. "I always knew Giles was a shade too wild for his own good, but I never would've pictured him doin' such a thing as this. You sure there ain't been some mistake?"

"There was, and he made it."

The sheriff's face pinched hard. "What do you want of me?"

"You know it's Ranger policy to involve local peace officers whenever we can. I'd like you to take me out to Pritchard's place and assist me in the arrest."

Battles could see that Durham was wrestling hard with his doubts. Durham said, "I don't guess you know that Giles got married a year or so ago? I was at the weddin'. Alicia's about as pretty a girl as I ever met."

"I'm sorry Pritchard's a friend of yours. It doesn't change what he's done."

"His old daddy was one of the finest men I ever knew. I was a pallbearer at his funeral."

"It wasn't his daddy who killed the teller."

"The old man worried a right smart about Giles's streak of wildness. I'm glad he's not here to see this."

Slowly and with reluctance, Durham retrieved his hat from a rack in the corner. "It's ten miles out there. We'd better go down the street and get us some dinner before we start."

Durham had little to say on the long ride to the Pritchard place. He would begin to relate a story about something he and Pritchard had done together, or something about Pritchard's kindly old father. He would break off the stories before they were finished.

Battles said, "There must be a side to him that you never wanted to recognize. Flaws in him that you never saw."

"I always believed in givin' a man the benefit of the doubt."

"Give it to the wrong man and he's apt to kill you. At the least he'll leave you hurtin'."

"I've never known anybody who took as much pleasure in runnin' down outlaws as you do. I've seen you get damned near drunk on it."

"Bury enough friends and you'll get to where you hate them like strychnine. A couple of them snakes came in off of the railroad one time and killed my old daddy. Killed him for two dollars and a pocket watch. I tracked them down and shot them both like hydrophoby dogs. After that, I joined the Rangers." Battles scowled. "If it was up to me I'd stomp every last one of them like I'd stomp a scorpion."

He saw a small frame house ahead. By the dread in Durham's face, he surmised that this was Pritchard's home.

The sheriff said, "Knowin' your feelin's, I'd like to be the one serves the papers. I'd hate to have you shoot Giles when it's not necessary."

Battles was dubious about turning the responsibility over to a lawman so personally involved. "He's apt to be desperate, knowin' what he faces. You sure you want to do it?"

"He's my friend."

He's a murderer, Battles thought. *This is where friendship ought to end.* But his own liking for Durham caused him to waver. "All right, but watch him. He may not be as friendly as you think."

They rode up to a rough picket fence in front of the house. Durham dismounted. "You stay here, Fitz. I'll go talk to him."

Battles began having serious second thoughts as he watched Durham step up onto the narrow porch and knock on the door facing. "Giles, this is John Durham. I need to talk to you."

After a long minute that seemed like five, a young woman came to the door. She looked anxiously at the sheriff, then past him to Battles, who remained on his horse. "What do you want with him?"

"There's been some trouble over at Waco. I need to talk to him."

The woman's voice was shaky. "He's not here. He's out helpin' a neighbor work cattle."

Even at the distance, Battles knew she was lying. He had

seen through far better liars than this woman would ever be. He could tell by the sheriff's uncertain manner that Durham sensed it too.

Durham said, "I hate to do this, Alicia, but I need to look through the house."

"No, John, please." The woman turned quickly and shouted, "Run, Giles! Run!"

Almost before the words were out of her mouth, Battles was spurring his horse around the side of the house. He saw a man bolt from the back door and sprint toward the barn, rifle in his hand. Pritchard was feverishly trying to work the lever, but it appeared jammed. Battles overran him and leveled his pistol. He fired it into the ground in front of the fugitive. The bullet raised a puff of dust.

Battles said, "The next one goes in your ear."

Pritchard stopped and turned to face the Ranger. Eyes wide with fear, he dropped the rifle. "Don't shoot me. For God's sake, don't."

"I expect there was a teller in Waco said the same thing to you, or tried to. You shot him anyway."

Pritchard seemed so frightened he could barely control his voice. "Waco? Ain't never been in Waco."

"There's a witness back there who says different."

"What're you goin' to do with me?"

"Take you to Waco. Let you stand before your accusers."

Pritchard's eyes darted wildly back and forth. Battles thought he was probably already imagining that thick, slick rope around his neck, choking, strangling.

Durham hurried out the back door. He anxiously looked Pritchard over, his anxiety giving way to relief. "I thought Fitz had shot you. Damn it, why did you run?"

"I was scared. When Alicia hollered, all I could think of was to light out."

Battles observed, "If you were innocent, you had no reason to be afraid of us. You could've figured we stopped in for coffee."

"I'm always afraid when I see a Ranger. They been known to shoot a man for no reason."

Battles said, "You took time to grab a rifle."

"Instinct. I never had no intention of usin' it."

That was a lie, Battles thought. In his panic Pritchard had somehow jammed it. Otherwise he would have used it, or tried to. Of that, Battles was certain.

Durham said, "I hate to, Giles, but I've got to put you under arrest. Ranger Battles has got a warrant."

The young woman came out sobbing. She threw her arms around Pritchard. Durham was apologetic. "I'm sorry, Alicia, but I've got to abide by the law. Maybe the witness was mistaken. It'll all come out in court."

The woman's gaze moved to Battles, crackling with unspoken accusation. Battles wished he had an explanation that would ease her mind, but the law was the law. He was here to serve it. The longer she glared at him, though, the less he regretted not having something comforting to say. He considered her loyalty sadly misplaced.

He saw then the way the sheriff looked at the woman, and he thought he understood some of the reason for Durham's reluctance. *The boy has gone blind. He's in love with her himself. Hell of a note this is.*

Durham asked, "Do you want to go to Comanche with us, Alicia?"

Pritchard spoke quickly, "No, Alicia, you stay and take care of the stock. Send your brother to town."

Brother. Battles chewed hard on that. Nobody had identified Pritchard's helper, who had remained outside with their horses during the holdup. He was probably someone unknown in Waco. Witnesses had described him as a clean-faced boy, probably under twenty. The whole thing had happened so fast that nobody had taken a good look. Most had hunkered down, hoping not to be struck by a bullet.

Battles had found over the years that excited eyewitnesses to such affairs rarely saw everything the same way. He had known of black horses being described as white.

He was relieved that the woman would not be going to town with them. Women's tears had always been bad for his digestion. They were one reason he had never seriously contemplated marriage.

As they rode, Battles quietly asked the sheriff, "Do you know anything about her brother?"

Durham shook his head. "Never knew she had one. Could be a black sheep they don't like to talk about."

Black sheep. Possibly one who wouldn't mind being a partner in a bank robbery, Battles thought.

Durham was evidently thinking along the same lines. "I still can't believe it was Giles did that bank job. But if he did—*if*, mind you—then it might be that her brother was the one ridin' with him. Makes sense, sort of. I can't see Giles doin' such a thing on his own. If he did it, I'll bet her brother coaxed him into it."

Durham was still resisting the notion that his longtime friend was an outlaw. Battles thought it better for a peace officer not to have many really close friends. It put him in a painfully tight spot if he had to bring the weight of the law down on one of them.

He said, "If you're harborin' any doubts about Pritchard bein' guilty, you'd just as well put them out of your mind. He's got the rattlesnake smell all over him."

Durham continued to resist. "Somebody had to've led him astray."

"For your sake, I'd like to think you're right and I'm wrong." Battles didn't, though, not for a moment.

Durham said, "I feel awful sorry for Alicia. This'll be terrible for her."

"That teller may have had a wife. It's not easy for her, either."

Battles was tempted to say, *Look at the other side of the coin. With Pritchard out of the way, maybe you'll have a chance of winning her for yourself.*

He had the good judgment to keep his mouth shut.

Dusk was giving up to darkness when they led the handcuffed Pritchard into the jail. Battles gave the cell door all his strength so it would clang hard. The windows rattled, loose in their frames. The sound had a finality about it, like the dropping of a trapdoor in a gallows. The sound had always brought him a warm satisfaction when he locked away an outlaw.

Sheriff Durham stared through the bars at his friend. "Giles, if you needed money I wish you'd come to me. You and Alicia could have anything I own, and I'd go on your note if that wasn't enough."

Pritchard slumped on the hard cot. "Damned old dry ranches, I don't see why anybody would want one in the first place. First they work you down to a nub, then they starve you the rest of the way to death."

To Battles that was as good as an outright confession, but he knew Durham, though swaying, was still looking for a different answer.

Durham's aging jailer turned the key in the lock. He said, "John, I expect you and the Ranger are hungry. You-all go get you somethin' to eat. I'll be here."

Durham shook his head. "I couldn't eat. Low as I feel, I'd choke on the first bite. Fitz, you and him go."

The jailer was a gangly old man, thin as a willow switch, and looked as if he needed a meal. Several of them, in fact.

Battles cast a glance back toward the prisoner. "John, I know he's been your friend, but you can't look at him that way anymore. The longer he thinks about what's ahead of him the more desperate he'll get. He'd kill you if it meant he could get away."

Durham nodded a sad acceptance. "I won't give him the chance."

"All right." Battles jerked his head at the jailer. "Come along. I'm hungry enough to eat a mule."

The restaurant—that term was too high toned to fit the reality—was manned by a chuckwagon cook who had decided he liked life in town better than camping under the open skies every night. The food was tasty and filling, though far from fancy. The jailer lit into it as if he had not eaten in a week. Battles wondered what kind of wages Comanche County paid its employees.

The jailer said, "Odd name, Battles. Where'd you get it?"

"From my daddy and granddaddy. They said it came over from Ireland with some of my ancestors. Said they were fighters of the first water. Guess that's why they took the name Battles."

"Or maybe they favored strong drink and the name was supposed to be Bottles."

"That's possible. I doubt they were much hand at writin' and spellin'."

Battles was never one to eat heavily. He was used to long rides, and those were best taken on a lank belly. He leaned his chair back and watched the jailer finish everything on the table. It had been a stressful day. He was about ready to find a bed somewhere.

He heard the shots and knew instinctively where they came from. He jumped up, knocking his chair over, and took three long strides toward the door. He hit the dirt street on the run. Down toward the jail, people were shouting. Against the lamplight he saw two dark figures jump upon horses and spur away. One looked back just long enough for Battles to know he was Giles Pritchard.

He drew his pistol but realized a shot at this distance would be useless. More than likely he would simply hit some innocent bystander. There were not enough innocent people in the world as it was.

He saw that the second rider was slumped in the saddle. Pritchard brought his horse up even with him and held him in the saddle.

Battles ran for the jail, gratified that John Durham had hit one of them, anyway. It stood to reason that Pritchard's helper on the bank robbery had broken him out.

Send your brother, Pritchard had told his wife.

Several townsmen were inside ahead of Battles. Two knelt over Durham, stretched out on the floor. Battles felt a chill as he saw blood pumping from a hole in Durham's chest. He knew the sheriff had no chance.

One of the men saw Battles's badge. "You a Ranger?"

"I am."

"One of the boys went for the doctor. Don't you think you ought to be out chasin' whoever it was done this?"

"I'd just lose them in the dark." He dropped to one knee and leaned over Durham. "How'd it happen, John?"

Durham struggled to speak. The words came slowly and painfully, with long breaks between as he struggled for breath. The gist of it was that Pritchard's partner had burst in from the street, face covered by a neckerchief, pointed a pistol and demanded that Pritchard be set free.

"Anybody you ever saw before?"

Durham weakly shook his head. "Couldn't tell." He coughed. "I opened the cell . . . grabbed my gun . . . then he shot me."

"Pritchard?"

"His partner." Durham coughed again, spitting up blood. "But I hit him . . . I know I did."

Battles raised up, voice raw with impatience. "Where's that doctor at?" Even as he spoke, he knew a doctor could do little.

Battles clenched a fist. Outlaws! He wished he could string them all up, one at a time, slowly, letting them kick and choke to the last feeble heartbeat. He blinked away the burning in his eyes.

The doctor came, carrying a small black bag. Nothing in it was going to help much. A rattling sound came from Durham's chest. His hands flexed, he groaned, and life left him. The doctor closed the sightless eyes and looked up. "Can some of you boys carry him over to the livery? I'll rouse up the undertaker." He turned to Battles. "What're *you* going to do, Ranger?"

"I'll follow their tracks as far as it takes, even if that's plumb to Argentina."

"You'd better get yourself some sleep, then. It's a long way to South America."

Battles considered rolling out his blankets on hay at the wagonyard, but he knew he would never go to sleep. The images of Durham and Pritchard and the woman Alicia would keep running through his mind, along with the imagined face of Alicia's brother. If Durham's aim had been up to his capabilities, Alicia would have two men to mourn— her brother and her husband. He wondered if she was aware of Durham's feelings for her. If so, that made three.

Either by gun or by rope, Giles Pritchard would pay for this.

Several townsmen had chased after the fugitives. Battles reasoned that they had probably trampled out any nearby tracks that might have been helpful. Sleepy-eyed, his stomach in a turmoil, Battles played a hunch and rode in darkness, westward in the direction of Pritchard's place.

He figured it was a good bet that Pritchard and his partner would head there to pick up provisions and, more than likely, the Waco loot. Pritchard would know he could no longer remain here. It was anybody's guess where he would try to go. Mexico, perhaps, though it was far to the south. The Pecos River country, maybe, and beyond it the Davis Mountains. Or he might head north for the Red River and Indian Territory.

He would go to hell, if Battles had his way.

Dawn's first light revealed the Pritchard house ahead. Battles drew the rifle. It was more dependable than the six-shooter except at close range. He considered firing it into the house to try to rattle Pritchard if he were still inside. He decided that would present too great a danger to Alicia. This was none of her doing. She had made a poor choice in picking a husband. She had had no choice in her brother.

Battles bent low in the saddle to present as small a target as possible and let his horse plod on toward the house. The rising sun was at his back, a point in his favor. A rifle flashed in a front window, and he jumped to the ground, running for the protection of a large oak tree. He fired at the window, regretting the danger to Alicia Pritchard but seeing no alternative.

The tree's trunk was not thick enough to hide him completely, though it made him less of a target. He waited for a second shot, then fired immediately upon seeing the flash. He heard a cry and hoped it was from Pritchard or his partner, not from the woman.

Several long strides carried him to the small porch and into the house. Holding his arm, Pritchard sat on the kitchen floor amid shards of glass. Blood seeped between his fingers. "You busted my arm," he screamed. "Busted it all to hell."

Battles picked up the rifle Pritchard had used. The barrel was hot. "One arm'll do you where you're goin'. Where's your partner?"

"My partner?" Pritchard blinked at him, eyes watering.

"The man who was with you. Your wife's brother, if my guess is right."

Pritchard cried in pain but jerked his head toward a doorway that led to the bedroom. Battles checked the load in his rifle, then dashed through the door, holding the weapon ready.

On the bed lay Alicia Pritchard, her oversized shirt soaked with dried and drying blood. He could not bring himself to touch her. The clay-like color in her face told him she was dead.

Trembling, he returned to Giles Pritchard. "The blood's too old. My shots couldn't have killed her."

Pritchard gritted his teeth, his voice bordering on a shriek. "John Durham, damn him. All he had to do was let me go. He didn't have to grab a gun. Wasn't nothin' she could do but shoot him."

Battles's jaw dropped. "*She* shot him?"

"And then he shot her. I had to hold her in the saddle all the way here."

"I don't understand. Where was her brother?"

"She never had no brother. It was her all the time. Kept her hair hid under her hat. Covered her face before she went into the jail."

The rest of it came clear to Battles without Pritchard having to tell him. Alicia had been his partner on the Waco trip, passing herself off as a boy. She had held the horses while he robbed the bank.

The irony of it made last night's supper rise up in his throat, burning like Mexican peppers. John Durham had been in love with her, but she had killed him.

At least Durham would not have to live with the fact that he had killed her as well.

"Why did you let her do it?" he demanded. "How could you turn your wife into an outlaw?"

Pritchard's face twisted in agony. He looked as if he might faint. "*Let* her? It was her fault all the time, wantin' things this little old ranch never could pay for, whisperin' about how easy it would be to rob a bank somewhere that we wasn't known. A demandin' woman, she was. But I loved her all the same."

Battles started to say he was sorry, but the words stuck in his throat. Like hell he was!

He declared, "Every damned hoodlum I ever knew blamed somebody else for his troubles. I wish just one of you grubby sons of bitches would stand up like a man and accept the responsibility for what you've done."

His hatred for the breed swept over him like a brush fire out of control. He did a rough job of wrapping the shattered arm while Pritchard whined and cried. He intended to save Pritchard's life so the authorities in Waco could hang him.

When he got time, Battles would take pleasure in writing *apprehended* alongside Pritchard's name in his fugitive book. When the hangman had done his job, Battles would add the word *executed*. Then, with the warmest satisfaction, he would scratch a heavy line through the name.

One more down. But there were still so many to go.

IRON DOLLAR

by Loren D. Estleman

Loren D. Estleman's career as a western author is becoming legendary. Winner of many awards in the western field, his Journey of the Dead *won both the Western Heritage Award from the National Cowboy Hall of Fame and the Western Writers of America Golden Spur Award for Best Western Novel of 1998. His newest western is* The Rocky Mountain Moving Picture Association. *His series character, Deputy Marshal Page Murdock, was a natural for this collection, and he's crafted another dandy story for awards committees to ponder for 1999.*

Tim Boone, his brother Lloyd, and six men stuck up the express office in Deer Lodge September 6, 1882, and lit a shuck north with eight thousand in cash and securities distributed among their saddle pouches. Before they left, the gang stood the three clerks present against the wall opposite the safe and shot them each twice, in the head and chest, to eliminate witnesses. All this would have been meat for the county sheriff except one of the bags they took contained mail. That made it federal business.

Since I was in town at the time, delivering a prisoner to the territorial penitentiary, Judge Blackthorne wired me from Helena to head up the manhunt. The text was brief, in keeping with our six-year association:

DEP. US MARSHAL PAGE MURDOCK
DEER LODGE, M.T.

BOONE IS YOURS

H. A. BLACKTHORNE

The Judge, who hated to spend taxpayers' money on unnecessary verbiage, was telling me in his economical way to round up the entire gang. This was a compliment of sorts. The brothers Boone, who claimed a first-cousin relationship to the late great Daniel, had been bothering banks, trains, and Wells Fargo offices throughout the High Plains for a couple of years. They had outridden and outshot several *posse comitati,* and were held responsible for the death of an army major named Craddock who had taken it upon himself to try to collect the reward offered for the Boones' capture dead or alive. With Jesse James in the ground and his brother Frank in custody, Tim and Lloyd had begun to attract the attention of journalists back East, one of whom had written a blood-and-thunder yellowback novel entitled *The Boones of Bozeman* that had sold out its print run in six weeks, notwithstanding that it was full of stretchers concocted by a penman who had never met them or for that matter ventured west of Camden, New Jersey. If Deer Lodge was any indication, the desperadoes' new notoriety had made them bolder and more bloodthirsty. I made a note to thank the Judge for his faith in me, if I survived.

One of the clerks lived long enough to describe the Boones to a good man with shorthand, which was all I needed to start. I got together a dozen locals and tracked the gang for ten miles until we came to a place where a trailherd had obliterated the signs. We headed for Missoula, where Tim Boone was known to keep company with a woman known as Doubtful Mary. But when I knocked at the door of the Queen Anne house by the river where I'd been directed, the proprietress assured me that I'd missed my quarry by twenty-four hours. I paid for an interview with Doubtful Mary, a scrawny blonde whose bones stuck out under her thin muslin shift, who convinced me he was indeed gone and had not told her his destination. We searched the place anyway, and in the process lost two of the posse to the charms of the residents.

The balding Negro at the livery reported that a man answering Tim's description had traded a roan mare for a black gelding the previous morning and ridden out by way of a westbound street. The man was unaccompanied, and the stable hand hadn't observed any other strangers around town, so the likelihood was the gang had split up somewhere between Deer Lodge and Missoula. The black gelding had been freshly shod; we picked up tracks left by new shoes just past the western limits, but lost them in the Mission foothills, where three more of our group called it quits and went back to town to rest up for the trip home. The rest of us made camp and discussed our options.

"If he's as smart as they say, he's on his way to Canada." Ralph Pollard, who sold dry goods in Deer Lodge, lit his stump of greasy black pipe with a splint from the fire. He had hard eyes in folds of fat.

Kilmartin, the goat-faced Scot in charge of the general mercantile, picked coffee grounds from his whiskers. "He's smart enough to know we think he's smart enough to do that. That's why he's headed west."

"I wouldn't risk crossing the Bitterroots in September,"

said Lyle Stype, a shotgun messenger with Wells Fargo. He was the brother-in-law of one of the clerks the Boones had killed. His skin was cracked all over and dark as tobacco. He claimed to be twenty-nine and I believed him. About the only thing no one lied about west of the Rockies was his age. "I'd run to ground and wait for whoever's chasing me to give up. That's started already."

There was an argument, which as usual in those cases came to nothing. We listened for a while to the coyotes, a sound that never failed to put me on edge. One of them was always out of tune.

Our best tracker was a half-breed Blackfoot called Tom Shorthair, who ran errands between manhunts. Looking sleepy beneath the curled brim of his filthy bowler, he opened his mouth just wide enough to let words out. "Lorenzo Bliss and Charlie Whitelaw holed up at Clawson's for a month once."

"Clawson's what?" I asked.

Pollard ground his teeth on his pipestem. "Wheat farm on the Big Blackfoot, or it was. Clawson went bust and skedaddled back to Nebraska owing me for ten rolls of barbwire. He couldn't get the gauge he wanted in Missoula, worse luck for me."

"I know that place." A skinny fellow I never caught the name of fingered his prominent Adam's apple. "Last time I was by there, the roof on the house had fell in."

"Barn's still standing," said Pollard. "Them squareheads build them sound as forts."

"Where is this barn?" I asked.

Tom Shorthair opened his eyes. "Damn close."

The house had deteriorated further since the skinny fellow had last seen it. The walls were splayed and the rest had collapsed into the foundation. We reached the farm an hour after dawn and spent the better part of another hour surrounding the barn on foot, using junipers and scrub pine for cover. As Pollard had promised, the structure was a solid medieval affair built of cedar blocks mortised and tenoned together with a shake roof sealed with black pitch. If it escaped fire it would stand for half a century without maintenance.

Tom Shorthair motioned me over to where he was standing, just below a ridge overlooking the barn. He pointed out the print of a new horseshoe at his feet.

I crawled on my belly up to the ridge and waited until I was sure everyone was in position. We were down to a half-dozen now, two more men having stolen away in the night. The nearness of an actual face-off with a killer tends to put out the lesser lights.

I rose on one knee behind a jack pine that had been split down the middle by the weight of some heavy snowfall or other and rested the barrel of my Winchester in the *v* of the split.

"Tim Boone!" I called out. "I'm a deputy United States marshal! We've got the barn ringed in! Come out or we start shooting!"

A mourning dove hooted in the silence that followed.

I was about to repeat my demand when a windowpane parted with a clank and smoke and fire spat out through the space. The ball chugged into the earth ten feet in front of the shattered pine. The rifle report came after, bent by the wind.

I sent three slugs into the barn, and then the rest of the posse opened up, Lyle Stype's big-bore Remington adding bass to the lighter pops and cracks of Ralph Pollard's Henry, Kilmartin's single-shot Springfield, and the skinny jasper's Spencer repeater. Tom Shorthair carried a short gun only, and his Colt sounded like twigs snapping. The rest of the windows fell apart, big holes punched through the siding, a horse screamed inside the barn.

That was the end of it. No more shots came from inside, and after a moment a long barrel poked out the original broken window with a white rag tied to the end. I shouted for the others to hold their fire.

"You bastards kilt my horse!" cried a voice from the barn.

"That was just for practice," I called back. "Throw out your weapons and walk out touching the clouds or we'll make it count!"

After another silence, a Winchester toppled out onto the ground, the surrender flag still attached. A revolver flew out behind it.

"Hold on! I'm coming out!"

The door hung by one leather hinge, the other having been shot away. It flopped open and a lone figure emerged from inside, bareheaded, with his hands high above. His fair hair looked white against his deep sunburn. He was lanky in a woolen shirt without a collar, striped pants, stovepipe boots, and a gun belt with an empty holster. He was clean-shaven, blue-eyed, and very young. His wanted dodger said he was twenty-four.

I saw movement out the corner of my eye. Lyle Stype came up from behind a juniper and shouldered his Remington. I snatched off his Texas pinch hat with a shot from the Winchester. When he spun my way, mouth open in a face black with rage, I levered another round into the chamber.

"He murdered my Annie's baby brother!" he cried.

"And he'll hang for it. Put down that meat-chopper if you don't want to see him in hell."

He hesitated. Then he lowered the rifle and let it drop to the ground.

"Now give me a hand trussing him up," I said.

"Do it yourself. I'm going back to Deer Lodge." He turned away.

"If you're going to do that, leave your pistol. I've got enough on my plate without a bushwhacker for dessert."

"What if I run into a bear?"

"Growl back at it."

He carried his Smith & Wesson Russian stuck under his belt. He drew it out carefully, then flung it to the earth and stamped away, pausing only to pick up his hat. A moment later hoofbeats started up and faded off.

I manacled Tim Boone's hands behind him and asked him where the others were.

"Go to hell."

I slung my Winchester's stock into his belly. He bent over and threw up at my feet. I turned to Tom Shorthair. "What's the nearest town?"

"Little shit place called Iron Dollar, ten miles upriver. Mining town."

"Got a jail?"

He nodded, smirking. "I said it was a mining town."

"It won't hold me." Tim spat and straightened partway, sounding hoarse. "If Lloyd don't get a wire from me tomorrow, he'll come looking for me. With help."

The skinny fellow with the Springfield cleared his throat. "I said I'd help track down the Boones. I didn't sign on to go to war with them."

I looked around the shrinking circle. "Anyone else feel that way?"

Pollard filled his pipe from a leather pouch rubbed shiny from use. "I've got a store to run. I didn't figure to be gone longer than a week."

"That go for you too?" I looked at Kilmartin.

"My wife's looking after the mercantile," he said. "I'd just as soon not to go back to either of them right away."

I thanked Pollard and Skinny for their help, and in another minute we were three. Tim Boone's baggy grin fell off his face when I gripped the Winchester in both hands.

You can tell a lot about a community by its jail.

Iron Dollar's was built stoutly of stone, with a slate roof, bars in all the windows, and thick wooden shutters that closed from inside, with gun ports in the centers. It was the only building in town that didn't look as if it would keel over with a nasty cough. Everything else was canvas and clapboard.

I didn't like the look of the town marshal half as much as I did the jail. He was a suet-gutted fifty, with tobacco-stained handlebars and soft hands, who didn't bother to get up when four men entered his office, one in manacles. The nameplate on the desk read "J. T. WADDELL."

"I got four cells, all taken," he greeted. "Somebody went and shot the town's only whore and the vigilance committee bust up two saloons taking him into custody."

I said, "Keep the shooter and throw out the drunks. This is Tim Boone."

He got to his feet with a grunt and glared at the man standing between Tom Shorthair and me. "That ain't Tim Boone. Both brothers are over six feet and bearded black as Lucifer."

"You've been reading *The Boones of Bozeman*," I said. "Try looking at those dodgers once in a while. It's just your job." I inclined my head toward a bulletin board papered all over with official notices. Then I showed him my badge. "Page Murdock. I ride for Judge Blackthorne's court. I need to put up my prisoner in your tin box for a day or two."

"Better not make it two," said Tim. "Lloyd'll be here tomorrow."

"That straight?" Waddell turned his scowl on me. He didn't look anything like Wild Bill Hickok on the front page of *Harper's*.

I said, "Your guess is as good as mine. If it is, I can't chance getting caught on the road. Unless I can count on a citizens' posse to help me get Tim to Helena."

"What's wrong with yours?"

"Not a damn thing, except you're looking at the bunch."

"Three men took Tim Boone? I reckon he ain't so much as the papers made out."

Tim said, "Too much for a fat gut like you, I'll warrant."

Kilmartin placed a foot against his back and shoved. Without the freedom of his arms to balance himself, the prisoner fell to his knees. "Shut up, you." The hard trail had put a strain on the Scot's temper.

"We had more to start out," I said. "You know how these things work, Marshal. After a week or so these bankers and storekeeps get to missing their wives and featherbeds. I'm requisitioning reinforcements. The pay's twenty cents a day and expenses, plus a share in the reward."

Waddell's eyes, dead brown in whiskey-shot whites, showed a spark for the first time. "How much?"

"Two thousand. It's a six-way split so far."

The spark guttered out. "Too thin. You won't find any takers in Iron Dollar. The Boones didn't steal nothing here."

"That was a relief, I bet. Seeing as how the whole damn town assays out to the price of a shave." Tom Shorthair pinched a tick off the crown of his bowler and put it back on.

Waddell glared at me. "You let this breed talk?"

"I'll shut him up when he stops making sense." I stuck a hand under Tim's arm and pulled him to his feet. "If you can't promise me volunteers, I'll need the hospitality of your jail while I wire Judge Blackthorne for more deputies."

Tim was unbowed. "They ought to get here just in time to bury your dead."

Kilmartin raised his foot again, but I shook my head and he put it back down. I wanted to hear what Waddell had to say.

"I can't give it to you. If Lloyd Boone and his gang are on their way here to bust out his brother, I can't put the town at risk. What happened in Deer Lodge don't mean nothing here."

"Now you're talking smart," Tim said.

I drew the English revolver I carried and shot him in the leg. The ball went through his calf and he fell down with a shout.

"What the hell!" The marshal grasped the ivory handle sticking out of the holster behind his right hip. I didn't have the words and we were all deaf from the explosion anyway, so I turned the pistol on him. He spread his fat soft hands, backing away a step.

"What do you think Lloyd's going to do to this town when he finds out his brother was shot in your jail?" I asked, when the ringing began to go away. Tim was groaning on the floor. "Throw out the drunks and get a doctor. Leave the keys."

"You ain't no lawman!" Waddell remained motionless with his arms out from his sides.

"How would you know? Do what I said or I'll make bookends out of you and Tim."

That made him move. He went down a short hall to the cells in back, and in a minute or so a train of men in need of baths and a flatiron came out, collected their belongings, and left, scratching their scalps. Waddell went out after them to bring back the doctor. Kilmartin, Tom Shorthair, and I got a grip on Tim and dragged him, howling and cursing, into a vacant cell, where we dumped him on a cot. The man seated on the cot in the cell opposite watched with curious interest. I figured they could compare notes about robbing banks and shooting whores until the marshal got back.

While I was there I made sure the high small windows were securely barred and noted there was no back door. The more I saw of that building the better I liked it.

"What makes you think Waddell won't come back with friends?" asked Kilmartin when we were back in the office.

I sat down behind the desk. "If he does and we can't handle them, we'd be no match for Lloyd anyway."

"What happens next?" Tom Shorthair asked.

"Maybe nothing. If I had a nickel for every thief who told me someone was coming to bust him out and no one came, I'd have a dollar."

"How much would you have for them that came?"

I stepped around it. "He'll send an advance man, someone whose picture isn't on a poster. He'll come in as a citizen with some story to keep our heads busy while he gets the lay of the place. He'll ask a lot of questions."

Kilmartin said, "Then we arrest him."

"It'll be someone Lloyd can spare. Since he plans to kick the place in anyway it won't matter. But he'll prefer having the lay. That's how the Boones have managed to hang on so long."

Tom Shorthair checked the load in his Colt. "What's our plan?"

Just then the marshal came in with a young consumptive in a black suit that hung on him like a wagon sheet, carrying a leather bag. I had Kilmartin inspect the doctor's clothes and bag for weapons, then sent him back to let him into Tim's cell. Waddell scowled at me in his chair but said nothing. He took a bottle from a warped oak file cabinet, swigged from it, heeled the cork back in, and returned it to the drawer. Then he wobbled over to a dried-out rocking chair in the corner by the barrel stove and plunked down into it. The flush on his cheeks told me he'd made a stop on his way to fetch the doctor.

I asked him if Iron Dollar had a locksmith.

"Blacksmith," he said, when he realized he'd been addressed and decided to answer. "I reckon he can put on a padlock."

"Even better. Get him, will you?"

"Get him yourself. I'm retired."

I sent the half-breed. Ten minutes later he returned with his gun in the back of a bullet-shaped hulk whose arms bulged out of a filthy pair of overalls. The man's face, burned a deep cherry color by the heat of his forge, was a stack of downturned lines with small sharp eyes glittering out of one of them.

Tom Shorthair said, "He didn't believe I'm with the law."

I looked at Waddell. He was glowering into some space the rest of us weren't part of. I flipped my badge onto the blotter where the blacksmith could see it. "The marshal's under the weather. I'm filling in."

The small sharp eyes took in the engraving on the nickel-plated star. He raised and lowered his sloping shoulders. "OK."

Tom Shorthair holstered his Colt. I said, "I want a padlock and an iron bar on the door and iron shutters on the windows in front. How soon can you do it?"

The lines on his face deepened. "End of the week. I got two customers ahead of you."

"Tell them to wait. I need it done by tomorrow."

"Cost you."

I hauled from my hip pocket the leather sack of coins I'd

drawn for expenses and laid a double-eagle on his side of the desk. He looked at it, then picked it up and bit it with his molars. He didn't have any teeth in front. He put the coin in his bib pocket. "I'll get my rule and start measuring." He left.

Waddell blew air through his nose. "All the iron in town won't keep Lloyd Boone out."

Kilmartin and the doctor came in from the back. "I dug a forty-five slug out of the muscle in his calf," said the young man, mopping his sallow face with a lawn handkerchief. "He says you put it there."

I said, "He's a thief and a killer, but he's no liar. How is he?"

"He'll limp, but he'll live." He opened his bag and stood a bottle of alcohol and a roll of gauze on the desk. "Change his dressing twice a day and call me if he takes fever."

I gave him a dollar from the sack. He bounced it on his palm, looking at me. "The human body is a miraculous machine, Deputy," he said. "It's a sin to tear it up with base lead."

"I expect to serve my full time in purgatory." I motioned to Tom Shorthair to let him out.

Kilmartin brought in our bedrolls and long guns and took the horses to the livery. He came back by way of the town's only restaurant with chicken-fried steak, peas, and a pot of coffee. The meat was tough and fatty, the peas hard enough to fire out of a cap-and-ball pistol; but the coffee was good and strong. I sent food and coffee back to Tim and the other prisoner and told the blacksmith he was measuring in the wrong place. "I want the padlock and bar on the outside, the shutters too. Put padlocks on them as well."

"The *out*side?" Marshal Waddell had gone back for the

bottle in the file cabinet, and this time he had brought it with him to the rocking chair. "What you doing, locking Lloyd out or you in?"

"Neither one." Finishing my coffee, I propped my feet up on the desk and tipped my hat over my eyes.

It was a noisy night, with all the hammering and clanging going on out front. I gave up sleeping around midnight and dealt a hand of patience from a deck of cards I found in the desk. Kilmartin couldn't sleep either, and I had yet to see Tom Shorthair even try, so I switched to poker and we pushed the same eighteen dollars and change back and forth across the desk for a few hours while Waddell snortled and blew out his mustaches in the rocking chair, dead to the world. I'd never seen the luck distributed so evenly.

I finally caught some rest about dawn, then sent Tom Shorthair out for breakfast. I was polishing off my eggs when the blacksmith came in and dropped his wooden box of tools to the floor with a clank. He was streaming sweat and staggering. "Well, I earned that double-eagle."

I went out for a look. He'd left the surface of the outside shutters unfinished; they were sandpapery to the touch, but nearly an inch thick, and swung smoothly on pivot-pins like a stove hatch. Hinged hasps bridged the seams where they met, with loops for the padlocks.

"I didn't put in no gun ports. You didn't say nothing about that."

"I didn't want any."

"The bar's elm. That much iron'd be too heavy, and soft to boot. A good stiff push'd bend it like a weed. A buffalo couldn't crack that grain if he hit it running. I reinforced it just to be sure."

It was six feet long and rock solid, with iron staples at

the ends and in the middle. It slid easily between the brackets he'd bolted on either side of the door, which was made of oak two inches thick and bound with iron, with bars in the window. When the door was shut and padlocked and the bar in place, even the most determined buffalo would choose to go around rather than through it. With the shutters folded back and the bar removed and laid along the base of the wall, the improvements were barely noticeable. I gave the blacksmith two more dollars for his good work and he picked up his tools and went back to his horseshoes and felloes.

Waddell was awake and drinking again when I went back in. "There's two tax dollars wasted. The Boone gang won't be scared off by no scrap iron."

"I hope not," I said. "If they are, you're right about the waste."

My first full day in Iron Dollar reminded me why I'd chosen Blackthorne's court over a soft job in town. To hear the dime novelists and the eastern newspapers tell it, you'd think someone was being shot on every corner of every mining town at every hour, with drunken prospectors throwing one another through saloon windows and hostile Indians riding whooping down Main Street and carrying off women for ruinous purposes. But the strikes in that vicinity weren't rich enough to fight over and all the Indians with any bark on them were either on reservations or hiding out in Canada. We spent the morning playing cards and watching the merchants across the street sweep the boardwalk in front of their establishments and chase away the occasional stray dog that stopped to lift its leg by a porch post. Waddell sat in on our game and drunk as he was took the pot with four treys over my ace high full house. He was a poor winner, crowing about how he got the bulge on the high-caliber federal from the capital and swigging from his bottle until he passed out again.

"How's a dub like that wind up pinned to a star?" Tom Shorthair wanted to know.

"Town law." I let my tone carry the meaning.

Things picked up just past noon. One of those stray dogs had bit a chunk out of the clerk in the assay office, a bald-headed Swede named Norgerson, who limped in demanding the marshal earn his twenty a month and shoot the animal.

"The marshal's under the weather." I raised my voice to be heard above Waddell's snoring. "Why not shoot it yourself?"

His blue eyes stood out under the shaggy white shelf of his brows. "We got an anti-firearms law in this town!"

"You mean if desperadoes raided the place you couldn't defend yourselves?" This from Tom Shorthair.

I told Norgerson I'd take the matter up with the marshal when he recovered. After the clerk left, Tom Shorthair said, "The town's a damn henhouse with the guard out drunk. I can't hardly credit it."

"Me neither," I said. "I didn't know civilization had got this far."

Kilmartin went back and changed Tim's bandage for the second time that day. When he came out he asked when I thought that advance man would show up.

"Tomorrow maybe. I figure Tim was bluffing about the time."

Tom Shorthair inspected his Colt. "I think maybe I'll go out and shoot that dog."

"Stick here. I could be wrong about the bluff."

At suppertime I was thinking of using my bowie on another chicken-fried steak when the half-breed, leaning in the open doorway looking out, said, "Well, I'm damned." He stepped aside and took off his hat for the first time since we'd met.

A woman came in, dressed all in blue with a hat pinned to

her hair and her skirts gathered in one hand to clear the threshold. The dress was costly, trimmed with lace at the neck and cuffs, and difficult to care for. It would be her best unless she were rich, which seemed unlikely in Iron Dollar. She had red hair, fine bones, large eyes with a green haze, an aristocratic nose. Good mouth with a touch of rouge on the lips. Her figure was good too. An old fight with pox had left marks on her face—her one flaw—but powder softened that. She was all refined lady except for her walk. Try as they might her hips couldn't quite manage that glacial rigidity the station required.

"Marshal?" She looked around, brows lifted, and settled on me with my knife and fork poised above my plate.

I set down my tools, snatched the checked napkin from my collar, and rose. "For the time being, ma'am, until the real article gets back on his feet." Waddell, sprawled in the rocker, had slid into a quiet coma.

"I'm Mrs. Austin Mulroney. My husband is a carpenter. We're strangers here. On our way in we saw that many of the miners are living in tents. We thought perhaps there might be a demand for proper housing."

"If you'll pardon my being forward, Mrs. Mulroney," I said, "you don't dress like a carpenter's wife."

Her eyelashes brushed her cheeks modestly, but I noticed she didn't blush. "I took the trouble to change in the back of the wagon. I hope to open a dress shop in town. It would be poor advertising to present myself in my plain traveling clothes."

I said, "You won't make expenses. You might have noticed there are mighty few women here."

"Where men go, women follow." She looked around again. "Such a stout structure for so temporary-looking a town. Is there a lot of rowdyism about? How many cells do you have?"

"I'm damned," Tom Shorthair said again.

I looked at him hard. "I hope you'll pardon my associate's coarse manners. He's a half-breed, and you're looking at the savage half. We have six cells. Two are occupied at present."

Kilmartin came in from the back, drawn by the sound of a female voice. Looking from him to me, she said, "So many guards for only two prisoners? Who is back there, Clay Allison?"

"No, ma'am," I said. "Just Tim Boone and a no-account."

"The bank robber? Goodness. Aren't you afraid he might escape out the back while you're all in here?"

"There's no back door."

She took that in with a nod, smiling. Then she gathered her skirts again. "Well, thank you, Marshal. I feel confident we'll be safe with you and your men in charge."

"Glad to be of service, Mrs. Mulroney."

Kilmartin and Tom Shorthair went to the door to watch her walk down the street. I asked if either of them recognized her.

"I ain't sure," said Tom. "It could be Red Hannah, that left Annie Osage's place in Deer Lodge last year heading east. She looks like she got prosperous."

Kilmartin said, "Shouldn't we follow her? She could take us right to Lloyd."

"Lloyd would like that," I said. "He'd blow us out from under our hats and come collect his brother without wasting a man. I have to hand it to him for style. An ordinary advance man wouldn't have cost him near as much."

Tom Shorthair realized he was still holding his hat. He jammed it back on. "You told her everything but how much ammo we got."

"I'd have told her that if she asked. I hate to disappoint a pretty woman."

"If you got a plan, you might share it," he said.

"I plan to arrest Lloyd Boone and any of the gang he brought with him." I ate.

It was almost dark when Marshal Waddell awoke and announced he was going home.

"Why now? You've been wearing a hole in that rocker for twenty-four hours." I spoke without looking up from my cards. For a storekeeper, Kilmartin was good at blackjack.

"I'm out of liquor."

Kilmartin said, "I wouldn't go out wearing that tin plate. Lloyd Boone might mistake you for a lawman and put a hole in you."

Waddell paused with his hand on the doorknob. "He's here?"

"I figure he's waiting for dark." I told Kilmartin to hit me.

"Well, what the hell are *we* waiting for? Them fancy iron shutters is hanging wide open."

Kilmartin dealt me a card. It put me over and I threw in my hand. "Shut the wooden ones, will you? We ought to look like we're putting up a fight."

The marshal shut them and threw the bolts. "What're you, in with him? Figure he'll cut you in if you give up his brother? He'll cut you in, all right. He'll see you get your share of the lead."

I looked at the fresh hand I'd been dealt and said I'd stand pat. Kilmartin took a card and turned his over. "Twenty-one."

I said, "If Waddell hadn't won all our money, I'd shoot you for dealing seconds."

"I'm just lucky."

"Well, your luck run dry when you throwed in with Murdock," Waddell said. "The Boones don't leave witnesses."

I told him there was a bottle of rye in my bedroll. He dug it out and went back to his chair.

Tom Shorthair came in from the cells, crossed the room in two strides, and peered out through a gunport. "Horses, lots of 'em," he said.

He had good ears even for an Indian. Another second went by before I heard hoofbeats. I got to the other window just in time to see a half-dozen or more riders come clattering past the jail and around the corner into the alley next to the harness shop on the other side of the street. Men and horses were loaded down with iron that gleamed in the coal-oil light coming from the store windows.

"Looks like they're fixing to set up in the harness shop," Tom Shorthair said. "Probably put one or two on the roof with rifles."

I told Kilmartin to douse the light. He blew out the lantern on the desk.

"Damn." Waddell's speech was shaky and already slurred. "Damn. I ought to of went home when I said."

Just then glass broke and something struck one of the wooden shutters with a thud. The report that followed was a hollow plop. The marshal cursed again, in a shrill voice.

"Shut up," I said. "That was a pistol. If it was meant to be more than just a warning they'd have used a long gun."

"You in the jail!"

A loud, bawling voice, the kind that carried a long way with little effort. After a pause I cupped my hands around my mouth and yelled back.

"State your business!"

"This here's Lloyd Boone! You got my brother Tim in there and I want him back."

"Burn 'em down, Lloyd!" Tim's voice carried as well, all the way from the cells in back.

I laid my pistol on the windowsill and got my Winchester and leaned it next to the frame. "Boone, this is Page Murdock! I'm a deputy United States marshal and I'm taking your brother back to Helena to stand trial for robbery and murder."

"Like hell!"

I flattened out against the stone wall just before another bullet smashed through one of the shutters and buried itself in the oak partition behind the desk. That one came from a rifle.

Kilmartin said, "I'd like to know why you spend all that money on iron shutters you won't use."

"Damn!" The bottle in Waddell's hand gurgled.

"Burn 'em, Lloyd! Make 'em crawl!"

I told Tom Shorthair to go back and quiet Tim down. "Use your pistol butt."

He went back. There was a loud grunt and then the thump of something heavy hitting the floor. The half-breed returned, border-rolling his Colt to put the barrel back out front.

"Last chance, Murdock!" bawled Lloyd. "I got more guns on you than Custer!"

"Do what you have to, Boone. I can't answer for your brother with all that lead flying around."

"Better a bullet than a rope!" he said, and the guns opened up.

Slugs punched long white splinters out of the heavy oak door, riddled the shutters, shattered the extinguished lamp, and clanged off the barrel stove. I heard the rockers on Waddell's chair creaking maniacally and knew he had flung himself to the floor. As my eyes adjusted to the darkness, I saw Kilmartin spread-eagled against the wall next to the other window, holding his Springfield with a sack of shells strung from his skinny neck by a strap. Tom Shorthair crouched beneath the bulletin board on the adjoining wall gripping his Colt. During a pause between shots I poked my Winchester out through the gunport, drew a bead on a silhouette slightly darker than the sky atop the roof of the harness shop, and squeezed the trigger. The silhouette disappeared, but I couldn't tell if I'd hit it or if my target had ducked; rooftop snipers aren't as easy to kill as you read in dime novels.

Kilmartin took aim through his gunport with the single-shot rifle and fired. He made a satisfied grunt afterward that suggested he hadn't wasted his bullet. He quickly extracted the spent cartridge and replaced it from his sack.

That's how it went for five minutes or so, which always seems longer when you're under attack: hails of lead from outside, with the occasional pause while we tried to return fire. My luck didn't improve and it didn't look as if the storekeeper from Deer Lodge had repeated his first success. Tom Shorthair, with his short gun and nothing to fire it out of, waited for his chance.

The next assault was determined and sustained. The stove binged and bonged; a heavy ball collapsed one of the short legs on the desk and it dumped over, hurling papers and the deck of cards and what remained of the lamp to the floor; another smashed through the door to the cells and twanged off a couple of the bars. The prisoner who had shot Iron Dollar's only whore called us all names at the top of his lungs. I put one through the same door high with my pistol and he shut up. Slugs struck the outside of the stone wall, knocking mortar loose inside. They must have brought enough ammunition to fight the Mexican War all over again.

I raised my voice above the gunfire to ask if anyone had a handkerchief.

Kilmartin said, "Hell of a time to blow your nose." But he produced a blue bandanna from his hip pocket.

"No good. I need a white one."

"Well, ain't you J. P. Morgan," said Tom Shorthair.

Waddell, however, understood. "I got one, but you're going to have to come get it."

I went over in a crouch, staying close to the wall. A bullet lanced in at a steep angle, carrying away part of my left sleeve and chunking into the floor at my feet. I checked to make sure I wasn't hit, then seized the handkerchief the marshal was waving. I went back to the window, tied the white cloth to the Winchester's muzzle, and slid it out through the gunport. I waggled it back and forth.

Little by little the shooting fell off. Finally Lloyd Boone called for the others to hold their fire.

"You got one minute, Murdock!" Then, with a sardonic edge, he threw my own words back at me. "State your business."

I said, "We're outgunned. You can have Tim if you'll let us go."

"You yellow son of a bitch," Tom Shorthair said. "What happened to all that bark you had before the shooting started?"

Waddell said, "Shut up, breed. This is the first time he made sense since I knowed him."

"Send him out and we'll be on our way!" shouted Lloyd.

"Too thin," I said. "You might hang back once you got him and plug us all when we come out. We'll leave you the jail and you can come in and get him yourself."

There was a pondering silence. Then: "Throw your guns out first. You might could hang back yourself and do us the same."

"It's a deal." I withdrew the Winchester, unlatched the shutters, and tossed the carbine on out through the broken window. It hit the boardwalk with a clatter.

"You must of won that star in a poker game." Tom Shorthair spat on the floor.

"Stop flapping your chin and stick your pistol under your belt in back. Hang your shirttail over it. Here." I put my English revolver on the floor and slid it his way.

He shut his mouth with an audible *clop* and hid the Colt. Then he picked up my pistol.

"Throw it out. They can count."

Kilmartin had already opened the shutters on his window and tossed out the Springfield. Tom Shorthair went over and tossed the pistol after it. Waddell contributed his own side arm, a Smith & Wesson American with cracked ivory grips. I called out to Lloyd that that was the lot.

"It better be. I'm keeping a man on the roof to make sure. Step out with your hands as high as they go. I know there are four of you and what you look like. If you try playing the shell game, I'll kill you all."

We lined up in front of the door, me in front with the half-breed last and the others in between. I opened the door and we walked out single-file, our hands in the air.

"Turn right and go to the end of the boardwalk," Lloyd called out.

We did that, and waited on the corner where a streetlamp was burning. Two minutes crawled by, then the door opened in the harness shop and a lanky figure came out. Lloyd was taller than his brother but built along the same loose lines. He wore a slouch hat and cowboy denims and carried a revolving Colt rifle. Behind him walked four men in dusters and canvas coats and broad-brimmed hats, except for one straw skimmer, weighted down with rifles and carbines and belly guns. Six men had accompanied the Boones into the freight office in Deer Lodge, so providing Lloyd hadn't lied about leaving one man on the roof, either Kilmartin or I had hit what we were aiming at earlier.

I spotted the man finally, crouching next to a chimney with his rifle resting on top. I nudged Tom Shorthair, who nodded. He'd seen him too.

The bandits took their time crossing the street, looking all around with weapons ready; plenty enough time for me to tell Kilmartin and Tom Shorthair what I wanted them to do.

"It could work," said the half-breed. "You'd have to be loco to see it coming."

Kilmartin said, "Let's hope that fellow on the roof is right in the head."

Waddell was listening in. "I don't follow you."

"You don't have to," I said. "Just stand here and try not to get shot."

"Don't try too hard on our account," said Tom Shorthair.

Lloyd sent a man inside the jail to look around. When he called back that everything was square, Lloyd and the others went in. The man in the straw hat backed over the threshold, covering the street.

"Now!" I said.

Tom Shorthair jerked his Colt, sighted quickly along his extended right hand, and shot the man on the roof. Without waiting to see him fall, he pivoted and shot the man in the doorway just as he was swinging his rifle our direction. Kilmartin and I were moving before he tumbled out onto the boardwalk. The storekeeper slammed shut the iron shutters on the first window and rammed home the padlock. One of the men inside snapped off a shot as I paused to shove Straw Hat's body out of the way with my foot, but the bullet went wide and I swung shut the door, secured the padlock, scooped up the iron-reinforced elmwood bar, and shoved it into the brackets. Kilmartin meanwhile closed and locked the other set of shutters. We scrambled away from the door as lead came racketing through it. Someone inside—Lloyd, probably—shouted for them to hold their fire, and then a heavy body struck the door from the other side with enough force to split the wood, but not the bar. It didn't even bend. Someone shrieked; the man with the shattered shoulder.

After a pause, the door was struck again, this time by someone swinging the marshal's rocking chair. One of the rockers stuck out through the bullet-torn wood and hung up there. By this time I had hold of Straw Hat's weapon, a Henry repeater; I sent a bullet in next to the rocker, then threw the Henry to Tom Shorthair, who caught it one-handed and put away his Colt to work the lever. I picked up my Winchester, Kilmartin retrieved his Springfield, and all three of us hammered away at the door until someone inside shouted my name.

It was Lloyd. I called for the others to cease firing.

"What can I do for you, Lloyd?"

"You can stand aside. I came for Tim and I'm going to leave with him."

"How are you going to do that, Lloyd?"

"Damn it, Murdock! You're outgunned. You said it yourself."

"I am. I did. But I can send for more guns, and you're not going anywhere."

"This tin box won't hold me!"

"I don't agree. Anyone can bust *into* jail, Lloyd; you just proved that. Busting out's the hard part. The blacksmith in this town is an artist."

He answered that by wasting a bullet. It went through the door and into the deserted harness shop across the street.

There was a wait after that. The Boones of this world don't give up until they run out of possibles. Someone shot at one of the shutters. We heard the bullet ricochet and then someone cried out that he was hit. Later something heavy struck the other set of shutters with a clang—the top half of the stove, I guessed—and the hasp bent a little, but held fast. Around dawn there was a noise inside as of a charging locomotive, and then the building shook and a big enough piece of board fell out of the door to expose the marshal's heavy oak desk, which made a formidable battering ram, but still not enough to crack the thick bar. Just in case, though, I discouraged them from trying again by ordering a fresh volley at the door.

Coming on noon someone got the gaudy idea of setting fire to the door. They slopped coal-oil over it from the ruined lamp and touched a match to it, but there was too much smoke. They coughed bitterly as they used blankets from the cells to slap out the flames.

Lloyd tried one last tack. "Murdock, there's a man in here we don't know. Ask the marshal how he feels about trading a citizen for Tim and me and the rest."

Waddell had finished the rye and brought a chair out from the post office next door to drink a fresh bottle from the saloon and watch the show. He answered Lloyd before I could. "Go ahead and kill him if you like. Every single man in town'll chip in to build you a statue."

That was the last serious attempt, although a couple of times something banged the shutters in frustration. When the sun started going down, I sent Kilmartin to the butcher shop for steaks and we built a fire in the street and started roasting them. The jail was downwind. Finally the Boone gang's bellies got the best of their stubborn nature and Lloyd asked for my terms. I offered him a home-cooked meal and a set of manacles for every man in the jail; except of course the man who shot the whore. He belonged to the town.

Most of the stolen money was recovered from the gang's saddle pouches. The territory paid two thousand apiece for the Boone brothers and an additional fifteen hundred for the rest, including the three who were killed. It got split up among the members of the posse. Marshal Waddell filed a

protest with Blackthorne's court when he wasn't cut in, but
he withdrew it when I wired to say I'd be glad to come back
and discuss it with him. Red Hannah, who really turned out
to have been married to a man named Austin Mulroney, was
apprehended in Missoula and charged as an accessory. As
manhunts go I'd had tougher, but not as tough as the Judge
when I tried to explain the blacksmith's bill on the expense
sheet.

ANNA AND THE PLAYERS

by Ed Gorman

Ed Gorman is about as close as you can come to a renaissance man in this business. He is a publisher of magazines and books, as well as the author of novels in the mystery, horror and western genres. His most recent western novels are Wolf Moon, Dark Trails *and* Trouble Man. *He continues to do work that stretches the form, as he does here with his Cedar Rapids lady Constable Anna Tolan.*

At least they didn't have her running out and getting lunch for them anymore, Anna thought. That in itself was a sort of promotion.

She yawned.

As the lone female on the ten-man Cedar Rapids Police Department in the year of Our Lord 1883, police matron Anna Tolan had spent the previous night studying the work of a French criminal scientist named Marie Françoise Goron. The field was called criminology and both Scotland

Yard and its French counterpart were expanding it every day. Using various methods she'd learned from Goron's writings, Anna had solved three murders in the fourteen months of her employment here. Not that anybody knew this, of course. Two detectives named Riley and Czmeck had been quick to claim credit on all three cases.

Anna yawned again. Her sweet landlady, Mrs. Goldman, had come to her door late last night and begged Anna to turn off the kerosene lamp and get some sleep. "You push yourself way too hard with this police thing, Anna."

Yes, and for what reason? Anna thought. It was doubtful she'd ever be promoted to full police officer. There were people in town who thought it was sinful for her to be on the police force at all. A woman. Just imagine. Tsk-tsk. They even stood before the mayor in city council meetings and quoted scripture to her that "proved" that God didn't want women police officers. Apparently, God had opinions on everything.

Thunder rumbled down the sky. The chill, rainy October morning was at least partly responsible for Anna's mood. Rain affected her immediately and deeply, made her feel vulnerable, melancholy. Even as a child back on the farm near Parnell, Anna had been this way. Rain always brought demons.

"There's a lady up front who won't talk to me," a male voice said. "Said she wanted to talk to the one and only Anna Tolan."

The half-bellow, the smell of cheap cigars and the dog-like odor of rain on a wool suit meant that Detective Riley was leaning in the door of Anna's office in the back of the station house.

"Something about ghosts," Riley said.

Anna turned in her chair and looked at him. Fifty pounds ago he'd been a good-looking man. But early middle-age hadn't been kind to him. He looked puffy and tired. Ten years ago, he'd pitched a no-hit game against Des Moines and had been town hero for several years following. Now, he looked like the bloated uncle of that young man, only the faintest resemblance showing.

"Ghosts?"

"That's what she said."

"Nice of you to give it to me."

Half the cops were nice to her and helped her in every way possible. They recognized her for the competent law officer she was. This, thank God, included the Chief. The other half gave her all the cases they didn't want. But she was glad to get even the bad ones, because otherwise her day would consist of checking the jail three times a day, walking around town in her light blue pinafore and starched white blouse and asking merchants if everything was going well with them— no break-ins, no robberies, nobody harassing them. One of the reasons that Cedar Rapids had grown so quickly was that it knew how to attract and keep businesses. Twenty-five thousand citizens. More than four hundred telephones. Electricity. In two or three years, there'd even be steam trolleys to replace the present horse-drawn ones. There was even an opera house that featured some of the world's most notable theatrical attractions. Chief Ryan once said, "It sure doesn't hurt to have a pretty little slip of an Irish girl—and with beautiful red hair yet—talking to the merchants to see that the town keeps them happy. It sure docsn't, Anna."

"I thought you wanted any cases we gave you," Riley said. "If you want me to, I'll give it to somebody else."

"I'm sorry. I'm just in kind of a crabby mood today."

"Trace Wydmore bothering you to marry him again?"

"I wish you'd leave him alone. He's a decent man."

"If he's so decent, why don't you marry him?"

"That really isn't any of your business."

"Tell him to give me some of his money. He's got plenty to go around, that's for sure."

Trace Wydmore was intelligent, handsome, pleasant, fun and kind. He was also very, very rich. About every three months, even though they'd long ago quit seeing each other, Trace would suddenly reappear and ask her to marry him. She felt sorry for him. But she didn't love him. She liked him, admired him, appreciated him. But she didn't love him.

She changed the subject. "You're right, Riley. I *do* want the case. Thank you for giving it to me. I guess I'm just in a bad mood. The rain."

"You and my old lady," he said. "If it's not her monthly visitor, it's the weather. There's always some reason she's crabby." Then he waggled his fingers at her wraithlike and made a spooky noise. "I'll go get the ghost lady."

Her name was Virginia Olson, a bulky, middle-aged woman with a doughy face and hard, bright, not terribly friendly blue eyes. She cleaned rooms at the Astor Hotel, a somewhat seedy place along the river. She wore a pinafore, not unlike Anna's in cut and style, but stained and smudged with the indelicacies of hotel guests. When she talked, silver spittle frothed up in the corners of her mouth and ran down the sides of her lips. She said, "Oh, I seen her all right."

"Anthea Murchison?"

"Anthea Murchison. Right in front of my eyes."

"She's been dead over a year now. Her buggy overturned over in Johnson County and she went off a cliff."

"I don't need no rehash, miss," she said. "I read the papers. I keep up."

"Then if you keep up," Anna said, staying calm and patient, "and if you think it through, what you're saying is impossible."

"That a dead woman was in the hotel last night? Well, she was."

Anna sighed. "Exactly what would you like me to do?"

"You're just as snooty as the men officers. You try'n give the coppers a tip and look what you get."

"I'm sorry, Mrs. Olson."

"Miss Olson."

"Miss Olson, then."

"Not that I never had no chances to be a *Mrs.*." She sucked up some of the frothing spittle.

"I'm sure you had plenty of chances."

"I wasn't always fat. It's this condition I have. And my hair used to be black as night, too. But then I got this here condition."

"I'm sorry. Now, if you'll just tell me—"

"She wore this big picture hat. You know what a picture hat is?"

"Yes." They were fashionable these days, hats with huge brims that covered half a lady's face.

"She also had some kind of wig on when she came in the hotel. That's why I didn't recognize her. Her disguise. But I was goin' to my own room—the hotel gives me room and board except the food is pig swill—anyway, later on I'm goin' to my room and I seen her door was partly open and I just happened to glance inside and there she was without her hat and her wig and I seen her. Anthea Murchison. Plain as day."

"Did she see you?"

"I think she must've because she hurried quick-like to the door and practically slammed it." She paused to suck up some more spittle. Anna wondered if the spittle had anything to do with the woman's "condition."

"You'd seen the Murchison woman before?"

Miss Olson smirked. "You mean when she was alive?"

"Yes."

"Oh, I seen her all right. Plenty of times."

"Where?"

"The hotel. That's why I recognized her so fast. Her and her gentleman friend used to come up the back way."

"When was this?"

Virginia Olson thought about it for a time. "Oh, six, seven months before she died."

"How often did they come there?"

"Once a week, say."

"They didn't check in at the front desk?"

"No. They had—or she had, anyway—some kind of deal worked out with Mr. Sullivan. The manager. Poor man."

"Poor man?"

"The cancer. He weighed about eighty pounds when they planted him. Liver. He was all yellow."

"That's too bad."

"No, it isn't."

"It isn't?"

"I mean, I didn't want to see him die that way—I wouldn't want to see *any*body die that way—but he was a mean, cheap bastard who never did a lick'a work in his life."

"I'm sorry to hear that. But let's get back to Anthea Murchison."

"They were havin' it on."

"I gathered that. Did you know who he was?"

"I almost got a look at him once. But he always moved real fast. And he wore this big fake black beard and this big hat that covered a lot of his face."

"Like her picture hat?"

"I never thought of that. But you're right. It was sorta like a picture hat except it was for a man. Like somethin' you'd see on the stage, I guess. That a villain would wear or somethin'."

She took a railroad watch from the pocket of her pinafore and said, "I got to get back. I'm just here on my break."

"I still don't know what you want me to do, Mrs. Olson."

"Come over there and look at her. See if it ain't Mrs. Murchison in the flesh."

The woman wasn't going to be Mrs. Murchison, of course. But it'd be better than just sitting here on this gloomy morning. And on the way back, she could swing past the jail and make one of her morning inspections. Make sure things were being run properly. Chief Ryan prided himself on his jail. He wanted it clean, orderly and without a whisper of scandal. He hoped to run for mayor someday, Chief Ryan did, and he didn't want some civic group pointing out that his jail had been some hell-hole like something you'd see in Mexico. Their jails were much in the news lately. A lot of men died mysteriously in those jails.

"I'll walk back with you," Anna said, standing up.

"I got to hurry," Mrs. Olson said. "Mr. Sanford's worse than Mr. Sullivan ever was. Now Mr. Sanford, I sure wouldn't mind seein' him get the cancer. I surely wouldn't."

Hotel rooms always saddened Anna. She'd seen too many suicides, murders and bad illicit love affairs within their walls. One problem with being a copper was that you generally saw the worst side of people, even in a nice little town like Cedar Rapids. The grubby hallway of the Astor's third floor told her that the room she was about to see would be grubby, too. The Olson woman had gone back to work.

The hallway offered eruptions of sounds on both sides—tobacco coughs, singing-while-shaving, snoring and gargling, presumably with "oral disinfectant" as the advertisements called it.

Room 334. Anna put her ear to it. Listened. Silence. Just then a door down the hall opened and a bald man in trousers, the tops of long johns, and suspenders peeked out and picked up his morning paper. He gave Anna a very close appraisal and said, "Morning."

Anna smiled, wanting to remain silent, and nodded good morning back.

She put her ear to the door again. If the woman inside was moving around, she was doing so very, very quietly. Maybe the woman had gone out the back way. While the desk clerk had assured Anna that the woman had not come down yet this morning, he obviously didn't know for sure that she was in her room.

Anna knocked gently. Counted to ten. No response. Knocked again. And still no response.

Sounds of doors opening and closing on all three floors of the hotel. Morning greetings exchanged. Smells of cigarettes, pipes, cigars. Men with leather sample bags of merchandise carted out here from points as distant as New York and Cincinnati and Chicago suddenly striding past her in the hall. A quarter to eight and the business day just beginning.

Anna knocked again.

One of the officers friendly to her had given her a couple of tools resembling walnut picks. Showed her how to use them on virtually any kind of door. He'd also given her several skeleton keys. She could get into virtually any room or house.

The room was about what she'd expected. Double bed. Bureau. Faded full-length mirror hanging on a narrow closet door. Window overlooking the alley on the east side of the hotel. What wasn't expected was the woman in bed. She lay in a faded yellow robe, with her arms spread wide. She was otherwise naked. Somebody had cut her throat. There was a necklace-like crust of dried blood directly across the center of her neck.

The woman was Anthea Murchison.

Anna's first instinct was to hurry downstairs and send somebody to summon the Chief. But then she forced herself to calm down. She wouldn't get much of a chance to scientifically appraise the room—the way her idol Goron would want her to—with other cops there.

She spent the next twenty minutes going over everything. In the purse, she found various documents bearing the name Thea Manners, obviously the name the Murchison woman used during the past year. But where had she been? What had she been doing? Anna inspected the bed carefully, looking for anything that might later prove useful. She found red fibers, hair strands that looked to belong to Anthea Murchison, a piece of a woman's fingernail. She checked Anthea's fingers. A slice of her right index fingernail had broken off. The piece Anna held fit the maimed nail perfectly. A couple of times, Anna noticed the small, odd indentation in the wooden headboard. She took a piece of paper and held it tight to the headboard. Then she scribbled lead over the indentation. It showed a symbol: H. The style was rococo, and a bit too fancy for Anna's tastes. She put the paper in her pocket. Then she started in on the floor. Down on her hands and knees. Looking for curious footprints, or something tiny that might have been dropped. She found a number of things worth dropping in the white evidence envelope she'd made up for herself. A plain black button interested Anna especially. She checked it against Anthea's clothes in the closet. There was no match. The button belonged to somebody else. The way fashions were getting so radical these days—an Edwardian craze was sweeping the country—it was impossible to know if the button had come off male or female attire.

Fifteen minutes later, the room was filled with police officers. Anna was pretty much pushed aside. She went downstairs to the porch and stood there looking out at the street. The rain had let up, but the overcast, chill autumn day remained. Wagons and buggies and surreys and a stray stagecoach or two plied the muddy streets. Somewhere nearby, the horse-drawn trolley rang its bell. Then she realized that the trolley could take her very close to where she needed to go.

She hurried to the corner. The trolley stopped for her. On a day like this one, the conveyance was crowded; bowlers on men, bustles on women bobbed as it bounced down the bumpy streets. Horse-drawn taxi cabs were busy, too. The rain had started in again.

Ten years ago, the large red barn had housed two businesses, a blacksmith and a farm implement dealer. It now housed The Players, a local theatrical group that did everything it could to create controversy, and thus sell tickets. Kevin Murchison was a dentist by day but at night he oversaw production of the plays. His partner was David Bailey, a medical doctor. The men had much in common. They were in their early thirties, literary, handsome and were widely held to have slept with half the women, married or not, who took roles in the various plays. Kevin was tall and pale and blond; David was short and dark and not without an air of not only malice but violence. His bedside manner was rarely praised. In fact, it was well known that most of the other doctors in town regretted ever letting him practice here. One practiced in Cedar Rapids only at the sufferance of the docs already in place. Many were called; few were chosen. David Bailey was generally regarded as a terrible choice.

The playhouse was empty when Anna arrived. She stood

at the back of the place, listening to the rain play chill ancient rhythms on the roof of the barn. The stage was set up for a French bedroom farce advertised outside as "DEFI-NITELY NAUGHTY!"—THE NEW YORK TIMES. Who could resist that? Word was this was the most success-ful play of the past three years, so successful in fact that both dentist and doctor were thinking of quitting their respective practices and joining The Players full-time.

"It's lovely, isn't it?" The voice definitely male but prac-ticed and just this side of being "cultured."

She turned to find three people standing there: Dr. Murchi-son, Dr. Bailey and Bailey's gently beautiful wife, Beatrice.

Anna said, "You've done a nice job."

Murchison said, "The finest theater outside Chicago."

Beatrice actually blushed at the hyperbole. "Or so we like to think, anyway."

There was no clue on their faces or in their voices that they'd heard about their friend Anthea. She was probably at the undertaker's by now.

Murchison, whose Edwardian suit complemented his clipped good looks and slightly European curly blond hair, said, "I'm sure you're here about Anthea."

So they did know.

"It's terrible," Beatrice said.

"I hope there'll be an investigation," Bailey said. His stocky form looked comfortable in Levi's and work shirt. The odd thing was, Murchison, who looked almost effete, had been raised on a farm. Bailey, who'd come from Boston money, could have blended in with a crew of railroad work-ers. "I was the one who pronounced her dead. I've got my reputation to think of." Then he made an awkward attempt to touch his hand to Murchison's shoulder. "I'm sorry, Kevin. You're grieving and all I can talk about is my reputation."

There was something rehearsed about the little scene

she'd just witnessed. Or was there? Theater people—or so she'd read in one of Mrs. Goldman's eastern magazines—sometimes carried their acting over into real life. *Ham* was the word Anna wanted.

"Did any of you see her last night?"

"No," said Murchison. "I wish I had. My God, I have so many questions for her." Tears filled his eyes and Beatrice, tall, regal Beatrice, took him in her arms and held him.

"Why don't we step into the office?" Bailey said. "We can talk there."

Theater posters lined the walls of the small office with the roll-top desk and the long table covered with leaflets for the present production. *Uncle Tom's Cabin, The Widow's Revenge, A Cupid for Constance* were listed as forthcoming. The Players were an eclectic bunch. They mixed tame fare with the occasional bedroom farce and seemed to be surviving quite nicely these days.

"She was dead when we put her in the ground," Bailey said. "I'd swear to that."

"You'll have to, Doctor. There'll be a lot of questions about the autopsy report you signed."

A tic troubled his right eyelid suddenly. Anna said, "You didn't see her last night?"

"I believe I already answered that question."

"I'd appreciate you answering it again."

"Neither of us saw her last night," Beatrice said as she came into the office. "Poor Kevin's lying down in his private office." She went over and took a straightback chair next to her husband's. "We worked at the theater until nearly midnight and then went home and went to bed."

"I see."

Beatrice smiled. "I was just wondering if you're even authorized to ask us questions. I remember you had some trouble with the city council and all."

"The Chief will back me up, if that's what you mean." Then, "I'm going to ask for the grave to be disinterred this afternoon."

"And why would you do that?" Bailey said.

"I want to see what's in the coffin."

"Well, obviously *Anthea* won't be." Bailey said. His eye tic was suddenly worse.

"How did Anthea and Kevin get along?"

"Just wonderfully," Beatrice said.

"There were a lot of rumors."

Beatrice smiled. "Of course, there were rumors, dear. This is a rumor kind of town. Anybody who shows a little flair for anything even the slightest bit different from the herd—well, rumors are the price you pay."

"Then they were happy?"

"Very."

"And there was no talk of divorce?"

"Of course not."

They weren't going to cooperate and Anna knew it. They had pat little answers to turn aside all her questions. And that was all she was going to get.

She stood up. "Where's Dr. Murchison's office?"

"Just down the hall," Beatrice said. "But he really does want to be alone. He's very confused and hurt right now."

"I'll keep that in mind," Anna said. "And thank you for your time."

As she was turning to the door, Bailey said, "You've been incredibly insensitive. I may just talk to the Chief about it."

"That's up to you, Dr. Bailey."

They stared at each other a long moment, and then Anna went down the hall.

Just as she reached Murchison's door, she heard a female voice behind it say, "Oh, Kevin, why lie about it? You sleep with all the ingenues and then get tired of them. That's what's happening to us. You're tired of me but you don't want to hurt my feelings by telling me."

"I just need some time to—think, Karen. That's all. Especially after this morning. My wife and everything."

"You should be grateful to her," Karen said. "She gave you a perfect excuse for not seeing me tonight." By the end, her voice had started to tremble with tears. "Oh, I was stupid to think you were really in love with me."

Anna had always been told that in amateur theater groups, the real drama went on offstage. Apparently so. She hated to embarrass Karen by knocking now but she had work to do. She knocked.

Murchison opened the door quickly, obviously grateful for any interruption. But he frowned when he saw Anna. "Oh, great, just what I need. More questions."

"I just need a few minutes, Dr. Murchison."

The word "ingenue" had misled Anna into picturing a slender, somewhat ethereal young woman. While Karen was still an exquisite-looking woman, her years were starting to do damage—the face a bit fleshy, the neck a bit loose, the high bustline a bit matronly now. She was a fading beauty, and there was always something sad about that. There was a wedding ring on Karen's left finger. But it was the other thing she kept touching, fingering—a large ornamental ring that was most likely costume jewelry.

"I'll talk to you tonight," Murchison said, "if Miss Tolan here doesn't put me in jail for some reason." He didn't even try to disguise the bitterness in his voice.

Karen whimpered, pushed past Anna, and exited the room.

"I suppose you heard it all while you were standing by the door," Murchison said, "and will run right down to her husband's office and tell him." Anna suspected that this was the real Murchison. The mild man she'd met earlier had been a mask.

"I don't even know who her husband is," Anna said.

"Lawrence Remington," Murchison said. "He has a very successful law practice in the Ely Building. On the second floor, in case you're interested." He smirked. "I only commit adultery with the upper classes. I guess I'm something of a snob." He took out a packet of Egyptian cigarettes. Nobody was more pretentious than certain amateur theater types. "She's not as beautiful as she used to be. But Remington doesn't seem to notice that. He's insanely jealous."

"Maybe he loves her."

But love didn't interest him much. He merely shrugged.

"I'm told that you and your wife were on the verge of divorce at the time of her supposed death."

He glared at her. "You don't waste any time, do you? Have you ever thought that I might be grieving? Here I thought my wife was dead—and then she suddenly turns up. And now she's dead again." She could see why he produced the shows instead of starred in them. He was a terrible actor.

"Did you see her last night?"

"I've already told you no."

"What if I said somebody saw her slipping into your house?"

He didn't hesitate. "Then I'd say you're lying."

Sometimes the trick Chief Ryan had taught her worked. Sometimes it didn't. She tried a trick of her own. "I found a cuff button in your wife's hotel room."

"Good for you."

"I'm sure you'd be happy to let me look through your shirts."

He met her eye. He seemed to be enjoying this, which did

not do much for her police officer ego. "Would you like to go to my place and look through my shirts?"

Once again, she changed the subject, now uncertain of herself and the direction of her questions. "The night clerk said he saw a man going up to her room late last night." One last attempt to trap him.

"Oh? Maybe you'd like me to stop by so he can see me." He laughed. "I'll cooperate with you any way you want, Miss Tolan. I have nothing to hide."

Maybe he didn't, after all. Or maybe he was clever enough to offer himself up this way, knowing she wouldn't call him on it. She felt slow-witted and dull. She was sure she'd been the brunt of many jokes told after-hours at the Players' notorious wine parties. She was just glad Chief Ryan wasn't here to see this sorry interrogation. She wanted to be home suddenly, in Mrs. Goldman's parlor, listening to Mrs. Goldman's stirring stories about the Civil War, and how the ladies of Iowa had worked eighteen-hour days making bullets and knitting sweaters and stockings and mittens for their Union husbands and sons and brothers. Mrs. Goldman said that they'd even loaded up the steamboats when no men could be found.

She angled herself toward the door. "I guess I'll be going now."

"I was just starting to have fun." Then, "You're very pretty, Anna. Have you ever thought of trying out for one of our plays?"

She knew she was blushing. His compliment had cinched his victory. He'd reduced her status from detective to simple young woman.

"I'll talk to you later," she said, and hurried out of his room. He laughed once behind her—an empty, fake laugh that was yet another example of his bad acting.

Anna was about to walk out through the front door

when she heard the weeping in the deep shadows to the side. She squinted into the gloom and saw nothing. But the weeping sound remained constant. Anna made her way carefully toward the far wall. A shape began to form. Karen Remington. She paused long enough to say, "Do you have a cigarette?"

Good girls don't smoke, Anna wanted to say. Or so her farmer parents had always told her, anyway. And Anna couldn't get away from their influence, much as she wanted to sometimes. Any woman she saw smoking a cigarette, she automatically downgraded socially if not morally. "I'm afraid I don't smoke."

"I must look terrible. My makeup."

Anna smiled. "Actually, I can't see you very well."

The Remington woman laughed. And that made Anna like her. "If that's the case, I should probably stay here the rest of my life. In the shadows. Then I won't have to see how old I'm getting." She paused, snuffled tears, daubed a lace handkerchief to nose and lips. "I've always read about women like myself—that's why I can't stand to read Henry James, I see myself in so many of his silly, middle-aged women. Vain and desperate." More snuffling. "I told myself that The Players would be good for me. My son was off to Princeton, my husband was always busy. I felt—Oh, it's all such a cliché. You know how I felt. So I decided to help out with publicity. Then I helped with costumes. Then I tried out for a part in a play. And then I got involved with dear Kevin. You know the funny thing? He not only seduced me—though of course I *wanted* to be seduced— he convinced me to give him money. And large amounts of it. My husband was furious when he found out. Even threatened to divorce me. I actually think he resented the money even more than he resented my being unfaithful. He's not a generous man. But I didn't care. Kevin and I were going to run off and start another theater someplace. I wanted to go east, to be nearer my son. Kevin led me to believe—"

"Nasty Kevin," a male voice said on the other side of the gloom. "Nasty, nasty Kevin."

It was Kevin, of course.

"I didn't 'lead her to believe' anything, Miss Tolan. She believed what she *wanted* to believe."

"Unfortunately," the Remington woman said, "that's true."

And promptly began sobbing again, even more violently than before.

Soon enough, Anna was on the trolley, headed downtown once again. The sun was out now; the temperature was up in the forties. Anna looked longingly at the stately buildings of Coe College, Main Building and Williston Hall, as they were known. She hoped to take classes there someday. She's seen photographs of college girls in crisp spring dresses. How intelligent and poised and professional they looked. Her secret dream was to be one of them. Anna Tolan, college girl.

Anna had no trouble with Chief Ryan. He understood exactly why she wanted the Murchison woman's coffin dug up. Judge Rollins, who could sometimes be a problem, also understood and approved her request.

At four that afternoon, Anna, Chief Ryan and two scruffy gravediggers stood over Anthea Murchison's gravesite. The air was fresh, cleansed by the recent rain, and the gravestones glistened as if they'd been scrubbed. Some of them dated as far back as the late 1700s, when some Frenchmen down from Green Bay, Wisconsin, had started trading iron kettles, cloth and knives for some of the Ioway Indians' animal skins. An influenza outbreak had killed at least a dozen of the French traders.

"If there's a body in there, Anna," Chief Ryan said. "I

want you to look away. Otherwise, it'll stay in your mind the rest of your life."

Chief Ryan was every bit as grandfatherly as he sounded, a big, broad, gray-haired man with the red nose of a drinker and the kind eyes of a village priest. His grandparents had come from County Cork two generations ago. Every Ryan male since had been a law officer of some kind.

"I'll be fine, Chief."

"You're not as tough as you think, young lady."

Remembering her wretched questioning of the glib Kevin Murchison, she had to silently agree.

The exhumation went quickly. The gravediggers knew their business. When they reached the wooden coffin with the cross in the center of the lid, the taller of the two jumped down into the grave with his crowbar. He was able to balance himself against the walls of the grave and open the coffin lid.

He pried it up and flung it back. "Empty, sir," he shouted up to the Chief.

When they got back to the station, Anna found a man waiting for her. She saw him around town frequently but didn't know who he was or what he did.

He doffed his derby and said, "My name is Peterson. Pete Peterson. I sell insurance."

"This is a bad time to sell me anything, Mr. Peterson."

He smiled. He had a boyish face emphasized by the youthful cut of his checkered suit. Salesmen, or drummers as they were popularly called, had come to favor checks. They felt that the pattern put people in a happier frame of mind than, say, dark blue or black. "I'm here about Anthea Murchison."

"Oh?"

"My company issued her a life insurance policy for fifty thousand dollars eight months before she died."

"Oh," Anna said, catching his implication instantly.

They sat in her office for the next hour. The day shift was winding down. Men called goodbyes to each other. The handful of night-shifters came on, their leather gunbelts creaking, their heavy shoes loud on the wooden floors.

"Insurance fraud is what we're looking at," Peterson said. "If we can prove it."

"Why couldn't you prove it?" Anna said. "The coffin was empty. And Dr. Bailey signed the death certificate. He had to know she wasn't dead."

"I think it was for that theater of theirs."

"The money, you mean?"

Peterson nodded. "The way I understand it, they couldn't get any more investors. They'd borrowed everything they could. The theater was going under."

"So they staged Anthea Murchison's death."

"And collected fifty thousand dollars."

"Your company didn't investigate?"

"Of course, we investigated. But as you said, we had a signed death certificate. There was no reason to go into an all-out investigation. We didn't spend all that much time on it. Now, it's obvious we were defrauded."

"They'll probably try to leave town."

"If they haven't already."

"I'm not sure how long I can hold them on what we have now, though."

"But we *know* what happened, Anna."

"Yes, we know it. But can we prove it? Defense attorneys are very creative people, Pete."

"Don't I know it. They've helped cheat my company out of millions of dollars." Whenever he spoke of the company, his tone became downright reverent. Like a cardinal invoking the name of the Vatican.

"I need to talk to the Chief about all this, Pete. There's also a murder investigation going on. He'll want to move carefully."

"What's he afraid of?"

"What he's afraid of, Mr. Peterson," Chief Ryan said, walking into Anna's office, "is that you'll get your fraud case all resolved, and we still won't know why Anthea Murchison came back to town last night—and why one of them killed her."

Peterson frowned. "So you're not going to arrest them?"

"Not right now," Ryan said, "and I don't want you approaching them, either. You understand?"

"My company isn't going to be happy."

"I'm sorry about that, Mr. Peterson," Ryan said. "But that's the way it has to be for a little while longer."

Mr. Peterson's checkered suit seemed to fade slightly in intensity. Even the magnificently bogus gleam in his eyes had dulled. His company wasn't happy, and neither was he.

"Now, if you don't mind, Mr. Peterson, Anna and I need to get back to work."

Mr. Peterson dragged himself to his feet. He looked weary, old. He took his faded suit and faded eyes to the door and said, "I'll have to go and send my company a telegram, I guess." And with that, he was gone.

A moment later, Chief Ryan said, "The mayor wants me to put Riley on the case."

"I figured that would happen."

"You know this isn't my decision. But there's an election coming up and he doesn't want to have an unsolved case like this hanging over his head." Ryan smiled. "But nobody can stop you from working on the case on your own, Anna."

Their usual bargain had been struck. Anna worked on the case and secretly reported back to the Chief.

Anna smiled. "I guess I do have a little time on my hands tonight."

"Glad to hear it."

After dinner with Mrs. Goldman, Anna took the evidence up to her room and started sifting through it. Goron had instructed would-be detectives to store all evidence in the same box, and to tag it alphabetically. Fingerprints were beginning to play a role in law enforcement. Even though officers in the United States were still skeptical of such evidence—and no court would allow it to be used—Goron insisted that all pieces of evidence remain as pristine as possible. She also insisted that fingerprints were the surest way to identify a killer. Find a print on a murder weapon and you had your man.

Anna worked till after midnight. On her bed was the button she'd found on Anthea Murchison's hotel bed, the sketch she'd made of some strange footprints on the hotel room floor, a cigarette made of coarse tan paper and heavy tobacco leaves, a man's comb with gray hair in it, a drinking glass across which were smeared two or three different sets of fingerprints, and then the curious H marking she'd found on the headboard of Anthea's hotel bed. The trouble with all her evidence was that she couldn't date it. It might have been in the room for a month. Even the cigarette butt didn't tell her anything decisive. A sloppy cleaning woman might have left it behind a few weeks ago.

There would be no trouble proving that the owners of The Players had perpetrated a fraud; proving that one of them had perpetrated a murder might be something else again.

Kevin Murchison had planned on only one drink at the River's Edge. He had four in less than an hour. On an empty stomach. Which was not exactly brilliant. With the law now having him under suspicion—even that stupid insurance investigator Pete Peterson should be able to figure things out now—he needed to remain sharp and clear-headed.

But somehow his fear (Oh, he'd do just dandy in prison, wouldn't he?) and self-pity (Why shouldn't a nice decent fellow like himself be able to get away with a little fraud now and then? Insurance companies had lots of money, didn't they?) and loathing (He hated the taverns of Cedar Rapids; all the silly yokel chatter; never a word about theater life or the latest Broadway scandal, which Kevin kept up on via *The New York Times*, however dated it was by the time it reached this little hellhole of a burg.)—somehow his fear, his self-pity and his loathing forced him to drink more.

By the time he was ready to walk home, he had to make himself conscious of his gait. Didn't want to appear drunk. Drunk meant vulnerable, and oh, how that pretty little piece of a police matron or whatever the hell she was would love to get him when he was vulnerable.

The autumn dusk was chill and brief and gorgeous, the sky layered in smoky pastels of gold and salmon. His Tudor-style home was dark when he reached it. He'd let the last of his servants go shortly after Anthea's "death." He could no longer afford the pretense. Anyway, he needed the town's sympathy—the bereaved husband and all that—to allay suspicion that Anthea's death had been suspicious. People in a place like Cedar Rapids were never sympathetic to people who had servants.

He reheated this morning's coffee and then went to the north wing of the house, where the den was located. He'd just touched a match to the desk lamp when the smell filled his nostrils. He wanted to vomit.

She lay over by the fireplace, the fire poker next to her

fine blond head. The tip of the poker gleamed with her blood.

He knelt next to her. Once or twice, he reached out to touch her. But then stopped himself. He didn't want to remember her flesh as cold. In life, it had been so warm and supple and erotic. He had never loved anyone as much as he'd loved Beatrice. They'd been planning to run away tonight, leaving her husband David Bailey to explain things to the police—the insurance fraud and Anthea's murder last night.

Now, he knew who had murdered Anthea. David Bailey. Anthea'd stopped by the house here late last night and demanded more money, said she'd been living in New Orleans but had run out of money. They'd been planning to divorce anyway at the time they faked her death—so she took one-third of the insurance money and fled, and they put the rest of the money into the theater. He'd lied to her last night and said he'd get her more this morning. Anything to get rid of her. So, apparently, she'd next gone to visit and blackmail Bailey. And he must have killed her. As he'd killed poor Beatrice tonight. Bailey, a jealous man for all his own unfaithfulness, had likely learned about Beatrice and Kevin. And killed her for her betraying him.

He wasn't given to tears and so his sobs were fitful. He leaned in. He couldn't help himself. He kissed her cold dead lips.

And then he stood up and knew what he had to do, where he had to go.

Right now, nothing else mattered. Nothing else at all.

"You could've killed Beatrice," Anna said.

"No, I couldn't," Murchison said. "I loved her too much."

"So," the Chief said, "you admit to the insurance fraud."

"Yes, of course. I've told you that already. We were just trying to save the theater."

"But not to murdering your wife," Anna said.

"Or Beatrice," the Chief said.

It was near midnight in the small back room of the station the police used to question suspects. The room was bare except for a few fading dirty words prisoners had scribbled on the wall from time to time.

Kevin Murchison had gone to Anna's and told her what happened. His version of it, anyway. Then she'd taken him downtown and used the telephone to call the Chief and ask him to come down, too. She still got a thrill every time she used the telephone. They'd spent the last two hours going over and over Murchison's story. The atmosphere wasn't hostile but it was certainly intense. The dancing light of a kerosene lamp threw everything into soft shadow.

"Who do you think killed them, then?" Anna said.

"I've told you that already."

"I wish you'd quit saying that," the Chief said, lighting his pipe with a stick match. "We're well aware we keep asking you the same questions over and over."

"It's damned annoying is what it is."

"So," the Chief said, "who do you think killed the two women?"

Murchison glared at him. Sighed. "I've told you and told you. David killed them."

"Why would he kill them?"

"He's got a terrible temper. Anthea must've seen him last night and demanded money. The same way she did from me. He got angry and killed her."

"But why would he kill Beatrice?" Anna said.

"Because he found out about us. Not only that we were lovers but that we were running away together."

"And so he killed her?" Anna said.

"You'd have to see him lose his temper to understand how easily he could kill somebody. He's terrifying when he's like that."

A knock. The Chief said, "That's probably Henning, Anna. Why don't you take it? I'll keep on questioning our friend here."

"I didn't kill either of those women," Kevin Murchison said, sounding like a sad little boy. "I really didn't."

Anna opened the door. Henning was one of the older officers, a big, bald man with bushy eyebrows and a chin scar from a long-ago altercation with a hobo. Anna stepped out into the hall. "Bailey wasn't at home."

"Did you find a train schedule?"

Henning nodded, handed her a pamphlet.

"Thanks," she said.

"I need to make my rounds."

She nodded. There was a train leaving for Chicago in forty-five minutes.

She opened the door and peeked in and said, "I'm going over to the train depot."

"Good idea," the Chief said. "You know where my Navy Colt is. Take it."

"I probably won't need it."

"Take it, anyway."

While Anna didn't much like firearms, the Chief had turned her into a fair marksman. She preferred to think of herself as a Goron-type of peace officer. "Brain power" Goron often said was more important than "brute power." But she reluctantly went into the Chief's office, went to his desk, opened the wide middle drawer, and took out the Navy Colt.

Cedar Rapids had a crush on its train depot, one of those crushes that made folks just about absolutely goofy. Some folks would bring their own chairs to the depot just so they could sit and watch trains arrive and depart all day long. Other folks even brought picnic lunches, just to sit and watch the panoramic show that trains put on. People loved everything about trains, the bold colors of the engine cars, the gray billowing smoke, the stink of coal, the smell of oil, the clatter of couplings. They were especially interested in the fancy dining cars and parlor cars. "The envy of sultans!" as one advertisement boasted. They liked to see exotic strangers disembark, New York people or Chicago people or Boston people, fancy people stepping down to stretch their legs before the train roared away again, women in huge capes and big important hairstyles, and men in dove-gray vests and top hats and spats, money and culture and a self-confidence that Cedar Rapids folks could only daydream of.

Because the temperature had dipped several degrees, most of the waiting passengers were inside the depot, on the benches close to the potbellied stove. The fog had discouraged them, too, a damp, thick, gritty fog. There weren't many people inside, mostly drummers on to the next burg, derbys down on their faces as they snored off weariness and whiskey.

She searched all the obvious places inside. Bailey wasn't in any of them. She described him to everybody she saw. Nobody had seen him. Not even the ticket seller recalled seeing him.

She'd been there fifteen, twenty minutes when the drunk came reeling in. She'd arrested him a few times. His name was Henry. He'd used so many aliases neither he nor the police were sure of his last name. He was mostly a small-time grifter preying on elderly folks. He was a decent-looking man but you couldn't tell it beneath the layers of grime and bar liquor.

He went over to the ticket window. Moments later, he was shouting at the ticket man. Anna went over.

"Where the hell is he?" Henry wanted to know.

"Where is who?" the ticket man said several times. "I don't know who you're talking about."

"That doctor."

"What doctor?" Anna said.

Henry turned awkwardly and glared at her. He looked to be near collapse, the final stages of this particular bender. He'd stay dry for a few months, working his grifts, and then do another bender again for five, six weeks. "You got no call to arrest me."

"I just want to talk to you."

"That's what you said las' time."

For a drunk, he had a good memory. She took his elbow, angled him away from the ticket window. "Who's the doctor you're looking for?"

"None of your damn business. I got rights, you know."

"You keep it up, Henry, and I *will* arrest you. Now who's the doctor?"

He needed a shave, two or three baths, and his dirty black suit needed all sorts of sewing. He glared silently at her as long as he could. Then he sighed and said, "Bailey."

"I thought so. Why're you looking for him?"

"He promised me five dollars." Five dollars would buy a lot of bad liquor.

"For what?"

"For buying his train ticket."

So that's how Bailey had worked it. He knew the police would be watching the depot. "Where'd you see him last?"

Henry nodded eastward. "Out by the baggage carts."

The plan was becoming obvious. Bailey had sent Henry in to buy a ticket. That's why nobody had seen Bailey. Then he'd wait till the very last minute and jump out of the shadows and board the train. He'd hide somewhere aboard until the train was thirty, forty miles down the line.

"Where was the ticket to?"

"Chicago."

A good place to get lost in, Anna thought.

"He said he'd pay you five dollars?"

"Yeah. But he only paid me two. Said that was all the cash he had on him. I went over and started drinkin' and the more I thought of it, the madder I got. So I come back here."

"I appreciate this, Henry."

"You see him, you tell him he owes me three dollars."

"I'll tell him, Henry. Don't worry."

Things were working out for Bailey. A heavy autumnal fog was even heavier, rolling in, snaking silver across everything. You couldn't see more than a yard or so in front of you.

She started making her way down the platform. She'd decided to use the Chief's Navy Colt, after all. She gripped it tight in her right hand.

She heard somebody walking toward her. She ducked behind an empty baggage cart, one as large as a small horse-drawn utility wagon. She raised the gun, ready to use it if necessary.

An older couple, the Mayples, appeared out of the fog. Selma Mayples had on the tiny straw hat with the merry red band she wore whenever she left the house. Stout Sam Mayples was carrying a small suitcase. Selma must be visiting her sick sister in Rock Island again.

After they passed, she resumed her search. She walked up and down the platform twice, searching in, under and around anything that looked even vaguely like a hiding place. She had no better luck outside than she'd had inside.

She was just about to give up when she heard a horse neigh somewhere in the gloom. The cabs. This late at night, there'd be only one cab working. But a couple of the drivers always left their cabs here. The livery was close by. They'd just walk their horses over in the morning and they'd be ready to go.

She found the shapes of three empty cabs down by the wagons. In the fog, the wagon beds resembled coffins. She had her gun drawn, ready.

Night sounds. Player piano music from a tavern somewhere. The rail-thrumming buzz of a distant train. Fog-muted conversation from inside the depot.

She walked up to the first wagon. Checked out the bed. Empty. Moved on to the second wagon. Also empty.

Was just moving to the third wagon, when he suddenly lurched from the murk—the smell of whiskey, the rustle of his wool suit—and brought the handle of his six-shooter down on the side of her head. But she'd just been turning away from him and so the impact of his blow lost most of its effectiveness.

Bailey made the mistake of trying to hit her a second time. He moved too far in and this time—despite the pain he'd inflicted—she was ready for him. He found himself facing the barrel of her Colt.

"Give me your gun."

He hesitated. Then she put the barrel of her weapon directly against his left eye and slowly eased back the trigger.

"Your gun."

He handed her the gun.

"The Chief wants to talk to you," Anna said.

"For what?"

"For killing Anthea last night, and your wife Beatrice tonight."

She couldn't see him well enough to read his expression. But when she mentioned Beatrice, an animal cry seemed to stick in his throat. "Beatrice? Beatrice is dead?"

"You don't know anything about it, of course?"

"My God. You're talking about my wife. I would never kill her."

She thought of Murchison saying essentially the same thing about his own wife's death. They were both apparently reading from the same bad play.

"I didn't kill her, Anna. I really didn't."

"We'll talk to the Chief about that."

She took his shoulder, turned him around so that he faced the depot. "We'll walk to the depot then take the alley over to the station. Just remember I have a gun."

"He must have done it."

"Who?"

"Kevin. He thought she loved him. She must've changed her mind and then he killed her. He was never satisfied with just seducing them. They had to fall in love with him, too." His words were bitter yet tired, the force of them fading in the fog. "The way he got Karen Hastings to fall in love with him. He thought that was such a conquest."

"Who's Karen Hastings?"

"You met her yesterday. At the theater. In Kevin's office."

"I thought her name was Remington."

"Oh—sorry. Hastings was the name she used at the theater. It was her maiden name."

"C'mon, now. Move."

"But I didn't do anything. I really didn't."

"You're part of an insurance fraud if nothing else."

She nudged him with the gun.

The tracks thrummed louder now. The train was approaching. Passengers were drifting to the platform, carrying carpetbags and suitcases and even a trunk or two. This late at night, and the fog so heavy, the festive air common to the depot was gone. The passengers just wanted to get on board and be gone. A couple of Mesquakie Indians shivered inside the colorful blankets they had wrapped around themselves.

And then Anna saw the woman they'd just been talking about, Karen Remington. She was just now hurrying out the depot door to the platform. She wore a vast picture hat that did a good job of concealing her face, as the Russian-style greatcoat concealed her figure. Anna wouldn't have recognized her but Bailey did. "Karen!"

The Remington woman swung her face away from Bailey and tried to hurry to the edge of the platform. Obviously, she didn't want to be seen. Bailey started to reach out for her but Karen Remington raised her hand to keep him away.

And when Anna saw the large, pale hand—and the ring with the H on the large, pale hand—she remembered the indentation on the headboard in Anthea Murchison's hotel room. A ring had put that indentation in the headboard, probably when the hand was flung against the wood as the killer was wrestling with Anthea. A ring with the letter H on it. Karen Hastings Remington was the killer Anna was looking for.

It was dawn before Karen Remington told Anna and the Chief what had really happened. When Karen learned that Anthea was back in town, she was afraid that Anthea would steal Kevin back. So she killed her. Then when Kevin spurned her for Beatrice, she decided to end his life in an especially nasty way—kill the woman he loved, and see to it that he was hanged for that murder.

Anna used the new typewriter to pound out a confession for Karen Remington to sign. By this time, Karen's blustery husband was in the station making all sorts of threats to the Chief and talking about what an outrage it was to even *suspect* a woman of such high reputation of murder. He even summoned a few more of his firm's lawyers to come to the station and badger the Chief.

Anna reached home about noon. Mrs. Goldman fed her warm tomato soup and a cheese sandwich Anna took the latest Nick Carter suspense story upstairs with her. She didn't get much further than the part where Nick disguised himself as a blind Chinese wise man so he could infiltrate the Tong gangs that had been plaguing the city.

Nick would have to wait. So would everything and everybody else. She slept.

WOOLLIES

by James Reasoner

James Reasoner's career has too long been buried beneath pseudonyms, but in recent years that has begun to change. Now he is the author of Manassas, *the first of a planned eight books about the Civil War, and this dandy little tale about a railroad detective which sort of takes him back to the form he started with, the private eye story. His* Texas Wind *(1980) is a cult favorite in the mystery field, but James is reaching beyond cult status now.*

A knot of angry men waited on the platform of the train station. Dan Boyd leaned out the partially open door of the last freight car and looked along the tracks toward them as the train began to slow. The settlement behind the station was small, a single street with half a dozen buildings on either side. The men who had gathered here today to meet the train were not from the town. They had ridden in from the ranches scattered across the Wyoming grasslands that rolled all the way to the mountains in the distance.

Boyd moved back away from the door and bent to pick up his shotgun. He was a medium-sized man in boots, jeans, and, appropriately enough, a sheepskin coat. Prematurely white hair showed under his broad-brimmed black hat with its Montana pinch. His tanned face was deceptively mild, with plenty of laugh lines around his mouth and eyes.

The big Baldwin locomotive's brakes squealed as it shuddered to a halt. The single passenger car was lined up alongside the platform, with the freight cars behind it. The ranchers streamed down the steps from the platform and stalked along the tracks.

Boyd stepped into the doorway again, the greener tucked under his arm. "Howdy, boys," he said in a commanding voice.

The ranchers stopped short and looked up at him. One of them in the forefront of the group demanded, "Who're you?"

Boyd shifted his body so that the left side of the sheepskin coat pulled back to reveal the badge pinned to his black corduroy vest. "Just doin' a little job for the railroad."

"Damn it, you'll step down out of there if you know what's good for you."

Boyd smiled faintly and said, "You know, I've always had a problem figurin' that out."

The rancher who had assumed the role of spokesman cursed and stepped forward, and the twin barrels of the shotgun moved slightly and somehow wound up pointing right at him. One of the other men reached out and caught the sleeve of his coat.

"Wait a minute, Carl. That fella looks familiar. Think I saw him back in Kansas once . . ."

"I've been there," Boyd allowed.

"And he was wearing a badge then, too, but it wasn't no railroad detective's badge." The second rancher was beginning to sound worried. "I think he was a real lawman then."

"Deputy United States marshal," Boyd said. "Retired now. Name's Dan Boyd."

That quieted the muttering. There was silence except for the hiss of steam from the engine and the bleating of the sheep behind Boyd. After a minute, one of the ranchers said, "The fella who broke up the Walsh gang?"

Boyd nodded. "I was in on that job. Had a lot of help."

The second man pulled again on the sleeve of the first. "We better not do this, Carl."

Carl waved a hand toward the freight car. "He's got a bunch of damned woollies in there! You want those monsters on our range?"

"These sheep aren't being unloaded here," Boyd said. "They're bound for Bitter Rock. And I'm bound to see that they get there."

The conductor came along the tracks and asked, "Any trouble here, Mr. Boyd?"

Boyd looked at the ranchers. For the most part, the fight had gone out of them. Boyd said, "I don't think so."

"You ought to be ashamed of yourself," Carl said. "You're ruinin' the range for honest cattlemen. And from the looks of you, you might've herded a few cows yourself sometime."

Boyd said, "I'm workin' for the railroad now, and I intend to see that these critters get where they're goin'."

Carl leaned over and spat, then turned and walked away without looking back. One by one, the other ranchers followed him.

The conductor took off his cap. Despite the cool wind blowing across the plains, he had beads of sweat on his forehead. He wiped them away with a handkerchief and said, "I sure wish word hadn't gotten out about these damned sheep."

"They say bad news travels fast," Boyd said.

He had fixed up one corner of the freight car for himself, with a stool to sit on and a barrel to serve as a table of sorts. After the train had taken on water and pulled out again, he sat down and slipped a deck of cards from an inside pocket. The top of the barrel wasn't hardly big enough, but he managed to lay out a game of solitaire. He would have sighed, but that would mean taking a deep breath, and to tell the truth, the sheep really didn't smell very good.

Boyd wished Carl hadn't said that about being ashamed of himself. The rancher's guess had been right: Boyd had worked as a cowboy for quite a spell down in Texas before becoming a lawman. He had been a top hand, too, had even been foreman on a couple of spreads. But that was a long time in the past.

In the years since, he had carried a badge first as a county sheriff, then a deputy marshal, and finally now as a railroad detective, working for an agency that was kept on retainer by the Union Pacific and dozens of smaller lines. He enjoyed the work. It took him all over the country, and he had always been the fiddle-footed sort. And tracking down lawbreakers was what he did best.

So now what was he doing? Guarding a bunch of bleating woollies, probably some of the stupidest creatures on God's green earth. But that was the job he'd been given, and Boyd was going to do his best to carry it out.

He glanced over his shoulder at one of the animals that was in a pen by itself. A massive ram, thick-bodied and taller than the other sheep, with a pair of magnificent horns that curved up and out and back over its head. All the way from

England it had come, bound for the sheep ranch of some Scotsman who had settled here in Wyoming. And worth a pretty penny, too. All the other sheep could be replaced, but not that ram. It was to be the basis of the Scotsman's herd.

The massive head swung toward Boyd, as if the ram knew he was looking at it. Boyd doubted that; that would be giving the critter credit for too much sense. But he had to admit, the ram had a certain . . . dignity . . . about it, much like the same bearing Boyd had seen in longhorn bulls in the past.

Boyd chuckled and turned back to his game. "Better watch it, Danny boy," he said aloud to himself. "Keep it up and they'll be calling you a sheepman."

He had just laid a red jack on a black queen when he heard the loud boom toward the front of the train.

The explosion must have been a big one for Boyd to hear it over the clattering of the car's wheels on the tracks. He came up off the stool and snatched the shotgun from the floor. As he started toward the door, the whole train jolted violently. Boyd was thrown off his feet.

The sheep had grown accustomed to the rocking of the train, but this being jerked around was something new. Their bleating became panic-stricken, and the caterwauling assaulted Boyd's ears as he rolled over and came up on his hands and knees. He had dropped the greener, and he was reaching for it when the whole freight car began to tip. The shotgun slid out the open door before Boyd could get his fingers on it.

Then the car went over, and what felt like a whole mountain of woolly bodies fell on him. That was the last thing he knew for a while.

Boyd fought his way up out of a blackness that stank of sheep. He felt hands pulling at him and managed to grab on to one of them. He opened his eyes and found himself sitting on the ground. The gravel-covered embankment of the railroad right-of-way was a few yards away.

"You all right, Mr. Boyd?" a voice asked anxiously. "Damn, I thought sure you were dead when I pulled you out of all those sheep carcasses."

Boyd's head hurt. He lifted a hand to it and the fingers came away sticky with blood. He had a gash on his forehead, but as far as he could tell, everything else was all right. He said to the conductor leaning over him, "Help me up."

The man took Boyd's arm and steadied him. Boyd pushed himself to his feet and looked along the tracks at the wreckage of the derailed train. The engine was lying over on its side, as was the coal tender. The passenger car had broken apart when it tipped, which was probably what had kept the freight cars from overturning completely. They were sitting at a crazy angle. The caboose was the only car that had remained completely on the tracks.

Dead sheep were lying everywhere.

"Anybody killed besides those woollies?" Boyd asked.

"No, we were mighty lucky. Weren't many passengers. If the car had been full, somebody would've been killed, sure as sin. As it is, they're mighty shaken up. Got a few broken bones and bad cuts."

Boyd walked a step or two to make sure all his muscles and bones worked right. They did.

"I was in the caboose," the conductor went on. "Reckon that's what saved me."

"Dynamited the tracks, didn't they?"

The conductor nodded. "The engineer never had a chance to stop in time. All him and the fireman could do was jump out of the cab and hope for the best." The man's cap was gone, lost in the derailment. He ran a hand over his balding head and said quietly but fervently, "The sons of bitches."

Boyd knew he meant the men who had caused the derailment, not the engineer and fireman. "You sent for help?"

"Yeah, the fireman was able to shinny up a telegraph pole and cut in on the wire. He's already sent a message on to Bitter Rock. No telling how long it'll be before a relief train gets out here, though."

Boyd walked slowly through the carnage, followed by the conductor. Some of the sheep had been killed outright by the crash, while others were injured and bleating piteously. Many had not been hurt at all and had wandered off. Boyd saw them dotted across the rangeland that bordered the tracks. Being sheep, they had already forgotten all about what had happened and were grazing on the sparse grass, which would be even more sparse when they were finished with it.

Boyd looked for the ram and didn't see it. He climbed carefully onto the side of the freight car and peered in through the open door. The ram's pen was empty. It was not among the dead animals, and as Boyd hopped down and looked out across the prairie for that distinctive set of horns, he failed to spot them.

"Got a pair of field glasses in the caboose?" he asked.

The conductor nodded. "Sure do."

"I need them."

He swept the field glasses over the plains, studying each group of sheep. The ram was nowhere to be seen. Boyd didn't think it would have wandered completely out of sight on its own.

"Did you see anybody around the spot where the tracks blew?"

The conductor shook his head. "No, but the engineer thought he saw some men on horseback after the locomotive went over."

"Let's go talk to him."

The engineer had a broken ankle from his desperate leap from the cab. He was white-faced with pain as he sat braced against a rock, but his voice was strong and angry as he told Boyd, "Yeah, I saw half a dozen riders. They came up out of that gully and rode alongside the tracks. I thought they might shoot me, but they didn't."

"Where did they go?"

The engineer shook his head. "Sorry, Mr. Boyd, but I don't know. The last I saw of 'em, they were rounding the back of the caboose."

"Must've been right after the crash," the conductor put in. "I hit my head and was knocked silly for a few minutes before I was able to get outside."

Boyd was anxious to take a look around, but the conductor insisted that he let that gash on his head be tended to. The conductor cleaned it with a rag soaked in whiskey, then bound a strip of cloth around it. Boyd retrieved his hat, knocked it back into shape, and gingerly settled it on his head. Then he went to look for hoofprints.

He had been taught to read sign by an old Texas Ranger who had once ridden with Captain John Coffee Hays and fought in the battle of Bandera Pass. But even a raw kid could have found the hoofprints and figured out the story they told. The only problem was that some of the prints had been obscured by the sharp hooves of the wandering sheep. Still, Boyd was able to tell which direction the riders had driven the ram.

"I'll be going after them," he said.

"On foot?"

"If I have to."

Boyd stripped off the sheepskin coat and draped it over his arm. The afternoon sun had grown warm. Without the coat on, the ivory-handled butts of the twin Colts he wore holstered on his hips were revealed. He started walking north, following the tracks left by the riders.

"What'll I tell the supervisor?" the conductor yelled after him.

Boyd paused long enough to call back, "Tell him I've gone after the men who did this."

He had spotted the thin plume of smoke about a mile north of the tracks before he ever left the wrecked train. The conductor had not seen it, his eyes not being as keen as Boyd's. The mile walk was enough to make Boyd's feet ache pretty badly, and he was glad to see the small ranch house and barn at the bottom of one of the rolling hills.

A couple of dogs started barking and rushed out from the house as he walked down the slope. They were fierce, bushy creatures, but they stopped barking and growling as Boyd approached. He had always gotten along well with animals. He wasn't particularly worried about the dogs.

He could not have said the same about the woman who stepped out of the cabin with a Winchester in her hands.

She was tall, honed down to the leanness that the frontier imposed on most people, male and female alike. She held the rifle like she knew how to use it, and her voice was flinty as she called, "Stop right there, mister."

Boyd smiled and lifted both hands a little. "I'm not looking for trouble, ma'am."

"Well, you've found it. We don't like strangers around here."

"Even ones who're afoot?"

"What happened to your horse?"

The big white gelding was back in Cheyenne as far as Boyd knew, in its usual stall at the livery stable. He hadn't figured he would need a mount on this job, just riding the train to Bitter Rock and back.

"I'm off the train that derailed a while ago," he said, not really answering the woman's question about his horse.

"I don't know anything about a train derailing."

"Didn't figure you did. I'm looking for the men responsible for the accident. Half a dozen or so of them. They came this way on horseback."

The woman shook her head. The breeze plucked at her short, fair hair. "It's a big country. Nobody stopped here today. They must've gone around."

"Yes, ma'am," Boyd agreed. "That's what their tracks show. I was just hopin' you might have a horse you could lend me. Or sell me, if need be."

She frowned. "You're a lawman?"

"Railroad detective."

"And you walked up here from the railroad tracks?"

"Yes, ma'am."

For the first time, she didn't sound completely hostile as she said, "Your feet must hurt."

"A mite. More than that, actually. I'd surely admire to sit down for a spell, but I don't have the time. Now, about that horse . . ."

The woman lowered the rifle but kept it pointing in Boyd's general direction. "Come on. We have a couple of horses in the barn. You're welcome to the use of one of them."

Boyd nodded and said, "Much obliged, ma'am. And by the way, I'd appreciate it if you'd tell the boy not to shoot me. I don't know if he heard you or not."

She looked surprised for a minute, then turned and waved her free hand at the small figure crouched in the shadows just inside the open window of the hayloft in the barn. The barrel of another rifle was pulled back into the barn.

"You knew all along, didn't you?" the woman asked as Boyd walked into the small yard between the cabin and the barn.

"Yes, ma'am, but it's my job to notice things." Like how this place was a little run-down, he thought, as if there was no man around to keep it fixed up. Chances were something had happened to him, and the woman and the boy were trying to keep the spread going by themselves, probably because they didn't have any other place to go back to.

"I'm Sarah Lennox. Mrs. Lennox. My husband Tim's out on the range, ought to be back any time now."

"Yes'm." Boyd nodded, letting her continue the fiction if she wanted to. "What's your boy's name?"

"She's not a boy. Her name's Roberta."

The girl came out of the barn. She was ten, maybe eleven, and the rifle she was carrying was about as big as she was. She looked at Boyd and asked, "What happened to your head?"

"I hit it accidentally," he told her, "when some bad men wrecked the train I was ridin' on. I'm after them now."

"I hope you catch them," Roberta Lennox said solemnly.

"So do I, honey, so do I." Boyd turned to the girl's mother. "I reckon I'd better see about that horse."

Sarah Lennox sent her daughter in the house and followed Boyd into the barn. While he was saddling the horse he picked out, a decent-looking black, he talked to the woman and found out a few things.

"How many head are you running?"

"We . . . we don't have cattle. We have sheep."

"Had any trouble with the ranchers over them?"

"No, not since—"

Boyd drew the cinch tight. "Killed your husband, did they?" He had already spotted the marker under the tree behind the barn.

Sarah Lennox's hands tightened on the Winchester.

"They said nobody meant for it to go that far. They were trying to rimrock our herd. Tim got in front of them to try to head them off, and one of the rams knocked him over the cliff. He broke his neck." She lifted her head defiantly. "I reckon they were ashamed of what they'd done, especially when I told them they'd have to kill me and Roberta, too, to get rid of us. Otherwise, we were staying. It takes us both to handle the sheep we have left, but we'll make do. Roberta's a hard worker."

"I'll bet she is," Boyd agreed. He finished adjusting the stirrups for his longer legs. "What did the law say about your husband's death?"

She laughed humorlessly. "The cattlemen *are* the law out here. Nothing was ever done about it. I don't know why I'm telling you all this. You work for the railroad, and the railroad and the cattlemen are thick as thieves."

That hurt, the way she lumped him in with all the others, but he couldn't really blame her, either. And he didn't have the time to try to set her straight.

"I'm obliged for the use of the horse. I'll bring him back safe and see that you're paid, too."

Sarah Lennox shook her head. "It doesn't matter. I just won't see a man afoot."

Boyd swung up into the saddle and tugged on the brim of his hat before he rode out of the barn and took up the trail again.

They weren't expecting anybody to come after them, that much was clear to Boyd's experienced eyes. Once they were out of sight of the wrecked train, they had slowed down and taken their own sweet time. The trail turned to the west, paralleling the railroad tracks. By nightfall, Boyd had made up a lot of the lead they had on him. Off to the southwest somewhere was Bitter Rock. To the northwest was the range claimed by the Scotsman, MacPhee.

It was getting dark when Boyd's nose caught the faint tang of woodsmoke. He didn't need to be able to see very well to follow that trail. He kept riding, letting the black pick its way. The terrain had grown more rugged and rocky, and Boyd was careful not to let the horse make too much noise.

When the smoke smell was strong and he heard the faint murmur of voices, he reined in and dismounted. After tying the black's reins to a greasewood bush, he started forward on foot. He caught a glimpse of a small orange glow in the darkness and closed in on it until he could see the campfire and the men gathered around it.

Their horses were tied nearby, and on the opposite side of the fire, tied to a stake, was the ram. Most sheep would have been bleating in annoyance and fear, but not the ram. It just stood there, not even grazing, balefully regarding the men grouped around the fire.

". . . goes against the grain, that's for sure," one of the men was saying.

"I know what you mean," another man agreed. "If it was up to me, I'd just shoot the damned thing and be done with it."

A third man snapped, "That's not what we're being paid for, and you know it. The boss said if that ram was to live through the wreck, we had to bring it with us to collect the rest of the money he owes us."

"How would he know what happened? We could tell him the blamed woolly got itself killed."

"And risk him findin' out later?" The third man snorted in contempt. "I don't reckon so. Just hush your complainin'. He'll be here 'fore long."

That bit of information was enough to make Boyd wait patiently atop the small hill where he was hidden. He slipped his coat on, since the night was getting chilly. His fingers moved over the sheepskin lining for a moment.

Half an hour later, he heard horses approaching. He lifted his head so that he could see over the crest of the hill. Two men rode into the small circle of light thrown by the campfire.

"I see ye found 'im," one of the newcomers said without preamble, in an accented voice.

"That's the one you wanted, ain't it?" one of the men asked. "We figured it had to be, with those horns."

"Aye." The man reached into his coat. In the firelight, his face was bony and red under the brim of a hat. He took out a pouch and tossed it to one of the men around the fire. "There's the rest o' yer pay."

Boyd came to his feet, stepped up onto the top of the hill, and shouted, "MacPhee!" It was a damn-fool play and he knew it, but he was too angry to do anything else.

The red-faced man twisted in the saddle and bellowed, "Whoever he is, kill 'im!"

Both of the ivory-handled guns flickered out of their holsters. The left-hand gun put a slug in the middle of one of the men who had wrecked the train. The right-hand gun blasted a couple of shots around the feet of the horses. Spooked, the animals tore loose and stampeded, knocking down a couple of the men and thundering through the campfire, scattering sparks and ashes. Boyd fired the left-hand gun again and saw the red-faced man sag in his saddle. He darted back, putting the hill between him and the guns of the other men, and turned to race back to the black.

He jerked the reins loose, then swung up and kicked the horse into a run. In the back of his mind, he was chiding himself for acting so rashly. For most of his life, he had been able to stay cool and calm, no matter what the provocation; that was the only way he had lived so long. Yet the sheer callousness he had witnessed today was more than he could stand.

Using his instincts to guide him, he circled wide around the fire and started in. Shots were banging on the far side of the camp as some of the men pursued where they thought he was. They were wasting bullets. Boyd drove the black ahead and suddenly a horse loomed up in front of him. A muzzle flash split the night. Boyd sensed the slug whipping past him as he fired. The man groaned and pitched off the horse. Boyd lunged the black past the now-riderless horse, slowing only long enough to reach over and snag a Winchester he had spotted sticking up from a saddle boot.

The shots brought the rest of the gang hurrying back. Boyd heard them coming and lifted the rifle to his shoulder. He didn't know how many rounds were in it, but he fired into the darkness as fast as he could work the Winchester's lever. The shots were deafening, but as their echoes faded, he heard a man yell, "That's enough! I'm gettin' out of here!"

The Winchester was a .44, like Boyd's Colts. Boyd took cartridges from the loops on his shell belt and fed them into the rifle. He kneed the black forward. The campfire was just scattered embers now, but they gave off enough of a red glow for Boyd to see the dark shape sprawled on the ground.

"Did . . . did ye get 'im?"

The raspy whisper came from the man on the ground. Boyd said, "No, MacPhee, they didn't."

He heard horses running in the night, the sound of the hooves fading. The other men had caught their mounts and were pulling out. Dynamiting a train was one thing, but they hadn't been paid enough to fight it out with a crazy man, especially one who could shoot and move like Dan Boyd.

MacPhee didn't say anything for a long moment. He might have been dead, had it not been for his harsh breathing. Finally, he asked, "Who are ye?"

"The man who was supposed to deliver that ram safely to you."

"Th . . . th' railroad man . . . why . . . why did ye do this?"

"Why did you pay those owlhoots to wreck the train and then bring the ram to you if it lived through the crash?" Boyd didn't wait for MacPhee to answer. "You planned to sue the railroad for the cost of the herd. If the ram was killed or lost, the cost would go up that much more. But you still wanted the ram."

"Th' bloody thing's worth . . . ten thousand dollars!"

"So you pocket the payoff from the railroad's insurance company and with a little bit of luck still get the ram, and all you had to do was wreck the train and risk the lives of everyone on it."

MacPhee started to laugh, a bubbling sound that showed how badly he was hit. "Ye must think . . . I carried a Scotsman's thrift . . . a wee bit far . . ."

"It doesn't have anything to do with you being a Scotsman," Boyd told him. "You're just a greedy, coldblooded son of a bitch."

MacPhee found the strength somewhere to jerk up his arm. The pistol in his hand cracked, the bullet taking a chunk out of the brim of Boyd's hat. Boyd fired the Winchester one-handed from the back of the horse. MacPhee flopped back on the ground. He didn't move again.

Boyd walked the black over to the ram, which had stood there stolidly through the entire fracas. All the lead that had flown around had missed the ram somehow. Boyd dismounted and pulled up the stake, then, holding the lead rope, swung back into the saddle.

"Come on, you damned woolly," he told the ram.

"You never found them?" the supervisor of the rail line asked in disbelief as he sat in his office in Cheyenne with Boyd two days later.

Boyd shook his head. "Nope. Bein' afoot like I was, there was nothing I could do but turn around and come back."

The supervisor leaned forward and shuffled some papers on his desk. "As it turns out, Alexander MacPhee was killed in a hunting accident the very same day as the train wreck."

"First I've heard of it," Boyd said.

"Under the circumstances, we'll be lucky if his estate doesn't bring suit against us for the animals that were killed or lost."

"I wouldn't worry about that." Boyd had already done some straight talking to MacPhee's lawyer, whose office was just down the street. The man had agreed that MacPhee's family back in Scotland wouldn't want the truth to get out. It seemed, according to the lawyer, that MacPhee had always been something of a black sheep.

Boyd had almost laughed out loud when the lawyer said that.

"Well, I must say I'm disappointed in you, Mr. Boyd. You have a reputation as a man who seldom fails in his duty."

Boyd shook his head solemnly. "I reckon nobody can come out on top every time."

"I'll be speaking to the head of your agency."

"Yes, sir. I expect you will."

A few minutes later, Boyd stepped out into the brisk morning air and grinned. One good thing about getting a little older, he reflected, was that winning and losing no longer

mattered quite as much. He had experienced enough tri-
umphs in his lifetime; he could swallow one defeat.

Especially when he thought about what the looks must
have been like on the faces of Sarah and Roberta Lennox
when they found that ram in their barn the next morning,
along with the borrowed horse and a note of thanks from
Boyd. The postscript to the note, scrawled on a scrap of
paper with the stub of pencil he always carried, had read:

"Found this critter up in the hills. It doesn't seem to belong
to anybody, so I figured you folks could give it a good home."

MAINTIEN LE DROIT

by Tim Champlin

Tim Champlin has long been a favorite of mine among Western novelists, and he has written too few novels. I was very pleased when he agreed to contribute to this anthology, and even more so when he chose to write about the Northwest Canadian Mounties. His most recent novels are Swift Thunder *and* Shadow Catcher.

Constable Derek Barker threw back the bearskin cover and sprang from the bunk, clad only in wool socks and longjohns. He caught his breath as the heavy cold in the one-room log cabin shocked him like a plunge into an icy stream. Clenching his teeth and shivering violently, he opened the wrought-iron door of the squat stove and thrust a handful of long splinters into the banked coals. In the several seconds it took for them to blaze up, he glanced at the dull gray light filtering through the small window. Frost an inch thick covered the glass pane from top to bottom. But he didn't need to see the spirit thermometer hanging under the eave just outside to know that it showed a reading of minus thirty or lower.

"Probably at least ten below in here," he muttered aloud.

The thin splinters flared up and he quickly added three hunks of split, dried oak from the wood box. He briefly considered jumping back into the warmth of the feather tick and bearskin, but forced the temptation aside and grabbed his clothes hanging from a nearby chair. He knew he would never toughen himself to the cold if he continued to give in to his whining flesh. He pulled on his breeches and long boots, then the red tunic and, until the fire drove the cold into the corners, his long sheepskin coat and his peaked, straight-brimmed Stetson. Then he proceeded to add more wood to the stove and fix breakfast, setting some pre-sliced strips of venison in a frying pan on the stove lid to thaw, along with a blackened coffee pot filled with solid ice.

The other man assigned to this outpost, Sergeant Cecil McKee, was an early riser and would have had all this done, but he was gone on patrol downriver and not expected back until sometime tomorrow night.

Just yesterday, Barker had turned the page on the wall calendar to April 1899 and he reflected that he was close to surviving his second winter in the Yukon with nothing worse than a mild case of cabin fever—no scurvy, no frostbite, no broken bones, no lacerations from ricocheting axes or the slashing fangs of his half-wild sled dogs, no madness brought on by the isolation of weeks of darkness on this frozen tip of the planet. It was more than could be said of most men who chose to winter in the subarctic. He smiled grimly to himself, knowing that the flood of prospectors, along with foreign settlers and tradesmen, expected members of the Northwest Mounted Police to be bigger than life, to have the solutions to all problems and to be even-handed dispensers of justice. It was as if the red uniform endowed them with some special powers.

He stepped outside into the biting cold and, taking the short axe from the woodpile, chopped some hunks of frozen fish from the cache beside the cabin and threw one piece to each of the sled dogs who were sheltering in a lean-to behind the cabin. Then he scooped a bucket of clean snow and added some chunks of icicles from the low roof to thaw for water.

As he went about his routine chores, he pictured the sun passing a little higher across the sky each day. In its strengthening rays, icicles were beginning to form on the south-facing side of their cabin. The spring breakup was still several weeks away, and winter had not yet shown any real signs of relaxing its iron grip, but Barker knew he had weathered the worst of it. As he chewed his beans and venison, he thought again of requesting a transfer to Regina Barracks or Fort Macleod, or one of the more southern posts. They still had bitter winters, but those forts would seem almost tropical by comparison to the lonely outpost he and McKee shared on the Stewart River. They'd been on detached duty for two years, responsible for patrolling hundreds of square miles. At age thirty-one, he was a ten-year veteran of the Northwest Mounted Police. But, for many months, he'd ridden nothing but sleds or canoes. At the forts to the south, he would lose his independence and be subject to much external discipline, routine mounted drill, and would be dealing with persistent whiskey traders and horse thieves, who were as hard to stamp out as ticks in summer.

The rush to the goldfields had forestalled the dissolution of the force by the Canadian Parliament, and now it was rumored the law would be amended to allow men to retire from the mounted police with a pension after twenty years service or on disability. Should he try to wait it out? Or should he resign while he was still young enough to find another occupation? He had no other skills or interests. Sighing deeply, he drained his cup of tepid tea. For better or worse, he was astride this horse, and determined to ride until he was thrown.

He finished eating and donned his coat again, then his fur hat to go outside and split more firewood for the voracious stove. As he opened the door he heard the unmistakable sound of a whip cracking and the distant yell of a human voice. He knew that hail. It was Julien Beaudoin, the half-breed mail carrier approaching from upriver. Until this winter, when Beaudoin had been hired to haul the mail, he and McKee had performed this additional duty—for no extra pay. He had to admit the half-breed kept to a much better schedule, even in the most extreme weather.

Barker stepped outside as Beaudoin swung his dog team in toward the cabin. Barker caught a glimpse of white teeth flashing in a dark face. "Constable!" The man's face was nearly hidden in the fur hood and the wreath of steamy breath.

"Julien!" Barker raised a mittened hand. "Come inside for a cup of hot tea."

The half-breed grinned his appreciation, and threw a loop of rope around the wood-splitting stump to anchor his sled before starting for the door.

"Whew! She ees frosty!" he exclaimed, pulling off his mittens and raking at the ice in his mustache.

"Thirty-six below, according to my thermometer," Barker stated. "Spring is just around the corner," he added, grinning. He handed the mailman a mug of steaming black tea. The half-breed helped himself to a spoonful of sugar and began stirring it.

"Any news?" Barker asked, shrugging out of his sheep-skin coat.

"When I left Seely Creek there was one beeg ruckus."

Barker arched his eyebrows in silent query.

The half-breed threw his hood back and was standing as near as he dared to the hot stove. Melting snow dripped from his mukluks to the bare board floor. "Claim jumper," he replied. "Cheechako. Man name Arnold Klegg." Beaudoin sipped the scalding tea and Barker waited patiently for him to continue. "Gunnar Herbert caught him stealing from hees cache, too."

Barker gave a low whistle. "Trouble. Herbert isn't one to let that slide."

Beaudoin brushed his shaggy black hair from his forehead with stubby fingers. "Herbert ees a bad man."

"Intolerant, maybe," Barker said. "Never gives an inch. Did he send you to tell me so I can arrest Klegg?"

"Oh, no, m'sieur. They weell hold miners' court today or tomorrow."

"We know what the outcome of that will be," Barker mused, staring at the mug in his hand. "They'll hang him, sure. They should have sent for me."

"Ees eet not justice?"

"Only if there's no established law available. And, if Herbert is running things, it'll be more like vengeance. I've got to get there before it's too late." He reached for his coat. "You got time to help me hitch up the dogs?"

"Don't tell heem I sent you, m'sieur," Beaudoin said. "Herbert weel keel me."

"As far as he'll know, I'm just on routine patrol." On a sudden impulse, he reached up to a shelf for his sabretache—the square leather case that hung from his saber belt when he was on mounted parade. The brass, convex badge of the Mounties was worn attached to this sabretache. The badge was beautifully wrought with the embossed head of a bull buffalo in the center. Surrounding this head were the words "NORTHWEST MOUNTED POLICE— CANADA"—and, across the bottom, "*Maintien Le Droit*"—Maintain The Right. The head and inscriptions were enclosed in a cluster of maple leaves topped by a crown. He unfastened the badge, polished it on his pants leg, and pinned it prominently to the front of his fur cap.

Both man and dogs were fresh and the thirty-three-mile run to Seely Creek took only six hours. The sun had been covered by a gray pall of clouds almost as soon as it cleared the horizon and Barker guessed the temperature had risen to only ten below by noon. The sled was unburdened and the snow dry, so they made good time, following mostly in the backtrack of the mail carrier. He ran behind to keep warm, alternately riding the sled to rest. Several times, to make even more speed, Barker took the team off the trail onto the frozen river where the runners fairly sang along the ice, cutting through patches of powdery snow here and there. He rode the backs of the runners with the cold wind stinging tears to his eyes and blood to his cheeks. It felt good to be out on the trail again after nearly a week indoors.

After two short stops to rest the dogs, he arrived at the cluster of cabins on Seely Creek about mid-afternoon. He rapped with the butt of his whip on the whipsawed plank door of the largest cabin.

The latch was lifted and a face thrust out. "Yeah?"

Barker had opened his long coat so that his scarlet tunic was plainly visible, to go along with the badge on his fur hat. "Constable Barker on patrol," he announced, although Gunnar Herbert knew him on sight. "Mind if I have a look inside?"

"Ain't nothing here to see," Herbert growled.

"Nevertheless, let's have a short chat, then. I've come a long way and my dogs need some rest," he replied, evenly. "You wouldn't have something hot you could offer a man to drink, now would you?" He knew Herbert couldn't refuse to provide the customary hospitality without incurring suspicion. The policeman moved forward to enter, but Herbert stood his ground in the doorway.

"We're kinda busy just now, Barker. Maybe on your way back through . . ."

"This won't take long," Barker persisted.

Herbert squinted at him in the long rays of the declining sun shooting through a break in the clouds. The Swede was ruggedly handsome, Barker thought. Blue eyes, angular jaw and strong nose, eyebrows so blond they were almost invisible against the pale skin. Blond hair with a reddish tint. A big, rawboned man at least three inches taller than Barker, and probably tipping the scales at more than two hundred pounds. His clean-shaven face was flushing pink in the biting cold.

"Shut the damn door! We just got it warmed up in here!" a voice yelled from inside.

Reluctantly, Herbert moved aside for the Mountie to enter. "Well, if you have to . . ."

Before his eyes adjusted to the dimness, Barker's nose sensed a miasma of unwashed bodies and damp wool, mingled with wood and tobacco smoke. He slid along the wall, just inside the door, hand inside his coat near the flap of his holster. Slowly his eyes adjusted and he counted nine men in the room, most of whom he recognized—bearded miners he'd favored with help at one time or another. But now their eyes were hostile and suspicious. Then he saw why. He'd apparently interrupted preparations for a hanging. A thin man with black, curly hair was bound with rope and was being escorted toward the door by two miners. A third man carried a coil of rope with a hangman's noose fashioned in one end of it.

"What's going on, boys?" Barker asked, a hard edge to his voice.

No one answered at first. Then Herbert said, "We just had a trial. This cheechako was convicted and is about to hang for robbery and claim-jumping. Caught in the act," he added, as if that eliminated any doubts.

"If he's a newcomer, it might've been an honest mistake," Barker suggested, blandly.

"He ain't *that* new!" Herbert snapped.

"I thought the usual punishment for thievery was banishment," Barker suggested.

"Robbin' a cache can leave a man to die in the wilderness. You know that. Same as stealin' a man's horse. And that's a hangin' offense."

"Since I'm here, I'll take custody of him. You can press charges at his trial in a Canadian court." He looked at the prisoner. "What's your name?"

"Arnold Klegg," the man answered. Barker thought he'd never seen such a piteous look of gratitude.

"Too late, Barker. A miners' court has duly tried and convicted the sneaky son of a bitch. Everything legal and above board. Bring him outside, boys."

"Hold it!" Barker's voice cracked like a shot and the stirring among the miners instantly stopped as they looked from the policeman to Herbert.

"Let's talk outside," Barker said, edging toward the door. "I need to check my team."

The door closed behind the two men. Barker noted it was already getting dusk as the lowering sun had disappeared behind a leaden overcast. "I'll arrest that man, Klegg, on your say-so and take him with me," Barker said.

"We'll deal with him in our own way."

Barker shook his head. "I represent the law here. You or any of the others can come and testify when the time comes. Or, you can write out your statements, sign 'em and I'll take your affidavits with me."

"How much do they pay you, Barker?" Herbert looked away from him. "Last I heard a constable got about a dollar-fifty a day. Why, hell, even a miner on wages or a laborer gets at least three times that much. Is it really worth it—all the work and danger and responsibility—for starvation pay?" He shook his head. "Tell you what . . ." He slipped a rawhide bag half the size of his fist from his coat pocket. "Here's a poke of gold dust that will more than compensate you for your time and work. Call it a little bonus for all your trouble. But we don't need you here. Take it and go." He looked directly at Barker. "We'll feed and water your dogs and you can push on tonight. Or you can go on down the trail a ways and camp. Get a fresh start in the morning."

"I'll pretend I didn't hear that offer of a bribe," Barker said quietly, wondering how far he should push this man. He sniffed the breeze that had sprung up from the northwest. A definite smell of snow on the air. Even though he had a Winchester carbine on the sled and a Smith & Wesson .38 on his hip, he was outnumbered and outgunned. But the history of the mounted police, with the exception of the Métis uprising, was not written in blood. It was a history of good accomplished and crime deterred mostly by force of personality and a calm insistence on fairness. He made a quick decision. "Postpone the hanging and I'll camp out here with my dogs. We'll talk again in the morning when we've had a chance to sleep on it."

Herbert looked almost relieved to have avoided an immediate confrontation. Barker knew that Herbert wasn't personally afraid of him. It was the uniform, the force of law represented by the badge, that made the Swede hesitate.

Herbert nodded, opened the door and announced the delayed execution. The men dispersed, grumbling, to their cabins. Then, at Herbert's invitation, he and Barker sat down to supper, waited on by Herbert's half-breed wife, Tanna. She was a plain, dark-skinned woman who looked to be in her twenties. Barker guessed that her figure, under the shapeless wool dress and leggings, was stunning. She served them from a pot of caribou meat and beans on the stove, and cut thick slices of sourdough bread. Herbert must have planned ahead, or rationed his supplies carefully, Barker noted, to still be so well supplied this late in the winter season.

The men ate and discussed topics of mutual interest as though nothing had transpired between them. They ignored the prisoner who sat tied to a chair on the other side of the room near the stove.

Herbert had a reputation as a violent man when aroused. But he could be most amiable if he chose, and Barker realized once again why this man, in addition to his physical strength and endurance, was a natural leader of men.

After supper, they smoked their pipes, then Barker said good night and went to make up his camp. He didn't go far—only a few yards into the trees behind the cabin, to make sure Klegg wasn't executed before dawn. He took a tarp from his sled and made a lean-to between two trees to block the wind and reflect the heat of a campfire he built with the Swede's wood. He cut some low-hanging pine boughs to form a dry, springy base for his bed, then sat for nearly an hour, staring into the flames and thinking. Whether Klegg was guilty or not, he deserved to have his day in a real court. But if persuasion failed, how would he get custody of the prisoner? It would have to be at gunpoint. But that would be a last resort. If Herbert and the other miners were adamant about hanging this man, blood could be shed, and it might very well be his own. As Herbert had put the question, "Is it really worth it?"

He sighed and loosened the collar of his tunic, nodding wearily after hours on the trail. He pulled the wolfskin cover off his nearby sled and spread it on the pine boughs, then stretched out and covered himself with the long, sheepskin coat, his feet toward the fire. Just as he turned down the flaps of his fur hat and prepared to sleep, he noticed some snowflakes drifting down in the light. From somewhere in the distance came the mournful howl of a wolf. Then he remembered no more as sleep took him.

The next thing he knew he was awakened by some movement close to him. He opened his eyes in the dark. The fire was nearly out. Instantly alert, his hand went for the pistol still strapped to his hip. A dog, a wolf, a prowling wolverine perhaps? A chill went up his back and he lay perfectly still, senses straining to identify the presence. He caught a faint musky scent, then some essence of grease and old wood smoke.

"Meester Barker!" a low voice hissed.

"Who is it?" His eyes couldn't penetrate the blackness, but a figure moved in front of him, blocking the red glow from the few remaining coals in the fire.

"Tanna."

He sat up, keeping a hand on the butt of his revolver. "What do you want?"

"How long since you had a woman?" she asked, moving closer until he could feel her breasts rubbing his arm and shoulder.

His mind was in a sudden whirl. Now was not the time or place. Was this some kind of trap? Had Herbert sent her out here so the Swede could catch him in the act of seducing his wife and have an excuse to shoot him?

There was a slight gust of wind and he could feel wet snowflakes on his face. He thought the temperature had moderated.

"You make love to me?" she asked, taking his free hand and drawing it to her. She was wearing a cotton shift of some sort under a heavy fur coat thrown over her shoulders. He caught his breath at the touch of her warm flesh.

"Why do you want me?" he asked. The question sounded stupid, but he could think of nothing else to say.

"He theenk maybe you go 'way. Leave prisoner."

So that was it! What gold couldn't buy, maybe sex could. Herbert was going to try everything.

"Where's Gunnar?" he asked in a low voice.

"Sleep."

"Did he send you out here?"

She ignored the question.

Barker felt himself stirring at her touch. What did it matter? He could have this woman, and still arrest Klegg and take him back. Yet, deep down, he knew his honor would not allow him to take her body, any more than his honor had allowed him to accept the poke of dust. But the gold dust was only cold metal. Here was a warm woman who was his for the taking, right here, right now. The desire was strong and he wavered, considering, his heart beating faster.

Then an idea flashed into his mind. How loyal was Tanna to Herbert? Maybe Barker could enlist her help in getting the prisoner. But he remembered the intensity of her silent regard for Herbert during supper. She had shown him fawning looks of love. Or had Barker completely misinterpreted what was really submissive servility? He wished he'd been more attentive. Herbert was a strong, rich man. Did she really love him, or had he just purchased her from some tribe as an unwanted, half-breed girl child of a French trader?

"No," he managed to articulate. "You are a very attractive woman, but you belong to Herbert," he said. "I am the law. I must arrest Klegg." If this made any impression on her sense of loyalty or duty, he couldn't tell. He suspected her standards were far different from his own. He had nothing to offer her as an inducement to aid him. "You help me get Klegg."

There was silence for several seconds, as she finally let go of his hand and he withdrew it into the warmth of the sheepskin. He could feel the snow falling harder. In spite of the fact that she was lightly clad under the coat, she didn't seem to be shivering.

"I get Klegg, you take me weeth you?" she whispered in a husky voice.

He was stunned at this stroke of luck. Apparently her life with Herbert wasn't as happy as Barker had assumed.

"Yes," he heard himself saying. "You help me get the prisoner and we'll all leave here together—now." It was a terrible gamble. Not only was he taking Herbert's prisoner, but also his woman—enough to enrage the hot-tempered Swede twice over.

He stood up, stretching his stiff muscles, and stamped his feet to restore circulation. Without a word, Tanna was gone, and Barker set out to rouse up his dogs from where they lay curled in the snow, bushy tails over their noses.

A strong gust whirled the dry snow up around the cabins, and he hoped the wind would carry away the sound of the snarling and whining as he rousted the dogs, one at a time. They had finished a run of more than thirty miles only a few hours before, and were in no mood to be harnessed again. But he'd hitched and unhitched this team in the dark so often that he managed it now with little trouble. While he worked, the snow squall passed, and he looked up. The night sky glittered with stars like millions of ice crystals.

Suddenly he saw two figures ghosting toward him, silhouetted by the aurora borealis that wavered its eerie, silent light just above the horizon. It was Tanna and a very willing Arnold Klegg.

"By God, let's get out of here," Klegg said in a loud whisper. "I'm sure as hell not hankering for a rope in the morning."

"I'm arresting you for claim-jumping and robbery," Barker said. "You're not going free."

"Fine with me, Constable. I'll take my chances. I didn't have *no* chance with them."

"You got enough clothes on?" Barker asked.

"Yeah. Let's go." Klegg flung the hood of his parka up over his shaggy head.

"You ride," Barker said to the girl. "Klegg, you travel afoot for now to save the dogs."

"I weel walk," she replied with pride in her voice. "Strong."

"Okay," Barker replied, appreciating her more all the time. "But stay close. I don't want to lose either of you," he cautioned as the stars were blotted out and another heavy snow squall gusted down on them.

The snow was falling so thickly that he guessed, even in daylight, the visibility would have been only a few yards. He grabbed the handles of the sled and rocked it to break the frozen runners loose from the snow. "H'ya, Soot!" he called softly to the big, black leader and the dogs lunged into their harnesses. He held the coiled whip in one mittened hand, but didn't use it for fear of the noise. Guiding the team down around the cabin toward the river, he guessed at the location of the trail and started. Barker jogged behind the sled, one hand on a handle while the other two followed, single file, behind him. The snow was already very soft underfoot and he knew it wouldn't be long before the wind would cause the trodden trail to be drifted over completely. He briefly considered traveling the river where the ice alongshore was smoother from partial thawing and refreezing. But he dared not risk the danger of springs or other faults in the ice.

But the weather suddenly ceased to be his main concern as a clamor of barking and howling erupted behind them. Somehow Herbert's dogs had been aroused and were setting up a racket that couldn't fail to awake the men in the camp. The noise gradually faded into the distance as they rounded a bend and the moaning of the increasing wind blotted out the barking.

Barker estimated they'd gone less than a mile when he drew the dogs to a halt to wait for Klegg to catch up. Tanna was right on his heels with no apparent distress. But the prisoner finally came staggering up, gasping. Barker knew immediately that Klegg was going to slow them and he had a decision to make. The snowstorm was intensifying to a full blizzard, he realized, the wind roaring through the giant spruce and fir trees, the snow blowing sideways, stinging their faces. The dogs were having a difficult time keeping to the trail and had floundered off into deep snow several times. And twice the sled had upset.

Barker looked back. As yet, there was no sign of the pursuit he knew was coming. If he put Klegg on the sled, it would only burden the dogs even more. But Klegg was the reason for this trip, and Barker was paying a high price for him, so he had to insure he got the prisoner back to the outpost.

"Get on the sled, Klegg."

Breathing hard, the man obeyed, covering himself with the wolf pelt.

"Mush!" Barker popped the whip over the dogs and they surged ahead. He was unable to see, so had to trust the dogs to somehow sense the grooved trail. Protected from the wind by the side of a hill, they were able to keep the trail for about an hour longer. Then they dipped down into a swale and the running dogs floundered into deep snow. Barker, jogging with his head down, was caught off guard and pitched over the sled as it careened sideways. Klegg staggered to his feet. "I'm . . . fr-freezing!" he chattered.

Barker struggled up in the thigh-deep drift, brushing himself off, feeling the icy pack of snow down his neck and up his sleeves. "Run alongside for a while. That'll get your blood pumping!" Barker snapped with no sympathy. He was perspiring from exertion, and knew he couldn't stop long for fear of becoming dangerously chilled. He waded in among the snapping dogs, beating them away from each other with the butt of his whip as he strove to untangle the snarled harness in the dark. When he finally got them lined up again, he realized he could see the vague shapes of the dogs and the sled as the light of dawn struggled to penetrate the heavy snow clouds and the thick, swirling flakes.

The half-breed woman still showed no signs of fatigue as she averted her hooded face from the stinging blast and waited patiently for them to continue. He could see her now in the half-light and noticed a dark bruise on her left cheekbone. The mark had not been there the night before at supper, and he began to sense her desperation.

Day sneaked up through the flying blizzard, but it was only a gray pall to show that night was gone. The party moved at a slower pace now as the deepening snow slowed the tiring dogs. The trail was completely obliterated. Barker could only stay roughly between the white expanse of frozen river to his left and the irregular line of dark evergreens on the slope to his right. Finally he saw that he would have to break trail. He pulled his snowshoes off the sled and put them on, at the same time instructing Tanna to take the whip and be ready to drive the dogs, if they needed any urging.

Barker went out front to break trail for the animals who were unable to make any progress against snow that was above their bellies. He dreaded the ordeal that was coming—a test of man's conditioning and endurance, and ultimately of his heart and will. The snow was now more than knee-deep and with each step he had to lift his leg straight up, swing his foot forward and set it down, flattening the soft snow and creating a path the dogs could negotiate. Then he repeated the process with the other leg—up, forward and down; up, forward and down, with his feet far enough apart to keep from stepping on his snowshoes. Ten steps, forty steps, a hundred steps. He slitted his eyes against the biting wind that froze his eyelashes and numbed the exposed skin of cheeks and nose. In spite of this, sweat was soon soaking his inner clothing. Cold air whistled through his clenched teeth, searing his straining lungs. He'd always been blessed with great lung capacity. The doctor who'd examined him when he enlisted in the mounted police had even commented on his unusual chest expansion. It was a trait that had brought him through many exhausting ordeals since then.

But he floundered to a stop after only a few hundred yards, realizing he could not keep up this pace. He stood for several seconds, head tucked down into his fur collar, sucking air into his burning lungs, legs trembling. The bitterest thought was the realization that he was also breaking trail for Herbert and his team of rested huskies. The big Swede had a reputation as one of the best sled dog travelers in the territory. Barker knew he would have to make a stand and fight. It was too much to hope that the storm had discouraged pursuit.

He staggered back to the sled and reached under the wolfskin for the Winchester in its leather scabbard. He worked the lever to be sure the action wasn't frozen. It was stiff, but still operable. He let the hammer down and shoved the weapon back under the cover. As his breathing slowly steadied, he considered stopping for a rest, possibly building a fire and making tea to restore their energy. He estimated they'd covered barely ten miles—hardly a third of the distance. No. He would just keep going until they had to stop and camp for the night. It didn't appear they would be able to reach his cabin while daylight lasted. His strength was ebbing and the falling snow had not let up. If anything, the storm had grown fiercer, with visibility down to only a few yards. It had become a silent world from which all wildlife had fled to shelter.

Then Barker thought he heard something unusual. He raised the ear flaps of his fur cap and turned his head this way and that. He knew heavy snow was like thick fog in its ability to deflect, muffle and confuse sounds. He heard nothing. Probably a tree limb snapping under its weight of snow, he decided.

Then he heard the distinct crack and he instantly knew it for what it was—the popping of a dog whip. This was followed by a faint shout, and he looked back to see, through the whirling white, a dog team and sled.

"It's Herbert!" he shouted. He reached down and quickly

yanked off his snowshoes. "Make for the river! That way!" He pointed left. "Haw! Soot! Haw!" He grabbed the handles and threw his weight against the sled, tilting it, muscling it around as the team followed the lead dog and plunged away to the left. The unseen river was out there in that swirling whiteness. But how far? Two hundred feet? Two hundred yards? The trail roughly paralleled the water but never at a constant distance. If they could reach it quickly, they could make faster time, especially if the wind had swept the ice clear of snow in places. He knew there were dangerous faults in the ice that covered a swift-flowing current, but they would have to take that chance. What was coming from behind was no chance—it was a sure thing. He heard the boom of a heavy rifle. He yelled at the dogs and cracked his whip over their heads, leaning forward on the handles and running.

Suddenly, there was the river, like a wide, white high-way. The dogs' tongues were lolling out of open mouths, but they seemed to sense the desperation of the chase and lunged into their collars, the sled bouncing crazily over the steep lip of the riverbank and out onto the ice.

"Both of you—get aboard!" He grabbed Klegg by the back of his coat and flung him headfirst across the sled while Tanna leapt nimbly onto the backs of the runners and held on. Free of the deep snow at last, the team burst ahead, stretching their stride with renewed vigor. At the last instant, Barker dove and caught the wooden side of the sled, dragging alongside. He scrambled to pull himself up, losing his whip, but managed to snatch the Winchester from the sled before letting go. Tanna was yelling at the dogs, urging them on, as his sled disappeared into the whirling flakes.

Barker slid to a stop on his knees. He turned around,

thumbing back the hammer on the rifle. He wiped a sleeve across his face just as the wind tore a massive rent in the curtain of snow for several seconds. He saw the team coming, bushy tails bobbing over their backs, the sled yawing from side to side on the ice behind them. The figure of the broad-shouldered Swede showed above the back of the sled. He was trying to hold on and raise his rifle for another shot. Then the curtain of snow fell again, blurring the image.

Barker scrambled, slipping and sliding, toward the riverbank as Herbert swiftly approached. He slid behind a tangle of driftwood frozen in the ice. His eyes were watering as he squinted down the barrel at the dark, fast-moving figure. Herbert was now lying across the top of the sled, and raised his rifle just as Barker drew a bead. Both weapons roared simultaneously.

Barker felt as if an invisible fist had hit him in his left side, knocking him backward. Then came the searing pain. Gasping, he fumbled with the fastenings on his sheepskin coat. Then he unbuttoned his tunic and saw the red wetness staining his white longjohns. With his knife, he slit the underwear and examined the wound in the half-light. He let out his breath in a long sigh of relief. From the soreness and the look of it, the bullet had apparently been deflected by a rib and grooved a path along the flesh without entering his body. He blotted the blood with his cotton bandanna and padded the rib that was probably broken. The blood was coagulating quickly in the cold as he gingerly fastened his clothing back over it.

Picking up his rifle, he went to look for Herbert. He found him unconscious on the ice, his sled and team gone. Barker's bullet had apparently hit the brass receiver of the Swede's rifle, throwing the weapon back against his head and knocking him out. He had a gash and a purpling bruise on his forehead. He flung the ruined rifle away, then pulled the big man's belt off, looped it around Herbert's neck and began dragging him. The pain in his side was excruciating, and his breath was coming in short gasps, but he didn't have far to go before he came upon the Swede's winded team that had slowed and finally stopped.

Barker was checking the sled for some rope when he heard a grunt. He turned and swung the stock of his carbine. But Herbert was already up under it and rolled a shoulder into the Mountie's legs, knocking him to the ice. Barker gasped, momentarily stunned by the stabbing pain in his side. Herbert clumsily, groggily, crawled up onto him like some shaggy beast. His assailant was too close for Barker to use the rifle, and Herbert pinned him down, preventing Barker from reaching under his coat for his revolver. He gasped for air as more than two hundred pounds crushed him. Piercing pain in his lower rib cage screamed the message that jagged ends of bone were jabbing the muscle sheath. Herbert slowly slid his hands up to Barker's throat and clutched for a choke hold. The Mountie was powerless against the big man's strength. Desperately, Barker twisted his head from side to side to break the deadly grip. This movement, along with Herbert's bulky gloves and Barker's thick collar, saved him from being strangled.

Suddenly, the ice under them cracked with a report like a pistol shot. Herbert raised his head. Another loud crack and Barker felt the ice give slightly. Herbert let go and pushed himself up, eyes wide with alarm. Barker jerked his arms free and swung the carbine with all his strength. Herbert caught the force of the blow on the side of his bare head and fell sideways. Barker rolled to his knees and leveled the weapon, jacking a shell into the chamber. "Get on that sled!" he rasped. "On your back!"

The Swede obeyed with a dazed look. Barker jerked the lashings off the Swede's bedroll and secured Herbert's wrists and ankles to the sides of the sled.

The dogs were whining and lifting their paws gingerly as if sensing the rotten section of ice beneath their feet. Barker carefully drove the team close to the bank, then cracked the whip and pushed the dogs as fast as he dared. But it took another half hour before he glimpsed his own sled in the distance through the thinning snowfall. He shouted and waved to Tanna. She stopped to wait.

"We heard shots. Figured he'd got you," Klegg said. "Damned glad it's the other way around."

"Let's get moving," Barker replied through gritted teeth, hoping no one would notice how he was favoring his left side. He pointed with his carbine. "We've still got a long way to go."

Sergeant Cecil McKee smoothed his mustache with the back of his hand and looked at the half-breed girl massaging her bare toes in front of the stove. "One helluva tale," he muttered to himself. Two men had been arrested and shackled to the bedpost. Both lay on the floor sound asleep under Hudson's Bay blankets. His partner, Derek Barker, wounded, had been bandaged and fed and was now lying exhausted in his bunk.

Both prisoners would likely spend some time in jail, but no one had been killed in the fray—thanks mainly to Barker. McKee resolved, as soon as he got all the details, to write up a report, commending Barker for his actions. The report would go to their superiors by the following week's mail. It was the kind of thing that men of the mounted police were expected to do all the time, but McKee felt that such deeds should be recognized. He glanced at Barker's fur hat that had been tossed on the table. The brass badge pinned to the front of it glowed dully in the light of the coal oil lamp. "*Maintien Le Droit*—Maintain The Right," McKee muttered, thoughtfully. The motto fit the man.

THE KID

by Douglas Hirt

Douglas Hirt is the author of Deadwood, Cripple
Creek *and, most recently,* Shadow Road. *In this story
he traces the rise of a troubled young man to the position of authority and importance.*

I think it must be the snow, on cold winter nights like this,
that makes me remember . . .

I was with Frank Hadley the day the marshal hired on
young Bill Cassaway. We had been making rounds that hot
summer morning when right in front of McGilly's Saloon
six or seven men clambered out the batwings and gathered
around something there on the boardwalk. I had glanced at
Marshal Hadley and he said:

"Look at that. The mines are complaining about being
short workers and look at them. Wasting away their day in
the saloon. And it isn't even nine o'clock."

"What are they doing?" I asked, squinting against the
morning glare. Then we heard the frightened screech of a cat
from somewhere amongst them. Someone yelped and
cussed and another said, "Here, give me that thing! I'll show
you how it's done. Randy, get a match ready."

I frowned and we started across Mercantile Street. We both knew how men can get sometimes when they have been drinking. Before we'd made six steps, a young fellow had pushed apart the doors and we heard him say, "Let the cat alone. It ain't done nothing to deserve that."

One of the men hooted. Another shoved the kid aside. That was the wrong thing to do to Bill Cassaway, for as we later came to know, the kid was tough as piano wire, with the nerves of rock and the grit of a grizzly bear, though he wasn't much bigger than a cub. His fists came up hard and fast and he plowed into them like a small tornado. Frank and I rushed to break it up. A cat leaped from the center of the ruckus and skedaddled across the street and under the board-walk to safety. Suddenly a firecracker exploded and one of the men howled, fanning his hand.

By the time we got there, two men were nursing bloody noses and another four or five were atop Cassaway thrashing the tar out of the kid. Frank broke it up and we dragged the men off him. Bill Cassaway sat up, blinked a couple times and looked dazed, but none the worse for wear.

"What was that all about?" Frank asked.

No one would say.

"They was about to hurt that cat," Cassaway said. The men drifted off, embarrassed at being caught at a cruel and childish prank. Well, they hadn't broken any laws so we let them go, and it was only Bill Cassaway, Frank and me left there on the walk in front of McGilly's.

We asked his name and he told us. He'd drifted into town a week before and hadn't found a job yet. He didn't like mining, and was figuring to drift out again.

"What were they going to do to the cat?" Frank asked.

"Shove a firecracker up its ass."

Frank winced and shook his head. "You like cats?"

"Not particularly. But I don't like hurting things either."

That made an impression, even though Frank remained pokerfaced. When he gave me a look, I knew what he was thinking. We'd been shorthanded since Walter Haskin married Lilla Ecker and up and quit on us, claiming that now he was a married man, he had to find another line of work. We all knew that was just Lilla talking, but it left us shy a man just the same.

"What sort of work you looking for?" Frank asked.

"I can do most anything."

"Ever use a gun?"

He shook his head. "Not much."

"Want to learn?"

"What's in it for me?"

"Twenty-six dollars a month."

His eyes didn't exactly brighten at the offer, but it got young Bill Cassaway interested. Seeing as he looked hungry, we hauled him down to The Milly's Mineshaft Café and put breakfast in his belly, then marched him into Frank's office, read him a deputy's job description and swore him in.

Bill Cassaway was a quiet fellow and never let on much about his past. Not that a seventeen-year-old would have much in the way of a past anyway. He didn't seem to have any family; leastwise none he ever talked about. He was generally amiable though not overly ambitious. Cassaway had what I called "an eye for the detail." He'd stand and just study people, or take special notice to the way a heel print left a track in mud and wonder if it was worn away to the right or to the left. Cassaway discovered the marshal's books on "modern police methods" that first day and devoured every one of them. He had his quirks too, and we learned early on he did not like being woken up. Especially when Frank made his late night rounds about eleven o'clock. Seeing that he didn't care for the task, Frank set about to made it a point of calling Bill for the job each night.

"Why me again?" the kid complained one evening, glaring at the marshal. I'd been reading a copy of *Harper's Weekly* at the time and Cassaway pointed a finger at me. "Why not him?"

"Because I say so." Frank could be flint when he had a notion, and a reason.

Scowling, Cassaway tugged on his boots and threw his arms into the sleeves of his jacket. He still didn't own a gun so he took down one of the scatterguns from the rack. Frank always toted a scattergun when he made night rounds. When they came back an hour later and Frank went home to his wife, the kid sulked to his cot declaring that he hated night rounds more than anything.

Bill and me, we slept in the jail house. I usually took a cot in one of the cells when we didn't have any lockups, which was most of the time. Drunks made up nearly all of our callers, and then mostly on the weekends.

I remember once, after one of their rounds and Frank had gone home, Bill Cassaway looked over at me and said, "I know what that old man is up to."

"Oh?" I asked, glancing up from the Deadwood Dick novel in my hands.

"He's out to break me."

"Break you? You mean like a man goes out to break a mustang?"

"I mean, he just wants to see how much I'm gonna take before I quit."

"Why would he do that?"

" 'Cause deep down inside he's got a mean streak. That's why. Just like my Pa had."

It was the first I had ever heard him mention his family. "Not Frank," I said. "There is not a mean bone in that man."

Cassaway yanked off his boots and slammed them to the

floor. Then he curled up on his cot, pulled his blanket over his head and turned his back to me. What I had told him was true far as I knew. I'd never seen Frank do a mean thing in his life. He was a hard man, and he had his ways about him. But mean? I couldn't buy that.

Shortly after that we got word of another stage holdup down below Gunnison Pass. It was not too many days later when Horace Allison and his two brothers, Warren and Christopher, rode down out of the high country and staked a claim at one of McGilly's tables, camping out there day and night. I knew the Allison brothers weren't looking for work. Mostly, they looked for trouble, and generally they found it. They made their way through Johnson Junction maybe three times a year. And everyone, except for McGilly, was glad when they finally moved on.

Cassaway was never what you might call "outgoing," and as the weeks passed he became more withdrawn. Just the same, he stuck to the job like tar to a sailor's heel—night rounds and all. It was drawing nigh the end of August when he come down with the ague, though I suspected it was only the vapors. Frank didn't rouse the kid up off his cot for rounds. I went with him instead. It had been almost two months since I'd done the night rounds with Frank and I'd almost forgotten how dark the alleyways could be, or that tingling at the back of your neck when someone is standing half-hidden in a shadow, watching you.

Mountain nights are always chilly, no matter how hot the day has been, and I was shivering as we strode the sidewalk to the livery at the edge of town, then crossed over Mercantile Street and started back up the other side. Frank was wearing a stern face that night. He was not the sort of man who took kindly to prying, but I asked him anyway what was troubling him.

"Cassaway."

"You thinking he's not really sick, only wanting to get out of night rounds?"

Frank frowned and shifted the scattergun in the crook of his arm. "No. I was thinking the kid has gumption. He's got a rock-hard head and determination when he sets his mind to do a thing." There was anger in the marshal's voice, riding just under the surface. "Cassaway could make something of himself if he wasn't so damned lazy. And if he would ever unload himself of that chip he carries around with him."

I saw something that night, something I had missed before. Frank was right about Cassaway. Deep down inside, the kid had the making of a man. But something had happened to him; something that had turned him bitter. Something he wouldn't let go of. And I thought I saw something else too. It was only a glimmer, but I had to wonder if maybe Frank didn't have deeper reasons for driving hard on the kid like he did. It occurred to me just then that like the kid, Frank had never once spoken of his family, or youth. I got to wondering if he ever had one. Was he ever really a boy with boy ideas and boyish ways. Did Frank ever in his life sleep past six-thirty in the morning? Had he ever played hooky from school when growing up? I'd have sworn not—not by judging the man. But something in his voice that night made me start to wonder.

We came to McGilly's Saloon and looked over the batwings. The smoky barroom beyond was crowded this night. Mostly miners between shifts. The Allison brothers were there too, hunkered over cards with two other men, and serious whiskey drinking all around. We'd had some trouble with the Allisons since they came into town; one or another of them had taken my cot in the jail on more than one night. Christopher, who fancied the handle "Kit," glanced up from his cards, saw the marshal and me standing there, and nudged Horace. The older brother looked across the smoky room and grinned at us.

"What does he have on his mind?" Frank said as the tall, slender fellow threw in his cards and swaggered across the room. He was wearing a Colt six-shooter on his hip in a black holster that matched his leather vest. Silvery buttons glinted in the hazy lamplight as he strode toward us. His tall black boots thumped the floor; big Texas rowels jingling.

"Come on in, Marshal," Horace Allison said over the top of the batwings, his dark eyes flashing, his voice bearing the bravado of a man with more confidence than good sense, and maybe a bit more whiskey than was prudent. Not that anyone would ever accuse the Allison brothers of being prudent men. "Let me buy you and your deputy a drink." A cold shiver ran through me when he slid those dusky eyes my way. Pure evil and cussedness is what I saw there. "Where is the kid?"

Frank grinned easily. "The kid's feeling under the weather." It surprised me when he accepted the invitation. We followed Horace back to a table and McGilly brought over a bottle without being asked. Apparently he was used to Allison's big spending ways and only too happy to accommodate them.

"You come to show me the inside of your fine jail house again?" Horace asked after McGilly had gone.

Frank gave a short laugh, and a small smile lifted the corners of his mouth. I wondered what he was up to, drinking with this man . . . and what Horace was about, giving the invite in the first place. "Why, have you done something I should know about?" Frank asked, softly rapping the whiskey glass on the scared tabletop.

"Me? I'm pure as the driven snow, Marshal."

I started to laugh, but choked it back real quick when Allison's black eyes darted my way. He was playing friendly on the outside, but inside he was all devil, and I wondered again what Frank was thinking of, drinking with a man like that. Except, Frank had yet to take his first sip. I belted down another long swallow to settle my nerves. Allison had killed a man, I'd heard, and pistol whipped another so bad it had put him in a wheelchair for the rest of his life. Him and his brothers, they fought dirty . . . and for keeps.

Allison said, "It's a comfort to know that you and your deputy are doing such a good job keeping the peace here. I remember when Johnson Junction was nothing but a wide open whistle-stop and it wasn't safe to walk the streets at night." He saluted Frank with his whiskey. "Figure I'd show my appreciation."

That was about the biggest tale I had ever heard. Horace was toying with us. Life in Johnson Junction must be getting tiresome for him, I mused.

Frank just grinned and eased back in his chair. "Glad someone appreciates our work." He studied his untouched glass of whiskey then added casually, "You boys have been spreading money around like you were expecting the Second Coming any minute now. Making McGilly smile a lot. Did a rich uncle die?"

Horace was cool as springwater, but the tick in his right eye gave him away. His smile went suddenly wooden, then the stiffness melted and he laughed like he had just heard the funniest joke in all his life. "Don't I wish, Marshal. Fact of the matter is, me and my brothers worked hard for this money. Washed about a hundred ton of gold-rock for a fellow up near Petersville. About wore our fingers to the bone. He had a high-grade vein. It made him rich and he paid us real good too. But we got weary of the work. Me and Kit and Warren are just relaxing before we go looking for a different line."

Frank nodded. "Washing gold-rock is a hard way to

make a living, all right." He was looking at Allison's hands. Allison saw it too and he casually folded his arms and stuck them out of sight.

"You're not drinking, Marshal."

Frank frowned at the glass in his fingers. "I like to keep a clear head when I'm working, Horace. But I appreciate your hospitality." And as if to show it, Frank took a small sip and set the glass down. "Good whiskey. Wish I had more time to chat, but me and my deputy have got our rounds to complete."

Horace was grinning as we left, but I couldn't help but think it was all an act. In fact, the whole thing seemed unreal . . . maybe that was just the whiskey working on me the way it does sometimes. Outside, I said, "What do you suppose that was all about, Frank?"

"Brave-making in front of his friends. Sorta like bragging, only without the words."

"Why?"

"I'm not sure."

I snorted. "Allison plays with half a deck. One thing for sure, if he did wash a hundred tons of gold-rock, he must have been wearing gloves."

Frank grinned over at me. "You noticed that too?"

"Pretty obvious. Especially the way he went and tucked his hands out of sight afterwards."

"I wonder . . . ," Frank began, leaving the thought just hang there. We'd come back around to the jailhouse by then and Cassaway was still curled on his cot, shivering slightly beneath his blankets. Frank put the scattergun in the rack and asked the kid how he was feeling.

"Like I'm sleeping on ice," he said. "Can't seem to get warm."

Frank built a fire in the potbelly stove, then went home for the evening. But he came back about an hour later with a kettle of soup he said his wife had fixed. Cassaway was surprised. I was too. I'd never known Frank to coddle one of his deputies. Cassaway took a bowl of it and said it helped some with the chills. Frank left the kettle on the stove, and later in the night the kid lit a lantern and helped himself to the rest of it. The next morning he was feeling a little better.

"Why did he do that?" Cassaway asked me.

"I don't know. Maybe Frank was worried about you."

The kid thought it over. He was confused by Frank's goodwill gesture, not sure what to make of it. "Or maybe he's feeling guilty for riding me like he does."

"Guilty? That wouldn't be like him."

Cassaway's expression hardened. "No, you're right."

Frank let him lay about all that day, but come time for the night rounds he took down two guns and gave one to the kid.

"Time to go."

Cassaway scowled. Frank ignored it.

The kid was still peaked around the gills when they left. I watched them through the window disappear into the night, thinking those two were never going to learn to get along. Yet somehow they were very much alike.

Two days later the Allison brothers rode out of town, and everyone but McGilly was relieved. But I could see that Frank was worried about something. When I asked, he merely said, "I liked it better when I could keep an eye on those three."

September brought a chill wind to the high country and nipped the leaves of the aspen trees that dappled the mountainsides. October dusted Johnson Junction with our first snow. A big storm hit in November, shutting off the roads and any news from the outside for two weeks.

Through it all, Frank kept a regular routine. Cassaway took to it like a square peg eyeing a round hole. The two of them began to spat like hungry dogs over a bone. Little things were getting to the kid . . . and Frank kept driving him.

In early December a rider from Carter's Grove made it up the pass with the first word we had had since the storm hit and a slide took out a mile and a half of telegraph poles. The big news was that a stage from Petersville was missing and it was only now that a search party could begin to look for it. Frank listened with knitted eyebrows and a frown deepening upon his face. Right away he volunteered Cassaway and me to help in the search. Cassaway jumped at the opportunity to be out from under Frank's thumb for a few days, but all I could see waiting ahead for us was a lot of cold riding and infrequent meals.

The kid and I joined up with the searchers and rode the deep snow back toward Petersville. It was slow going and just like I feared, a cold and hungry ordeal. But Cassaway took to tracking right off, and in no time he was out front with old Caleb Miller, the sheriff of Summit County. I didn't think there was a lot of places a stagecoach could lose itself along that road, but we searched high and low all day and turned up no signs of it.

Hunkered around the campfire that night, trying to get warm, we conjectured upon its fate while clutching steaming cups of coffee in our hands. Cassaway thought we were looking in the wrong place. A coach that size had to have gone off the road somewhere, and if it did, then he reckoned we'd find it—or what was left of it—down some ravine, most likely buried by the storm.

Caleb Miller grunted his agreement and said, "Half of us boys should backtrack in the morning and test young Cassaway's theory." After that we crawled into our blankets and shivered the night away. The next morning me, Cassaway, Bob Grindel, Harry Sloan and Mr. Pat McCall, the newspaper editor, retraced our tracks keeping an eye open for any drop-off that might hide something as big as a Concord coach. And just as Cassaway predicted, we found it. It was easy to see how we had missed the coach for it had gone off the road and down an embankment, landing on its side. Then Mother Nature had stepped in, covering it with snow but for one corner, where now the morning sun glinted off shiny red lacquer.

We didn't have shovels with us so we dug with our hands down to the door and managed to heave it open. The passengers were all inside, and it was a gruesome sight. Cassaway was the first one to lower himself into the coach. At first we thought they had perished from the cold, but upon closer investigation the kid discovered that each one there, three men and two women, had been shot. Stunned, we left them alone while Pat McCall rode to bring the sheriff.

We dug down to the boot only to discover that it had been ransacked. There was suppose to be a chest of gold up under the driver's seat. It had been taken too. Cold and dejected, we built a fire and waited for McCall to arrive. None of us spoke much. Cassaway wore a strange, focused look, and he kept mumbling to himself and shaking his head.

"Why do some people have to hurt others?" he mused at one point. No one had a good answer for him, but it made me remember that first day when Cassaway came to the rescue of that cat, heedless of his own peril. A little later Cassaway returned to the coach and stalked around it as if looking for clues, then lowered himself back inside. I wondered what he was looking for. There was nothing there that I cared to see again, although I knew I would have to once the sheriff arrived and we began hauling bodies out. Cassaway reappeared a few minutes later, looking at something in his hand. Then he shoved it into his coat pocket and strolled back to the fire to warm his palms.

"What did you find?" I asked.

"Nothing much. Just an old button someone lost."

The tragedy weighed heavy on the folks of Johnson Junction for many weeks. One of the women murdered was wife to a miner named Jake Prescott who turned to drinking real heavy and wound up frozen in a ditch out behind McGilly's Saloon. We laid him next to his missus in a dugout, waiting for the spring thaw to bury them. An explosion in the Kelly Stamping Mill killed seven men that month and we were all feeling kinda low when near the end of December the cold finally drove Horace Allison and his brothers down out of the high country. Only McGilly was pleased to see them again, because when the Allisons were in town, his business boomed.

I had seen a change come over Cassaway after the stage-coach incident. He became thoughtful and moody, and seemed to be always looking for something. He began eyeing strangers closely, even men he had known for months. One day I woke to find Cassaway staring out the window at the gently falling snow outside. There was hardly any sign of life beyond the frosted panes. No horses nosing at the hitching rails, no pedestrians on the boardwalks. It was cold and the snow had drifted nearly knee-deep across the street; a first-class stay-at-home morning if I'd ever seen one.

"Good morning, Bill," I said throwing off my blankets and chucking another piece of wood into the stove.

"What's so good about it?" He looked at me over his shoulder, frowning.

"Something the matter?"

"Nothing." He went back to his staring. I took some coffee from the pot that had been sitting on the stove all night. It was bitter and I wondered if Milly Ralston was doing business at the café, or if the snow had closed it down. There wasn't much going to happen on a morning like this, so I told Cassaway that breakfast was on me. His eyes bright-ened. I didn't realize it then, but that was just what the kid needed to hear.

"All right. I'll go."

Milly had fresh coffee made and hardly anyone to serve it to so we sat there a long time talking. I learned that the day was Cassaway's eighteenth birthday, and he was feeling blue.

"I didn't expect no one to remember," he said. "No one knew. It just feels kinda empty inside, if you know what I mean."

I didn't understand exactly because both my Ma and Pa were still living and every year on my birthday I got a package and a long letter from them. But I could see how not having anyone remember might get a fellow down. I asked about his family, but he didn't want to talk about it.

Frank's horse was tied in front of the office when we got back. I told him about Cassaway once we were alone, and figured he'd make mention of it to the kid and maybe offer his congratulations, but he didn't. He acted like this was just any other day and that surprised me because Frank always had a favorable word for me when my birthday rolled around. I couldn't understand why it should be any different for the kid.

Cassaway spent the day in a funk. That evening when Frank took the shotguns from the rack Cassaway said he wasn't going with him.

"Getting too rough for you, kid?" Frank jabbed.

"Ain't nothing too rough for me!" Cassaway shot back. "And what do you know about hard times anyway?"

Frank lifted his eyebrows in surprise and said, "Suppose you tell me?"

"All right. I'll tell you 'bout hard times. I've been on my own for eight years now. Ever since my Ma died and the old man gave me one beating more than I was going to take!

Been making my own way in the world ever since I was ten. Most boys that age have at least one parent. Ever since I was old enough to understand such things, I knew my Ma thought me a burden on her life. The day she died the old man beat me with a leather strap and told me they had been happy before I came along. As if it was my fault I had been born. He said they should have stuffed me in a gunnysack and dropped me in the river. He said she'd be alive today if they had."

Cassaway heaved in a ragged breath. "He liked to hurt people, just for the pleasure of seeing them hurting. I never understood why some men are that way. After that, I run off. I know he never missed me, not for one day. He was better off with me gone, anyway. I never let any man push me around since . . . not until I took your damned deputy job. And I don't know why I put up with you bullying me as long as I have."

Cassaway tore the tin star from his shirt and threw it at Frank's feet. "You can have the job back. Been here too long as it is."

"You finished feeling sorry for yourself?" Frank retorted.

Cassaway glared at him.

"You think you're the only one who has ever had it hard?" The marshal leaned forward and narrowed an eye at the kid. Frank Hadley stood six-four and could intimidate men by sheer size alone. But the kid didn't cow before him and gave the stare right back.

"A real man finishes a job he takes on, and he doesn't expect to be nursemaided along just because life throws a few potholes in front of him. Maybe your old man treated you poorly, but that's no reason to carry it around with you the rest of your days, unless you enjoy how it feels. Maybe it makes you feel special? Well, you aren't. At least you started out with a Ma and Pa. Some of us never knew either.

Some of us spent our entire growing up being shuffled back and forth between kin who didn't want us, a burden to everyone. Trouble and misery aren't your very own private garden where you can run away to to feel sorry for yourself. Just because no one remembers your birthday and pats you on the back and tells you what a bully fellow you are doesn't give you the right not to be a man. So today you're eighteen. So what? That's no great feat. We all get there if we're lucky enough to live that long."

Frank's scowl deepened. "Now, pick up that badge. We've got rounds to make."

The kid and Frank locked eyes, neither giving an inch. Right then I could see they were two of a kind. I don't know why I hadn't noticed it before. Cassaway snarled and said, "Go to hell," and he grabbed up his coat and hat and went out into the cold, slamming the door behind him.

I was mildly stunned. Frank, he just stood there shaking his head. "I figured the kid had more gumption than that," the marshal said.

I finally found my tongue. "You rode him kinda hard, Frank."

He grimaced. "Some men are like horses. Hard riding is what it takes to make them useful." He snorted and shook his head, a deep sadness suddenly filling his eyes. "I was hoping the kid would make something of himself." He bent for the tin star and turned it over in his hand, looking at it. I thought he looked old just then, older than I ever remembered seeing him. He shoved the star into his pocket and drew in a long breath, shifting his view my way. "Get your coat. Got rounds to make."

I glanced out the window and watched Cassaway trudge through the snow toward McGilly's Saloon. I figured that to be the last I was going to see of the kid. I shrugged into my sheepskin and cradled one of the scatterguns in my arm. The night air was cold as we did a turn around the town. It was so quiet I could hear the fat snowflakes patting lightly upon my hat and shoulders. The noise picked up as we came near the saloon.

Frank moved closer to the building and peered through the window into the smoky barroom beyond. Cassaway was leaning against the bar with the glass in his fingers, looking across the tables, studying each man there as had become his habit since finding those murdered people in the stagecoach. The Allisons were at their table, drinking and playing cards as usual. The piano player was taking a break at the moment and through the glass I could hear the low buzz of men's voices. Frank and me were about ready to move on when Cassaway straightened up with a start, his view riveted on something.

The kid started across the room toward Horace Allison's table. I glanced at Frank. The marshal was frowning, a worried look cutting into his face. Allison didn't notice the kid at first, standing there, watching. But after a moment the dark-eyed man lifted his view from the cards in his hand. Cassaway said something we couldn't hear and all at once Allison locked the kid in a hard stare.

"What's Cassaway up to?" Frank wondered aloud.

I shook my head. The kid had never been one to strike up a conversation of small talk. And to have singled Horace Allison out now seemed mighty peculiar to me.

Suddenly Allison stood, knocking back his chair. He dropped his playing cards and planted his fists upon the table, his hard stare turning vicious.

Frank said, "I don't like the looks of this."

I said, "The kid appears to be calling Allison out. But he doesn't even have a gun."

Frank started for the doorway. We went through into the warm saloon, shutting the cold out behind us. The place had gone so quiet the thump of our boots sounded like a buffalo stampede in my ears. But nobody else seemed to notice. Nobody looked over. Every eye was trained upon the kid and Allison, and now we could hear their words.

"I don't like what I'm hearing in your voice, kid. You got something to say, do it straight out."

I'd have been shaking in my boots if it was me facing that deadly snarl, but Cassaway was cool; his voice even, unruffled. "Can't help but notice your clothing is beginning to look a bit ragged, Horace," he replied easily. "Now look at yourself. You must have been through some real rough country. You seem to have lost one of those fancy silver buttons off that vest."

"What's it to you?"

Cassaway shrugged. "I just figured a man like yourself would be more careful. Those are right pretty buttons. It's a shame to lose one of 'em, but I can see how it might be easy to snag one and rip it if you aren't careful."

I gave Frank a curious glance. He seemed to be following it in some vague way that was escaping me. His mouth had drawn out into a tight line, but a corner began to hitch up, like he was holding back a small smile. "The kid knows," he said softly as we made for Allison's table.

Brothers Warren and Kit were there too, concern written all over their faces. My heart climbed into my throat remembering the Allisons' reputation, and I thumbed back the hammers, mighty glad to be holding that short-barrel double in my fists.

Allison glanced at the front of his vest. "So I lost a button. What of it?"

"Have any idea where you lost it, Horace?" The kid asked easily, a thin crease of a grin on his face. I'd seen that grin before but couldn't place it right away.

Judging from his sudden look of alarm, Horace must

have had a real good idea where he had lost it. His hand moved for the Colt at his hip.

"He ain't armed," one of the men at the table warned Allison. The men scrambled out of their chairs, making room.

Then Frank and I were there. The Allisons had ranged out on one side of the table, the kid, alone and unarmed, on the other. The kid ignored us and said, "I can abide a lot of failings, Horace, but out and out meanness just ain't one of them. I seen the way you done them helpless folks. Even the women."

"Give him your gun, Kit," Horace ordered.

The younger Allison reached for his revolver. Frank's voice stopped him.

"Put that thing away."

"Your deputy is making accusations, Marshal," Horace growled, his narrowed eyes locked on the kid, his right hand rigid with anger near the Colt.

"So I heard. Is there any truth to them?"

"Whatever he has in mind, he is lying."

"You accused this man of something, Mr. Cassaway?" Frank asked.

"No, sir. Not yet, at least. I was just commenting on the sorry state of his clothes. Reckon he took offense to that."

"They do look a mite tattered," Frank agreed.

I didn't know what to make of it. Cassaway and Frank both seemed to be singing from the same hymnal, and I didn't even have a clue to what page they were on!

"I just said it was easy to snag a fancy button like what's on his vest and lose it. Like maybe while climbing in and out of a stagecoach?"

Frank nodded. "I can see how that might happen. Tell me, Horace. You recall where you lost that button?"

"No, I don't," he answered, his hand inching for the revolver.

The kid reached into his pocket and tossed the match to the button onto the table. "I found it among the pleats in the seat cushions of that stagecoach you and your brothers held up a few weeks back."

None of the brothers spoke right away. They looked at each other, licking their lips nervously. Then Horace said, "Take 'em!"

Guns leaped into their hands. I got a glimpse of Cassaway diving aside and Frank was moving too. I had all I could do just to keep my wits about me as I swung the scattergun out of the crook of my arm. Gunshots exploded; the sharp cracks of their revolvers, the deep-throated roar of Frank's shotgun. The air was instantly filled with gunsmoke. I wheeled toward Kit just as his revolver spoke and hot lead burned into my thigh, knocking me to the floor.

Frank's second barrel blasted to my right. A bullet splintered the floorboards near my ear and stung my cheek. Then Cassaway was at my side. Past him I saw Horace standing there, blood splattered all over that black vest of his, hate etched into his face. His revolver swung toward me as he thumbed the hammer. Then Cassaway threw himself in front of me to block Allison's shot, and at the same time he grabbed up my shotgun and squeezed both triggers. The gun bucked in his fists and beyond the billow of gunsmoke Allison's head disappeared in a haze of red mist.

Then the room got real quiet. My rasping breath stung my throat and a fire began to burn in my leg, raging into the worse awful pain I'd ever felt. I wanted to cry out, but I gritted my teeth against the urge and held it back. Footsteps came nearer as the men gathered around.

"They're all dead," someone said.

"How's the deputy?" another asked.

"Took a slug to the leg. One of you boys run for Doc Hildebrand."

"How you doing?"

I opened my eyes. Frank was there. "I don't know. Hurt god-awful bad, Marshal."

"You'll be all right." He slipped off his belt and wrapped it around my leg and twisted it tight. "The doc has been sent for."

I couldn't talk. I just nodded.

Then Cassaway bent over, concern in his eyes . . . and something else too. I don't know, maybe it was all the pain fogging my brain that made me think his eyes had changed somehow. There was a maturity in them I hadn't noticed before. But like I said, maybe it was just me at the time. "Just take it easy. It's all over," Cassaway said. His voice had the ring of authority to it. It sounded reassuring, sort of like he had taken all the troubles onto his shoulders and I didn't have to worry about it. Then the kid glanced at Frank.

"You ought to stay with him, Marshal."

Frank nodded.

Cassaway looked at the scattergun he was still holding. "Got extra shells?"

Frank took two cartridges from his coat pocket. Cassaway broke the action and thumbed them into the chamber, snapping the breech shut.

"Where you going?"

"Been thinking about what you said earlier."

"And what have you decided?"

The kid gave a wry smile. "I figure it this way. If a man keeps doing what he's always done, he'll keep getting what he's always got. I'm ready to make a change." He stood. "You can handle things here. I'll go finish rounds for you."

I blinked and shook to clear my head, wondering if my ears were working right.

Frank nodded again. Those two were reading from that

same hymnal again, but I was getting woozy in the head. It was more than I could ponder at the moment.

Frank said, "Here, you must have forgotten this at the office." He pulled the tin star from his pocket.

Cassaway grimaced, then took it and pinned it to the outside of his coat. "Yep, must have."

A faint smile came to Frank's face as Cassaway walked out.

We never called him "the kid" after that night.

I stood at the office window watching snow drifting down past the streetlights. There was no traffic out on Mercantile Street. The weather had closed businesses down early and Johnson Junction was quiet. Not that there was ever much trouble these days. What with the war on and most of the young men off to Europe to do their part in the name of freedom, we were pretty quiet. The mines had mostly shut down, silver being less important now than the molybdenum they had discovered over west of Petersville.

I glanced outside and up the sidewalk, figuring it was about time for the marshal to be coming back from his rounds. He was breaking in a new kid tonight, and one of the things the marshal was unbending on was keeping to a routine, and evening rounds were a part of that routine.

A Ford plowed its way up the street, headlights feebly fighting the storm, tires spinning on the ice. Then I spied a man coming up the sidewalk, caught momentarily in the machine's light. I blinked, thinking I was seeing a ghost, and I marveled at the similarities. Not in face, of course, or in size. The similarities were where it mattered: in that straight, bold way he carried himself, his determined confident stride and that thin crease of a smile that always made you think he knew more than he was letting on.

No, it wasn't Frank Hadley. It was only my imagination

again, and the remnants of those old memories that sometimes come back on snowy winter nights like these.

You see, we'd buried Frank some years ago, June of
1908, to be exact.

No, it was only Marshal Bill Cassaway, and the new kid,
coming back from evening rounds.

WHISKEYTAW FALLS

by L. J. Washburn

Livia Washburn is a past winner of the Shamus Award in the private eye field, and has produced many novels in the historical and western genres, like Riders of the Monte, Epitaph *and* Bandera Pass. *Her ex-gunfighter-turned-stunt man Lucas Hallum straddles both forms, and appears here in his young days as a Pinkerton.*

Hallam rode into town from the west, past Bare Butte, across the vast Waggoner ranch, and on into Wichita Falls. All the way, he looked at the oil derricks sticking up occasionally from the flat ground and suppressed the urge to shake his head in dismay. This wasn't the way the West was supposed to look.

He was a big man in range clothes, somewhere between thirty and forty. With his face cured to the color of old saddle leather by a lifetime of wind and weather, it was hard to say just how old he really was. But when he took off his broad-brimmed Stetson to sleeve sweat off his forehead, the gray streaks in his thick brown hair were revealed.

The broad, dirt streets of the town were lined with vehicles of all sorts: buggies, buckboards, spring wagons, and more than a few of those gas-burning contraptions that bounced over the roads on rubber tires. Hallam reined in and looked at the automobiles with a mixture of curiosity and disdain. He had seen only a couple of them before, but here in Wichita Falls there were dozens of them. If this kept up, the city fathers were going to have to pave the streets.

The sidewalks were clogged with men, all of whom seemed to be talking in loud voices and waving pieces of paper in the air. Speculators, thought Hallam. They were trading in oil field leases, trying to make a quick killing. Ever since the discovery of oil nearby, Wichita Falls had become a boomtown.

Hallam remembered when it had been a cowtown instead, fondly known as Whiskeytaw Falls because of all the saloons within its environs. The downtown area now sat smack-dab on the place where once old Dan Waggoner had built his branding fires at roundup time.

But all that was changing, and quickly, too. Cattle were still important hereabouts, but oil was doing its best to crowd them out. Hallam looked at all the men in town suits and fancy hats on the sidewalks and couldn't stand it anymore. He gave one long sigh for the past.

Then he swung down from the saddle, tied his mount's reins around a post, and shouldered his way into the saloon he'd been looking for.

It was a blind tiger, so named because the bartender couldn't see his customers. The bar was behind a counter and closed off from the rest of the place. The bartender stood behind an opening sort of like the window in a bank teller's cage, only there was no window, just a six-inch high slot through which he dispensed drinks. Hallam's sheer bulk enabled him to forge a path through the crowd in the blind tiger. When he reached the drink slot, he spoke loudly so as to be heard over the clamor in the saloon.

"Red draw."

A moment later, a hand belonging to the unseen bartender shoved a full mug through the opening. The mug was filled with an unappealing rust-colored concoction, a mixture of beer and tomato juice that was unique to Wichita Falls. Hallam dropped a silver dollar on the counter. The hand released the mug and scooped up the coin. Hallam picked up the red draw and took a swallow, grimacing as the stuff went down. It was an acquired taste.

This was the place he was supposed to meet the client; he was sure of that. The instructions in the wire he'd received at the hotel in Lubbock had been specific. He was here on the right day and at the right time, too. But as he looked around the saloon, studying the men at each of the tables and in the booths along the walls, he didn't see anybody who looked tough enough to be the famous Wild Bill McClanahan.

Something nudged his arm roughly. Hallam almost spilled the red draw. He looked around, expecting to see one of the oil field workers. Instead he didn't see anybody right next to him. Again, somebody poked his arm, and a voice that sounded like it was coming from the bottom of a well asked, "Are you the Pink? They said he'd be a big cowboy."

Hallam looked down and saw a man a head-and-a-half shorter than him. The fella looked to be about as wide as he was tall, and his shoulders stretched the fabric of the brown tweed suit he was wearing near to busting. A derby hat was jammed down on a thatch of hair the same color as the mixture of beer and tomato juice. The man's head was tilted back so that he could look up at Hallam with eyes set deep in pits of gristle.

"I'm McClanahan," the man said.

"Lucas Hallam."

McClanahan nodded. "Come on back to the hotel with me, and we'll talk about it."

Hallam had expected McClanahan to be a bigger man. McClanahan had a reputation as one of the toughest wildcatters in the oil business, or so Hallam's bosses at the Pinkerton office in Chicago had said in their wire. But as Hallam looked at McClanahan now, he could see that what the man lacked in height, he made up for in grit.

"Sure," Hallam said. "Let's go."

Dusk was settling down. Hallam went with McClanahan down the street to a three-story brick building with "HOTEL" painted in big letters on the wall of the second floor. The place was new since the last time Hallam had been to Wichita Falls. Hallam frowned as McClanahan led him into the elevator. He'd been in the things before, but he didn't like them.

McClanahan's room was on the third floor. His suite, actually, since there was a sitting room in addition to the bedroom. "Most expensive room in the house," the wildcatter said with a touch of pride as he ushered Hallam in. "Wild Bill McClanahan always goes first class. That's why I hired the Pinkertons. Not supposed to be anybody better when it comes to detectives."

"I reckon not," said Hallam. He hung his Stetson on a hat tree just inside the door.

McClanahan tossed his derby on a sofa and headed for a portable bar. "Want a drink?" he asked. "Something better than that swill in the blind tiger?"

"Not right now," Hallam said. "Why'd you have me meet you there, when you brought me back here in the open? I figured maybe you didn't want anybody knowin' you'd hired a detective."

"Yeah, that's what I was thinking at first." McClanahan splashed liquor in a glass, threw back the drink. "But it doesn't really matter now. I'm not going to be able to use you."

Hallam frowned. "What?"

McClanahan held up a hand. "Don't worry. I know you made a special trip over here. I'll pay your expenses. But there's no job here for you after all."

"I was told somebody's been sabotagin' your wells."

McClanahan's broad shoulders went up and down in a shrug. "Yeah, but I don't think there's going to be any more trouble. It's about played out now."

"How do you know that?" asked Hallam.

"Just a hunch. I follow my instincts. That's how I've always operated." McClanahan grinned. "And I've done all right for myself, if I do say so myself."

That was true enough, Hallam supposed. McClanahan was a rich man, with dozens of oil leases here in the Red River country and more down in East Texas. He was known for his stubbornness and reckless streak, as well as his ability to pick the best places to sink a well.

"All right," Hallam said. McClanahan was the client, after all. "What now?"

"I send a check to the Pinkerton office in Chicago, and you wire 'em and ask what your next job is." McClanahan poured another drink. "Because there's no job here."

"Sure." Hallam reached for his hat and put it on. He nodded to the wildcatter. "So long, Mr. McClanahan."

"Goodbye, Mr. Hallam."

Hallam stepped out into the hall and pulled the door shut behind him. He walked slowly down the hall toward the elevator, thinking hard. Then he realized what he was doing and turned toward the stairs instead.

He had just started down when he heard the ding of the elevator door opening. He looked back, saw a woman come out of the elevator and start down the hall. She was mighty pretty, but the two men with her weren't. One was called Doss, and the other was Garney. Hallam knew them right away, even though he hadn't seen them for nearly five years. The last time had been in a saloon in Big Spring, back when Hallam had still been wearing the silver star on a silver circle, the badge of the Texas Rangers.

Hallam had tracked Doss and Garney and a couple of other wideloopers to Big Spring, and they hadn't taken kindly to the idea that he was placing them under arrest. Lead had flown. The boys who'd been with Doss and Garney had wound up dead, leaking their life's blood onto the sawdust on the floor of the saloon, but Hallam had taken a slug and was losing some blood of his own. Quite a bit, in fact. Doss had been creased, but Garney was untouched somehow and had gotten himself and his pard out of the saloon and onto their horses while Hallam was trying to get back up. He was too late to stop them from riding off into the night, and then he was out cold. By the time he was back on his feet a week later, Doss and Garney were long gone. Their escape still grated in Hallam's craw.

But now, here they were in Wichita Falls, wearing expensive suits and fancy cream-colored Stetsons and tagging along with a gal who was pretty enough to be an actress. None of them paid any attention to Hallam, who was partially hidden from them by the wall of the stairwell. He started to grab the Colt on his hip and throw down on Doss and Garney, but something made him wait.

The gal said something to them, but Hallam couldn't make it out. Then they went on down the hall, and she stopped in front of a door and knocked on it. Hallam took off his hat and edged his head around the corner enough to see that it was the door of Wild Bill McClanahan's suite. McClanahan jerked the door open, exclaimed, "Darling!" and wrapped up the gal in a big hug. He took her into the suite and shut the door.

Hallam eased down a couple of stairs, leaned his shoulders against the wall of the stairwell, and said quietly, "Hell."

"Yeah, McClanahan's had all sorts of trouble," Rufus said. Hallam didn't know the driller's last name. "Pipelines broken, tanks set on fire, equipment stolen. Just about everything that can go wrong in an oil field has gone wrong for him the past few weeks."

That wasn't news to Hallam. It was McClanahan's trouble, after all, that had led him to hire the Pinkertons to find out who was behind it.

Rufus downed the rest of his red draw and made a face. "That's vile stuff. But it sort of grows on you."

Hallam had gone back to the blind tiger and had a few drinks, circulating among the crowd until he found the talkative sort of gent he was looking for. Rufus had worked in oil fields from Pennsylvania to Spindletop, and now he was here in Wichita Falls, following the booms.

After buying a couple more drinks and bringing them back to the table, Hallam said to the wiry, middle-aged driller, "Even with all his troubles, I reckon McClanahan has a few things to be happy about these days, what with that gal I saw with him earlier tonight."

"You mean Mrs. McClanahan?" Rufus took a healthy swallow from the mug, then wiped the back of his other hand across his mouth. "She's a looker, all right, but hell on wheels from what I've heard. Wild Bill don't back down from nobody and never has run from a fight, but that wife of his can break crockery over his head and get away with it."

"So they don't get along?"

"Get along? She's divorcin' him! Claims she's goin' to take him for everything he's got."

That didn't jibe with what Hallam had seen earlier. He said, "Are we talkin' about the same gal? Blond hair, nice figure, real pretty?"

"That's Katie McClanahan, all right." Rufus laughed. "She don't know what a light she's in for. Wild Bill never gave up anything easy, and I hear he's hired the best lawyer in Texas to help him get shed of Katie without havin' to pay her a dime."

Hallam stared down into his own mug. He had heard enough lies in his life so that he could recognize one most of the time. And McClanahan had lied to him earlier, he was sure of it. The wildcatter's troubles weren't over, not by a long shot. Throw in the presence of his wife, as well as Katie McClanahan's connection with a couple of hard-cases like Doss and Garney, whatever that was, and you had a mess.

Of course, he could ride away from it. McClanahan had made it clear that he wasn't going to be hiring the Pinkertons after all. Nothing was keeping Hallam here.

Nothing but his curiosity, and the fact that he didn't like being lied to.

He dropped a coin on the table as he stood up, and said, "Have another on me."

"Much obliged," said Rufus. "Enjoyed talkin' to you."

Hallam left the blind tiger and strolled back toward the hotel. He stood across the street from it for nearly an hour, in the shadows of an awning over the entrance of a hardware store that was closed for the night, before McClanahan and Katie came out of the hotel doors and turned to the right on the sidewalk.

Hallam watched them but didn't follow. Not until Doss and Garney emerged from the alley next to the hotel a couple of minutes later and took up the trail. Hallam gave them a lead and then fell in behind them.

Doss and Garney were watching McClanahan and Katie and never looked behind them. They had always been over-confident, thought Hallam. It had been pure luck they had gotten away from him in Big Spring five years earlier.

Trains ran between Wichita Falls and the main oil field to the northwest all day and all night, and they were always crowded. Coal oil johnnies, they were called. Hallam wasn't surprised when McClanahan and Katie went to the depot and boarded a train, nor did it come as a shock when Doss and Garney bought tickets and climbed into the passenger car behind the one in which the supposedly feuding couple was riding.

Hallam bought a ticket, too, but waited until the last minute as the train was pulling out of the station before swinging up on the platform at the rear of the caboose. The conductor looked at him in surprise and a little anger as he opened the door and stepped into the car. Hallam held out the leather folder in which his Pinkerton badge was pinned.

That made all the difference in the world. The relationship between the Pinkertons and the railroad was tight, maybe a little too tight for Hallam's comfort all the time. The conductor asked, "What can I do for you?"

"Bill McClanahan got on this train a little while ago with a pretty blond woman."

"Yes, sir. I saw 'em get aboard."

"That was Mrs. McClanahan with him?"

"Sure was." The conductor grinned. "Looks like they're back together again. I heard they were splitting up."

Hallam nodded. "Ain't it sort of unusual for a gent like McClanahan to be goin' out to the oil field at this time of night?"

"Drilling never stops," the conductor replied with a shake of his head. "You're liable to find Mr. McClanahan out there for forty-eight hours at a stretch. He likes to supervise his wells personally, even though that doesn't always sit too good with his foreman."

"Who'd that be?" asked Hallam.

"Fella named Mitch Belton."

Hallam filed the name away in his head. Might be important, and might not.

He didn't say anything to the conductor about Doss and Garney. The two owlhoots had robbed more than one train in the past and were still wanted for all those holdups, but Hallam didn't want to make his move against them until he knew how they were tied in with Katie McClanahan. He had a bad feeling about that.

The run to the oil field was short, less than an hour. Hallam spent it in the caboose, even after the conductor left to make his rounds. When the train stopped at the makeshift depot on the edge of the tent city that had sprung up, Hallam swung down from the caboose on the off side. He made his way along the train, watching between cars. He spotted McClanahan and Katie getting into a horse-drawn wagon. A tall, rawboned, dark-haired man was handling the team. He flapped the reins and started the wagon rolling into the forest of derricks.

The tent city was lit up brightly. Lamps and torches burned in front of most of the canvas structures. In that light,

Hallam had no trouble seeing Doss and Garney ride out on the trail of the wagon a few minutes later. They had rented the horses near the train station at a wagonyard and livery that consisted of a big corral with a tent pitched in front of it for the owner.

Hallam went to the same place and rented a big buckskin gelding. The owner was a small, sleepy-eyed gent. He yawned and nodded when Hallam said, "Busy tonight, ain't it?"

"Yeah. I don't usually rent too many horses this late. There some sort of get-together out at McClanahan Number Three?"

"What's that?"

"One of the wells. I've heard rumors they're about to hit pay sand."

"Goin' to come a gusher, eh?"

The liveryman shrugged. "You never know. Me, I'm just glad I don't have to get oil under my fingernails to make a livin'. Give me good honest horse manure any day."

Hallam grinned and swung up into the saddle he'd rented along with the buckskin. He understood how the man felt, even though he'd never been that fond of horse manure himself. Things were changing mighty fast in Texas these days, and Hallam wasn't convinced it was all for the better. But there wasn't a damn thing a fella could do to slow 'em down, either.

He rode after Doss and Garney, across flat, mesquite-dotted terrain that had once known only the hooves of buffalo and Indian ponies. Now the derricks, spider-like contraptions of wood and steel, rose all around and pierced the star-scattered sky. The night was filled with the growling and rumbling of the steam engines that powered the drilling rigs.

The derricks gradually thinned out. Prairie began to take

over again. The starlight was enough for Hallam's keen eyes to make out Doss and Garney riding several hundred yards ahead of him. He was sure they were still trailing McClanahan. They had to be getting close to the outer edge of the oil field by now. Hallam hadn't passed a derrick for quite a ways.

Suddenly, one thrust up into the air ahead of him. He saw a tarpaper shack nearby with a lantern burning in front of it. The wagon carrying McClanahan and Katie pulled up at the shack.

Doss and Garney veered their mounts off the road and vanished into the mesquites.

So did Hallam.

He halted the buckskin and dismounted. His hand went to the butt of the Colt and eased the gun in the holster. Just like old times, he thought. Here he was, trailing a couple of desperadoes through the chaparral. A grim smile tugged at his mouth for a second. A fella could almost forget it was the damned twentieth century now. Almost.

Hallam moved silently and carefully through the darkness, not wanting to trip over Doss and Garney. He made a wide circle around the oil well and the shack and almost stumbled into a huge pond of something that glistened blackly in the starlight. The stench that rose from the obsidian pool told him what it was: raw oil in a storage sump.

He went around the sump and slipped closer to the well. Where the hell were Doss and Garney? Hallam stopped and listened but couldn't locate them. They were like him, old enough to have grown up in a time when a man's life could depend on him being able to move quiet-like.

Hallam crouched behind a mesquite and peered between the branches, being careful not to rattle the beans. He saw McClanahan, Katie, and the rawboned man who had driven the wagon. The three of them were standing near the derrick platform. The younger man was holding the lantern, which he had brought from the shack.

"Damn it, Mitch, where are the men?" McClanahan demanded angrily. "Why isn't the donkey engine going? We're close to pay sand, I know it!"

Katie had hold of his arm. She said, "Don't be upset, sweetheart. I asked Mr. Belton to stop the drilling for tonight and send the men back into Wichita Falls. I wanted to see the rig without all that noise."

"Oh. Well, that's all right, I guess. Anything for you, darling. I'm just glad you're finally taking an interest in my work."

Hallam grimaced as he eavesdropped on the conversation. He didn't figure either of them meant a word of what they were saying. They were just fencing with each other, feeling out their opponent. Hallam had always preferred straight talk.

Evidently, so did Mitch Belton. The foreman said disgustedly, "For God's sake, Katie, stop playing up to him. You don't have to do that anymore."

McClanahan swung sharply toward Belton. "What the hell?"

"Don't be a fool, Bill," grated Belton. He reached behind his back and produced a pistol. Hallam saw it clearly in the light from the lantern in Belton's other hand. "You must've figured out by now how Katie and I feel about each other."

McClanahan looked at Katie, who drew back from him. "You told me you loved me, said you wanted us to put all our troubles behind us."

"What did you expect me to say? I had to get you out here some way," she said coolly.

"So you could murder me!" McClanahan accused.

Katie smiled. "I'll inherit all your leases, and Mitch can do a better job with them than you ever have—and without ignoring me for weeks on end!"

McClanahan glared at his wife and her lover for a long moment, then said, "I don't understand. If you want my wells, Mitch, why did you try to ruin them?"

The gun in Belton's hand shook a little as he replied, "I had to punish you for the things you've done to Katie. The wells are the only things you care about, the only way to get to you." He eared back the revolver's hammer. "But then she explained to me that we could have it all . . . if we just got rid of you."

Well, McClanahan had been right about the sabotage coming to an end, thought Hallam—but only because Katie and Belton had decided to kill him instead.

McClanahan sneered at Belton. "You won't pull that trigger. You don't have it in you."

For a couple of heartbeats, Belton didn't say anything. Then he lowered the gun and said, "You're right, Bill. I'm not a killer."

"But we found some men who are," said Katie. She raised her voice and called, "Doss! Garney!"

The two gunmen stepped out of the mesquite, about twenty yards to Hallam's right. Both of them were holding pistols. McClanahan glanced over his shoulder at them and laughed. "So you brought along your hired killers, did you?"

"They'll get rid of you," said Belton. "There are still places out here where a body can be hidden, places where it'll never be found."

Hallam slid his Colt from its holster. He had heard enough. Maybe McClanahan had decided not to hire the Pinkertons, but until Hallam's bosses back in Chicago officially took him off the case, he considered this his business.

Besides, he wasn't going to stand by and watch anybody be murdered.

"That's what I'm counting on," said McClanahan.

Hallam frowned. Maybe he hadn't heard enough after all. McClanahan didn't sound particularly worried.

"You see," McClanahan went on to Katie and Belton, "I don't particularly want *your* bodies being found any time soon."

"You're crazy!" Katie gasped. To Doss and Garney, she said, "Shoot him!"

"I don't reckon so, ma'am," Doss said coolly. "You see, you might've been a rich lady someday."

"But your husband's a rich man right now," Garney finished.

Katie flinched back a step. "You . . . you knew!" she said to McClanahan. "They told you!"

That cinched it as to why McClanahan hadn't wanted a Pinkerton around. Doss and Garney had double-crossed Katie and Belton, and McClanahan had manipulated the whole thing to get rid of his wife and her lover. Even now, McClanahan was stepping aside so his hired guns would have a clear shot—

Hallam stepped out of the mesquite and called, "Doss! Garney!"

It would have been easier to shoot them in the back. That's what most Pinks would have done. But Hallam wasn't most Pinks, nor did the passage of time always change a man the way it changed everything around him.

He let them turn, let them bring their guns around before he started firing.

Hallam's Colt crashed, the shots rolling out smoothly, unhurried. Doss went backward, folding up in the middle, the gun in his hand bucking as it sent a slug drilling into the sand at his feet. Garney was hit, too, but not as hard, and he stayed upright. Flame spouted from the muzzle of his gun as he fired. Hallam felt the breath of the slug as he squeezed off another shot. This one sent Garney spinning off his feet.

"Shoot!" Katie screamed. "Shoot him, damn it!"

She wasn't talking about Hallam. She was yelling at Belton, who still had the pistol in his hand. He tried to raise the gun as McClanahan lunged at him. McClanahan batted the weapon aside and barreled into Belton. His hands locked around Belton's throat, and the muscles in his huge shoulders bunched.

Hallam heard the crack as he turned toward them and knew from the limp way Belton sagged to the ground that McClanahan had just broken the man's neck with his bare hands. Off to the side, a gun cracked, and McClanahan staggered.

Katie had picked up Belton's gun. She pressed the trigger again, but this shot missed. McClanahan let out a roar and went for her. She turned and ran. McClanahan snatched up the lantern that Belton had also dropped, and went after her.

Hallam bit back a curse. He could shoot McClanahan, but he wanted the man alive. He wasn't sure how the law would look at everything McClanahan had done—breaking Belton's neck could be considered self-defense, after all—but somebody else was going to have to sort that out. He ran after McClanahan and Katie.

The woman's blind flight carried her toward the oil storage sump. Hallam saw the lantern bobbing through the mesquite as McClanahan pursued his wife. Hallam yelled, "McClanahan! Hold it!"

He didn't expect that to stop the wildcatter, and he was

right: it didn't. Branches whipped at Hallam's face as he plunged through the thick growth. He heard Katie scream, heard more gunshots. Hallam came out in the clearing that held that vast black pool in time to see Katie finish emptying the pistol into McClanahan. He stayed on his feet somehow, stumbling toward her, his final lunge carrying him into her . . .

They both went over into the sump.

It wasn't really an explosion when the lantern flame hit the oil, more like the striking of a giant match. The *whoosh!* was enough to send Hallam staggering back anyway as the heat pounded at him. He went down, rolling over in the sand. Mesquite trees burst into flames around him, the beans crackling as they burned. He scrambled onto his hands and knees and then to his feet, loping away from the fire until he could stand to stop and look back at the huge blaze. It was burning brightly enough, flames shooting hundreds of feet into the air, that folks could probably see it all the way back in Wichita Falls.

Hallam hoped the buckskin hadn't been spooked and run off. If it had, he would have a long walk back to town.

He explained it all as best he could to the authorities. Since he was the only one left alive, there was no one to dispute the story. The fact that he was a Pinkerton, and that Doss and Garney had been wanted outlaws, probably helped the sheriff to accept Hallam's story. It was well past daybreak by the time Hallam had a chance to find the Western Union office and wire his superiors in Chicago. He got an answer back quickly.

"MCCLANAHAN RETAINER ALREADY DEPOSITED STOP PROCEED IMMEDIATELY SWEETWATER STOP BANK ROBBERS FLED ON HORSEBACK

TOWARD CAP ROCK STOP PURSUE AND APPRE-HEND STOP."

Hallam looked up from the telegram with a grin. Chasing down a gang of owlhoots. That was more like it.

Wouldn't hurt to put off the future a while longer, he figured.

STANLEY AND THE DEVIL

by Wendi Lee

Wendi Lee is another talented author who toils in two fields, mystery and Western. Her series about Private Detective Jefferson Birch allows her to work in both at one time. Here, she creates an unusual member of the newly formed Secret Service and shows a talent for stories with a comic touch. Her most recent historical novel is The Overland Trail.

The bullet took him by surprise. Stanley fell to his knees. Then he looked down at the spot where the bullet had entered. Blood was seeping out of his shirt, but Stanley had the wild thought that it was a fairly neat hole, not much to look at considering how much of an impact it had had on his body. He felt himself going numb and he fell over on his side. His last thought before losing consciousness was that this was a lousy way to die, alone under the merciless New Mexican sun. And for what? A pair of lousy engravings.

• • •

It wasn't as hot as he'd been led to believe, Stanley Porter thought as he stood in the train station in Santa Fe. In fact, the weather was quite moderate with a light cool breeze in the air. Stanley squinted into the distance, taking in the sight of the low Sangre de Cristo range on the horizon. It was hard for him to believe that he was out West now. If his father had asked him to describe Santa Fe on the spot, Stanley would have to go with white. Everything appeared to be bleached white. And the buildings were strange. It was almost as if the alien pueblo structures were formations that had risen up from the very ground over thousands of years to become part of the landscape.

He thought about the fact that right now back in Philadelphia, it was most likely a cold, wet March day.

A large man with a handlebar mustache and a tin star on his dusty tan shirt loped over to him. This man was the first thing Stanley could say with certainty was not white. He was dusty. Now Stanley had two words to describe Santa Fe: white and dusty.

"You Stanley Porter?" the man asked.

Stanley nodded and stuck his hand out. "Yes, that's me."

The large man eyed Stanley, who was a small, thin man, impeccably dressed in his suit. "Sheriff Simon Wade at your service. Excuse me for saying so, but you look a little young and," he hesitated, "well, you look a little inexperienced to be in law enforcement, let alone an operative for this new Secret Service."

Stanley gave the sheriff a thin smile. "A lot of people say that, but the chief of the new agency handed me a badge all the same." He meant to imply that he'd gotten his badge through merit, but the truth of the matter was that Stanley Porter's wealthy and connected family had wanted him out of the way. They had paid for his way into a new law enforcement organization called the Secret Service. Two years ago, President Johnson and Secretary of the Treasury Hugh McCulloch had organized the Secret Service to catch counterfeiters. The fact that Stanley had been sent to this godforsaken town out West just meant that every day of their lives his family didn't have to see the son who failed law school.

But Stanley knew that he was still on trial. William Wood, chief of the fledgling bureau, was not happy to have Stanley, a "lily-livered lawyer-type," aboard. Stanley had overheard the chief saying the very thing to Stanley's father, when he could very well have hired a real lawman.

Ever since the Civil War ended, there had been a surfeit of false greenbacks and government bonds. Counterfeiters were a dime a dozen, and money was rapidly becoming worthless. Secretary of the Treasury Hugh McCulloch became concerned with the state of the treasury and approached President Lincoln with the idea of creating an agency to combat the counterfeiters. Lincoln agreed with him and on the day of April 14, 1865, he approved the plan—just hours before John Wilkes Booth fatally shot him.

While President Lincoln didn't have the opportunity to see the Secret Service formed, the plan went through quickly, even after his death. In July of the same year, William Wood, a former soldier who worked for the government, was sworn in as head of the Secret Service not too long after the new president, Andrew Johnson, took office.

And for two years, the Secret Service had been chugging along just fine without Stanley Porter. But when he was called into the president's office at Harvard and told that he was not going to pass that year, Stanley went home in disgrace.

And his father, fed up with his son's lack of enthusiasm

for the law, began a campaign to find suitable employment for his worthless heir. Stanley had not been happy about being sent away, a job paid for by his father to get him out of Philadelphia as quickly as possible. But once he heard those scorching words, "lily-livered lawyer-type," Stanley became determined to be the best damned operative of the new Secret Service that Mr. Wood had ever had. Pigheadedness was part of Stanley's nature. His father often told him it came from his mother's side. His mother wasn't able to disagree with his father anymore, God rest her soul.

"Let me show you your office here in town," the sheriff said, leading the way. He didn't pick up Stanley's bag, and for a moment, Stanley was at a loss—he was used to servants waiting on him. Rallying, Stanley grabbed his own luggage, hoisted it in one hand, and followed the sheriff to his new office.

Well, it was a corner of an office. It was housed in the Miller General Supply & Feed Store.

"This is it?" Stanley asked for the third time. He was thoughtfully rubbing his bifocals with his sweaty handkerchief and staring at the tiny one-drawer desk and straight-backed chair. He had envisioned a large office next to the jail, perhaps, or even better, next to the mayor's office.

"So I'm not going to be working someplace closer to the jail?" Stanley asked.

The sheriff had taken off his hat to reveal a white band across his forehead. "We thought about it, but Friday and Saturday nights get so crazy that we need the extra room for those cowboys who have to sleep it off. I didn't think you'd want to be moving in and out of there, and Tess offered—"

At that moment, a young woman strode in, a fifty-pound feedsack over her shoulder. Stanley admired her shapely shoulder, and then saw the rest of her. Tess Miller would look fine on his arm, dressed in diamonds and silks, attending a state ball. Her cheeks were rosy from exertion, and her eyes sparkled. Stanley hoped the sparkle wasn't from belladonna, a new fashion that had reached young ladies in Philadelphia recently.

The young lady before him dropped her load with a thud on top of a stack of half a dozen nestled up against the pickle barrel.

"Better watch out, Tess, your brother did that last month and that pickle barrel leaked all over the feedsacks," the sheriff said. "It was a terrible mess, as I recall."

Tess nodded shortly. "I'll remember, Simon." She turned to Stanley, curiosity lighting her face the way candlelight might grace her countenance during a late supper for two. "You must be the new agent Simon's been talking about for the last few weeks."

Stanley held out his hand and introduced himself. When her hand touched his, Stanley thought he'd been transported to heaven. Her smile was welcoming, too, he thought.

"I'm honored to meet you," he said. "And thank you for the space you're providing."

She waved her hand. "Oh, it's nothing. The government is paying rent to me for letting you hang your hat here." She gave him a keen look. "Do you have a place to stay?"

"I, I just got off the train."

Before Tess could offer Stanley something comfortable, maybe a room in her own home, the sheriff slapped him on the back, causing Stanley to cough and stagger at the same time. "Oh, don't you worry, Tess. I got a place for him to bunk when he's in town. He'll be out chasing down those counterfeiters most of the time. Maybe you'd best be getting things together for him—a bedroll, some utensils for camping, and some grub."

"Camping?" Stanley had almost forgotten that most lawmen and cowboys slept under the stars on a bedroll, a thin blanket folded in half and sewn together for a man to slip into. And what was it they used for a pillow? Oh, yes! Their saddle. Stanley shuddered at the thought.

The sheriff clapped Stanley on the back again. "While you're getting those things together, Tess, I'll just bring Mr. Porter over to the stables to get a horse."

Before they got out the door, Wade hesitated and turned back to Tess. "By the way, where is Harold?" the sheriff asked. He turned to Stanley and explained in a sotto voice, "The brother."

Tess's expression shut down and she crossed her arms. "Out to get supplies. Don't know when he'll be back."

As they walked out and crossed the street, which was little more than dirt, the sheriff said quietly, "Harold drinks a bit too much. Tess doesn't approve. Whenever he goes on a bender in another town, she tells me he's out getting supplies."

"How long have they lived in town?" Stanley asked.

"Oh, probably six months," Wade replied.

Stanley thought it was nice that Tess and Harold Miller had become such good friends with the sheriff in such a short time. Of course, it was clear that Wade was sweet on Tess, and Stanley couldn't blame him. He might be competition if he stayed here long enough.

As they approached the stable, Stanley's thoughts turned to the horse he was about to meet. He thanked his lucky stars that his father had insisted on riding lessons. When the two men entered the stable, which smelled as bad as every other stable that Stanley did his level best to avoid, the sheriff led him over to a mousy brown horse with a dun-colored mane and tail. Stanley thought the horse was kind of small for a lawman.

"This beauty would be ideal for your purposes," the sheriff explained, slapping a flank.

Stanley's eye was caught by a jet black horse with a glossy tail and mane. "What about that one?"

The stableman sidled up to him. "You mean Devil there?" He started laughing. It was hard not to notice that the stableman was missing a few teeth and smelled of drink.

Devil whinnied slightly, as if calling to Stanley to take him out of this hellhole. Stanley inched his way over there. Devil shook his glorious mane. "How much?" He turned to look at the stableman, who was squinting at him as if he was an idiot. Come to think of it, Sheriff Wade looked at Stanley as if he was destined for a straightjacket.

The stableman spoke up. "The government's payin' me. You just take that crazy horse outta here."

Stanley was puzzled. "Where is he supposed to stay when I'm not using him?"

The sheriff clapped him on the back again. "Don't worry, Mr. Porter. You'll be using him plenty for the next few days. You got an outlaw to track."

Stanley's heart dropped to the soles of his polished Italian leather boots. This was not what he had expected. He'd already planned out the next few days—organizing his day with what he'd do after breakfast (familiarize himself with the town and the people), after lunch (maybe a bit of correspondence and pitching woo to Miss Tess Miller), and after dinner (perhaps more pitching woo with Miss Tess).

"B-b-but I-I-I haven't even set up—" Stanley couldn't even find the words.

Sheriff Wade gave him a sidelong glance. It was the first time Stanley had the uncomfortable feeling that the sheriff knew exactly what stuff Stanley was made of.

"You sayin' you'd rather sit around here than go out and catch the bad guy?"

Stanley sighed. "No, no. I guess not."

Wade gave Stanley a nervous look, but didn't say anything else until they got back to the general store. Tess was pouring brine into the pickle barrel. She glanced over and smiled coyly. Stanley hoped the smile was meant for him. When she was finished, she set the large pickle jar down on the counter and, wiping her hands on the apron that covered her dress, walked behind the counter.

"This is the best I could do for a bedroll," she said, putting a grubby quilt on the countertop. "Emmy May down the street has offered to sew it partway up for you."

It was a colorful paisley pattern of green, red, and blue, very bright.

"Why, Tess, that thing'll glow in the dark when he's out there trying to bring in Bill Brockway."

"Brockway?" Stanley asked faintly. "William Brockway?"

Wade eyed him, clearly less enamored of Stanley than when they had originally met. Perhaps the sheriff sensed he was a rival for Tess's affections, Stanley thought.

"Yes. We got a telegram the other day that he's been seen in these parts. Do you know of him?"

"I believe he's the fellow everyone in the Secret Service would love to catch again—the 'King of Counterfeiters,' they call him," Stanley said. Chief Wood had brought Brockway to justice once, but now the "King of Counterfeiters" was out again, and counterfeiting paper money and government bonds as freely as before. He apparently disappeared almost overnight. Stanley couldn't understand why he'd been set free. Just because he turned on his fellow counterfeiters didn't mean he shouldn't be locked up as well.

Wade looked a bit appeased. "So you do know your stuff. I was beginning to think that you were about the dumbest greenhorn this side of the Mississippi." He turned back to Tess and sorted through the things she was putting on the counter—the cans of beans, the hardtack, the tin of matches, and the coffee, frying pan, and coffeepot.

Stanley refrained from mentioning that he had read an article in the newspaper back in Philadelphia about Brockway. He didn't want the sheriff to think any less of him than he already did.

Before Stanley knew it, Devil was packed up and ready to go. The sheriff handed Stanley a map. "This is of the area. I don't know exactly where he's gone, but I heard from the marshal in Albuquerque down south that he was headed this way." He handed Stanley the map, which Stanley couldn't make head nor tail of.

"Oh. Thank you." Stanley folded it and put it in his breast pocket.

"You might also want this," Wade said, handing him another paper.

It was a WANTED poster of Brockway. The engraving showed a clean-shaven man of about forty years old. The poster information went on to say that Brockway and his wife had eluded the Secret Service after testifying in the trials of fellow counterfeiters the year before back in New Jersey. Wood had been the agent to apprehend and question Brockway, who at first insisted he wasn't the counterfeiter. After five days of questioning, Brockway had broken down and admitted to his identity. He turned in a set of plates he had made, and turned on his fellow counterfeiters by providing testimony to convict them in return for a suspended sentence.

The problem was that Brockway had been clever enough to make two copies of the plates, and had only turned over one set to the government. Brockway's wife had hidden the second plates while Wood concentrated on questioning Brockway.

"And this." Wade handed Stanley one more item—greenbacks.

"I think I have enough money, thank you," Stanley said with a smile as he tried to hand it back to the sheriff.

"That's a couple of the counterfeit notes Brockway made," Wade explained.

Stanley made a show of studying it. "Oh. Oh, yes. I see now." He didn't, but he figured he'd have plenty of time to study the notes against one of his own. The paranoid thought that maybe all of his paper money was Brockway money flitted through his head. He resolved to change most of his money, with the exception of these counterfeit bills, into coins. He carefully put the Brockway bill in his right-hand vest pocket.

Stanley got on Devil and, after some spirited prancing and backing up on Devil's part, started to leave town. The sheriff grabbed hold of the reins.

"Mr. Porter?"

"Yes, Sheriff?"

"The town Brockway was last seen in, Leyba, is that way." He pointed in the opposite direction. With some difficulty, Stanley managed to guide Devil in that direction, toward the mountains.

Four hours later, Stanley was reflecting back on how he had managed to get out of town without being bucked off

Devil. His backside was sore from so much riding. Back in Philadelphia, he rarely spent more than an hour on horseback.

He had been traveling along the Pecos River for most of the time, and right now, he would give both his shotgun and Peacemaker for a sip of the cold stream that he traveled along. It burbled and tripped along beside him, making it impossible to ignore. His own canteen was dry as a bone.

Stanley spied a boulder, shoulder-high, near the stream. He guided Devil, with difficulty, over to it and stepped down onto it, keeping a firm hold on the leads, then led his horse, and himself, to water.

By his own reckoning, he was about ten miles from Leyba. He knelt to drink alongside his horse, making sure he was drinking upstream from Devil.

When he looked up, he couldn't remember which direction he'd come from, or where he was going. The place where he'd stopped had several tributaries branching off in different directions. He looked around for a landmark, but everything looked the same to him. Stanley clawed at his saddlebag for the map, took it out and stretched it on the boulder, then looked around again. It didn't help. How was he going to get anywhere? He tried to remember which way the sun had been shining when he left Santa Fe. But the sun moved all the time, so that didn't help him.

As if Devil understood Stanley's predicament, the horse came up to him and nudged him. Of course, Stanley thought. Horses have a sense of direction. He took hold of the reins, climbed back on the horse, and urged Devil forward. The horse walked in circles.

"This is ridiculous," Stanley said out loud. "I'll just have to pick a direction." He remembered that the water was on

one side of him, so he went that way. But the river mean-
dered, and he took out the map again and again over the next
few hours, becoming more and more frustrated as the sun
began to set. It was completely dark when he spotted the
campfire. He got off his horse and walked into the camp,
leading his horse. He'd read that advice in a dime novel:
When you enter another man's camp, lead your horse in to
make yourself as non-threatening as possible.

There was only one man sitting by the fire. His hat was
pulled low and he was stretched out against a fallen piece of
timber. His arms were crossed and his guns sat beside him,
resting comfortably nearby. His horse was tethered to the
ground with a stake and a long piece of rope. A pot of coffee
sat to the side of the fire to keep it warm. The temperature,
Stanley noticed, had dropped considerably and he was looking forward to getting his blanket out and wrapping it
around him.

Stanley cleared his throat. The man shifted positions, and
Stanley thought he looked up.

"Excuse me," Stanley said.

"What can I do for you, stranger?" the man finally asked.

"Um, I seem to be lost."

"Where you headed?"

"A small town called Leyba," Stanley replied. "I thought
I'd be there today, but I seem to be lost."

The stranger gestured for Stanley to sit by the fire.
"Come on over. I got some coffee brewing if you have your
own cup."

Stanley eagerly unpacked his cup—not without some
trouble from Devil—and sat down. He still hadn't had a
good look at the stranger's face, but he did get the impression the man had a beard. "My name's Stanley Porter."

"Nice to meet you, Stanley Porter." The stranger didn't
offer his own name in return.

"What should I call you and where are you headed?" Stanley asked.

The stranger hesitated, then replied, "Just call me John, and I don't have a particular destination. But I can tell you that if you follow the Pecos River to the bend, then head straight south, that's where Leyba is."

"You know these parts pretty well. Have you been in New Mexico Territory long?"

"Long enough to know where Leyba is," John said.

Stanley was going to make more conversation, but John stretched and dragged his saddle over to the log. "You best get some rest when you finish that coffee. Sun comes up pretty early around this time of year."

Stanley finished his coffee in silence then took his bedroll and saddlebags from Devil, not bothering to take the saddle off of the horse as well. He didn't want to saddle up Devil in the morning, and he figured nothing would happen between now and sunup. He'd tethered Devil in much the same way as the stranger's horse.

He tried to get comfortable, but his badge kept digging into his chest until he finally pulled it out and stuck it in his saddlebag. Then he pulled the saddlebag over and used it as a pillow. As Stanley was drifting off, he could hear the sounds of the high plains coming alive at night. He briefly wondered if he'd ever get a good look at his companion—the dimness of the campfire and the low pull of his hat had made it impossible to check the man's features.

Stanley woke up to a noise—not a loud one, just a whisper. He'd never been a good sleeper, especially out of doors like this. The morning light had not quite covered the sky yet when he slipped out of his bedroll. John was saddling up, his back to Stanley.

"Good morning," Stanley called out as he grabbed his badge to put back in his vest pocket and stood up to stretch to his full height. John turned and looked at him, then at the badge, and suddenly he had a gun in his hand.

Stanley caught a glimpse of John's bearded face just before he fired, then Stanley staggered back from the hit, unable to make a sound. As he fell to his knees in shock and disbelief, he had the odd thought that John looked familiar. He watched John pull Devil's tether stake up from the ground, climb into his own saddle, and ride off.

Stanley wasn't sure how long it had been since he'd fallen into unconsciousness. It could have been minutes or days. He only knew that being shot hurt, and he should by all rights be dead. Instead, he opened his eyes and began to move slowly. As he felt around the bullet hole, he discovered that it had been a clean shot, the bullet exiting from his back.

He pulled himself into a standing position and looked around, just in case John had come back to finish the job.

Devil was long gone, so Stanley picked up his saddlebags and started walking. His guns had remained on the saddle in special holders, but he did have some money with him. Then he remembered that most of it was counterfeit. At least he still had his badge. Stanley tried to figure out why John had shot him. He'd seen the badge—was he running from the law? It seemed to be the most likely explanation.

The day grew warmer—spring was finally taking hold and the temperature had soared. No gentle breeze cooled Stanley today. His stomach growled. He was still following the Pecos, so at least he didn't lack water, but he wondered if he'd ever eat again, see Santa Fe again, or the lovely Tess. He rested on the bank of the river, unable to walk any farther without food, weak from the loss of blood.

Would he soon be a pile of bleached bones lying prone near the river, just a warning to all travelers in this harsh land? His eyes were heavy, and soon he dozed off.

When he woke up, minutes or hours or days later, Stanley rubbed his eyes and stood up slowly. Something in the distance caught his eye. At first, Stanley thought it was one of those mirages. Then he realized it was a wagon in the distance. The wagon drew closer and finally pulled up next to him.

The figure holding the reins was that of a young girl. "Sir, are you all right?"

"No, I'm not," Stanley managed to say. "I've been shot and I need a doctor. I was on my way to Leyba."

"There's no doctor in Leyba," the girl said thoughtfully. "Besides, Santa Fe is closer." She hopped off the wagon, a little too sprightly for Stanley's liking, considering that he felt like an old man next to her. She gently helped him into the wagon, spreading out some half-full flour sacks for him to use as cushions. The wagon slowly jolted toward Santa Fe.

Later that day, they stopped to rest the horses. The girl's name was Elena; she was dark-skinned with black hair and flashing eyes. Her face was somber as she tenderly probed the area around the wound.

"Ow!" Stanley had hoped to maintain a dignified silence at the inspection, but his body contracted in pain when she touched a particularly sensitive area. It felt like a cross between a bruise and a hot poker.

"You may have the beginning of an infection," Elena said. She soaked a piece of cloth with water. "We must clean the wound."

Her touch was gentle, but even the touch of a feather would have hurt like hell. And when she poured whiskey over the wound, something she didn't even warn him about, he howled like a wounded animal, which was pretty much how he felt.

"Why ever would you use liquor on my bullet wound?" Stanley asked.

Elena shrugged. "When my uncle had an infection, this is what we did for him, and he's still alive."

"Isn't there another way to clean a bullet wound?" he asked testily.

She thought about it. "Well, I've heard of pouring gun powder on the wound and lighting a match. Or a hot poker would work as well."

Between cauterizing and using whiskey, Stanley decided the latter wasn't so bad after all.

It was dusk when they arrived back in Santa Fe. Elena drove him straight to the doctor's house on the edge of town.

The doctor, an older whiskered gentleman who smelled of whiskey, examined the wound. "I couldn't of done a better job myself," he called to Elena, who was waiting in the next room, the door between the rooms ajar.

"Thank you, Doctor," she called out.

He gave Stanley a bottle of rotgut.

"How many times a day do I pour this over the wound?" Stanley asked.

The doctor looked at Stanley as if he'd gone loco. "You're supposed to drink it. I'm gonna sew up the holes and you're gonna need to be passed out."

After the third shot of red-eye, Stanley thought it didn't taste half-bad. By the fifth shot, he closed his eyes to rest.

When Stanley came to, he was in a bed in a strange room. His head felt large and tender, but his bullet wound appeared to be better. He didn't feel the soreness there that he'd felt earlier. He got up carefully and sat on the edge of the bed.

A moment later, Wade poked his head in. "Hey, you're up. Feel like some breakfast?"

"What day is it?" Stanley asked as he stepped into his pants.

"You just slept through the night after Elena brought you here."

"How'd she know where to bring me?" Stanley followed Wade, walking stiffly from his ordeal.

"The badge," Wade said. "Most people in town know about you coming here. Tell me what happened at breakfast."

Stanley hadn't thought he was hungry, but he found himself devouring the flapjacks and eggs and bacon as if he hadn't eaten for a week. The sheriff's wife, whom Wade had introduced as Florence, kept his cup full of hot coffee. Maybe the sheriff wouldn't be competition for Tess after all, Stanley thought as he helped himself to some fried potatoes.

He recounted what had happened to Wade.

"Would you recognize that face if you saw him again?" Wade asked, stroking his mustache.

"Of course I would. In fact, he looked kind of familiar from the glimpse I got of him."

"Well, there are a lot of varmints out there, outlaws who'll take what they can from honest men. Why don't you stay here today and rest up? Take as many days off as you need. I'll telegraph your chief to let him know what's happened. The investigation will have to go on hold till you're better."

"Thank you, Sheriff," Stanley said as the sheriff left for the day. But Stanley couldn't get any more rest. Finally, he got up and dressed and went out to familiarize himself with the town. It didn't take long to find the sheriff's office and the Miller General Store. He walked slowly down the street, walking the stiffness out of his muscles.

As he passed the alley next to the general store, he heard a familiar sound. It couldn't be, he thought, but as he turned down the alley, he found that it was—Devil had come back. He went up to his horse and patted Devil on the nose. Devil actually nudged him with what passed for affection in an animal. Stanley checked the saddle still on Devil's back, and even though the shotgun was gone, his Peacemaker was still there. Whoever had left Devil out here unattended meant to come back soon. Stanley took his gun, gave Devil another reassuring pat, and tried to figure out what to do next.

Stanley's powers of deduction weren't high, but he fig ured out that the man who shot him was probably in the store. Fearing for Tess, but not wanting to endanger her life, Stanley decided to bide his time until the man came out in the alley. Once they were alone, it would be easier to capture him. And it would make him a hero in Tess's eyes.

Just to make sure he was getting the right man, and not some customer who came out here to relieve himself, Stanley found a wooden crate, dragged it over to a win dow, and peeked inside. There were only two people there, Tess and a man whose back was to Stanley. Tess was pulling a bolt of cloth down from behind the counter, talking to the man, who was kneeling by the bottom of the pickle barrel, doing something that Stanley couldn't make out.

The man wore just denims and a white cotton shirt with dark marks all over the sleeves and Stanley noticed that his hands were stained with something dark. When he straight ened up, it wasn't the stains on the man's hands that caught Stanley's attention, it was the fact that this man was the same one who shot him the night before. And what shocked Stanley was the fact that Tess not only knew him, she was in his arms, kissing him.

It wasn't a brotherly kiss, either. It was a passionate kiss, one saved for a lover or a husband. Stanley finally got over his shock and got a better look at the man's stained hands. It was indeed printer's ink. Stanley was pretty sure this was William Brockway, even with the beard, and his wife.

Stanley knew what he had to do. He got down from his crate and walked out of the alley.

"Good day, Tess," Stanley greeted the winsome woman as he strode into the store.

"Mr. Porter, I thought you'd gone out to track down that criminal," she said. Tess had to have been surprised to see him, but she covered it very well.

Stanley went over to his desk. "Yes, I was out there." He bent over and winced.

Tess came toward him. "Oh, you're hurt." She glanced off toward the side door, the one that led to the alley. "Can I get you anything?"

Stanley pointed his gun at her. "Yes, the plates. You can get me the plates."

A moment later, the alley door burst open and the bearded man came roaring at Stanley, who fired at him.

"William, no!" Tess screamed.

The counterfeiter crumpled at Stanley's feet. He pointed the gun at Tess and said to the three people who had come in off the street when they heard the gunshots, "Please be so kind as to fetch the sheriff." He flashed his badge at the crowd and one of the men nodded, turned, and went back out the door. The others backed out of the door, not wanting to be around any more potential gunplay.

Tess was bent over her husband, who was groaning. "Where are the plates?" Stanley asked.

She looked up. "What plates?"

Stanley shrugged. "They're somewhere here in your store. We'll take this place apart, board by board, and find them."

Her smile was cold. "I highly doubt it. What do you plan to do with us? You won't find the plates here. You have no proof that we were doing anything wrong. We were given a suspended sentence and we've just been living hand to mouth here ever since."

"You did have a printing press set up," he pointed out.

"We were starting a newspaper. That also explains the barrels of ink," she replied tartly.

Stanley shrugged. "My information source says that your husband made two copies of the plates and he's still printing greenbacks. That's why he's been seen in Leyba recently, isn't it? He's been buying things and passing the money around in other towns so you wouldn't be implicated." He nodded toward the back of the store. "That's where you set up the print operation, right?"

Before she could answer, the sheriff came in. "What's all the commotion?"

Stanley pointed to the couple. "Sheriff, meet Mr. and Mrs. William Brockway."

Wade's eyes widened, then he took them into custody. "What are the charges?"

Tess spoke up. "There are no plates, but he insists that there are. We've done nothing."

Stanley nodded to her. "Maybe not you, but your husband shot me. That's an offense right there."

The sheriff hauled a groaning Brockway out the door. Stanley hadn't shot to kill, only to wound, and the bullet had only winged Brockway. Tess glared at Stanley, then turned and followed her husband and the sheriff.

"I'll look after the place," Stanley called out.

He spent the rest of the morning doing a little paperwork, helped a few customers, and racking his brain trying to figure out where the plates were hidden. He was about to go to his midday meal when Elena came in the store.

"Good afternoon," he said to her. She was wearing a clean dress, her hair was pulled back in a chignon, and her eyes sparkled.

"I came by to see how you are doing," she said. He thought she was very pretty now that she wasn't pouring whiskey over his bullet wound.

"I must thank you for saving my life," he said, taking her hand in his own. "Are you hungry?"

She smiled. "I'd like that, but can we make it dinner? I must get back to my papa's house and help him with the ranch."

"I'll pick you up tonight and you tell me where we shall eat. I'm new in town," Stanley said as he walked her to the door.

After Elena left, he turned back to the store. He'd have to get the keys from the Brockways so they couldn't get into the store. Until he found those plates, a deputy would have to be stationed here at night.

Stanley went to the back of the store to inspect the printing setup. There were no plates in the press yet. Brockway had just been oiling the machine, readying it for printing phony money.

Stanley's stomach began to growl. He'd have to eat something soon. He spied the pickle barrel. The long rake-like scoop stood by it and Stanley used it to try to spear a pickle. The barrel was almost empty, but he remembered Tess filling it the other day. The pickle spear thumped the bottom of the barrel. Stanley judged the length of the handle, then looked at the outside of the barrel. Inside the barrel, he could see that the bottom wasn't quite as deep as the barrel. He also spied a pickle. Once he'd gotten his lunch out, he wrapped the pickle in newsprint and set it on the counter.

Kneeling on the floorboards was difficult for someone who'd been shot, but if Stanley was right, he'd have the plates in a minute.

"Mr. Porter?" Sheriff Wade came in. "What are you doing on the floor?"

Stanley just shook his head and thumped the bottom of the barrel. "Hand me a tool to pry this board off of here."

"But won't the brine spill all over the place when you pull the board out?" Wade asked.

Stanley looked up and smiled. "I don't think so."

Wade found an awl and handed it to Stanley, who pried a board from a secret compartment at the bottom of the pickle barrel.

He reached inside and came out with something wrapped in cloth. Wade helped him stand up.

Together, they unwrapped the package. Inside, the duplicate plates winked back at them.

"Now do we have enough to convict them both?" Stanley asked.

Wade clapped him on the back and Stanley winced as his insides felt as if they were shifting. "You've done a good job, Mr. Porter. I'm sorry I ever doubted you."

Stanley shrugged. "It's all in a day's work." He took a deep breath, feeling more like a member of the Secret Service than he'd felt when he first came on the job. Maybe he'd found his calling. He was looking forward to tonight, and what tomorrow would bring him. "And call me Stanley."

"I think you'll fit in here just fine, Stanley."

Author's Note: While William Brockway existed and was, indeed, the "King of Counterfeiters," there is no evidence that he ever moved west or had a second set of duplicate plates. However, it makes for a very good story.

Mama's Boy

by **Frank Roderus**

*Frank Roderus is a past winner of the WWA Golden
Spur Award and recently reprints like* Old Marsden
and Stillwater Smith *are joining his newer works like*
Jason Evers: His Own Story *on the shelves. He was
the first to respond to my call for Tin Star stories, with
this interesting tale of a mama's boy trying to change
his image.*

It wasn't cold. Not even a little bit. But he was shivering
so bad he was afraid his teeth were going to start chatter-
ing and give him away.

There was somebody in the alley behind the bank. He
was sure of that. It wasn't a stray cat this time or Mr.
Finkel's old dog. Three weeks he'd been on the job now and
he knew what those sounded like. He knew their noises, had
been frightened by them the first few nights, but no more.
Now he knew what those sounds were, and this was something different.

He was scared. The blunt truth of it was that he was
scared. He was supposed to be strong and brave and res-

olute—heck, people were trusting him to protect them—and the truth was that he was so scared he was afraid he might wet himself.

But he was even more afraid that people would find out how scared he was. If it hadn't been for that, well, he would have turned right around and skipped this block and pretended nothing happened.

Instead, shivering and trembling to beat the band, he took his gun out, using both hands to make sure he didn't accidentally drop it. Lordy, that would be all he'd need to make this mess complete. Drop the dang gun and it go off and wake half the town and people come running and find . . . what? Him. In the alley. Night Marshal Bobby Delane. Probably shoot himself in the dang leg and then where would he be? Still scared and humiliated too, laying there in the alley bleeding and making a mess of everything.

Bobby took in a few deep breaths, made sure he had a firm grip on the pistol and stepped around the corner and into the alley.

"Jeez, it's you. What the heck are you guys doing here? Don't you know it's the middle of the night? You been drinking or something?"

Bobby relaxed when he saw who it was back there making the noises he'd heard. He turned sideways, turning away from the slanting shaft of lamplight that came in from the street end of the alley, and stuffed his gun back into the holster. He hoped they hadn't seen that he was carrying the gun or they would guess how bad they'd scared him.

"You're s'posed to be checking the back doors down by the pool hall," the tallest of the noisy trio said in a grumpy, accusing tone of voice.

"I'm running kind of late tonight, Will." Bobby frowned.

"How'd you figure where I should be now anyway? And whyever would you want to?"

"You messed up, Bobby. You surely did." That was Terry Woodall. Bobby recognized him. Terry and Will Bayles and . . . he had to peer close to make sure . . . Albert Thompson. He knew them. Of course he did. Everybody knew everybody else in town and for thirty miles around to boot. After all, there weren't all that many folks that a body had to keep track of in order to do that.

"So what are you doing here anyhow?" he asked them. "If you're sneaking around smoking cigarettes or drinking whiskey you better do it someplace else, okay?"

Will Bayles looked at Terry and grinned. "He doesn't get it, does he? Doesn't have a clue."

"What would you expect from a mama's boy?" Terry said.

Bobby wished now that he'd turned around and gone somewhere else. For certain sure he did. These guys . . . for just about as long as he could remember they'd been deviling him. Ragging him. When they were kids they used to even beat up on him. Nowadays they mostly ignored him. He wished they'd ignore him tonight too, but he knew they wouldn't.

"Mama's boy," Terry accused again.

Bobby clamped his lips tight shut. He learned years ago there was no sense trying to argue back with them. He didn't have a father. He couldn't deny it. Everybody in the county knew the truth. He didn't have a father and his mama was never married, and they never let him forget it.

"How'd you get your job, Bobby?" Albert asked in a high-pitched, singsong voice. "Who'd your mama lay with so's they'd hire you, Bobby?"

"You gonna have a baby brother now, Bobby?" Will taunted.

"What's she gonna do when you want a better job, huh, Bobby?"

"Marshal Sam gave me this job," Bobby protested, heat rising in his voice and now behind his eyes too. "My mom didn't know anything about it."

"That's what you say," Terry laughed.

"That ain't what we heard."

"Hell, Bobby, maybe she didn't do nothing after all. Nobody else wanted that stupid job."

"It's a good job," Bobby snapped. The moment the words were out of his mouth he regretted saying them. Not because the statement was untrue—in fact nobody else had wanted the job as night marshal what with the lousy hours and meager pay the town could afford—but because here he was defending his job and he hadn't spoken up to defend his mother. He felt bad about that. "And I got it fair and square."

"Yeah, well, you shouldn't of," Will said. "It's a stupid job and that badge looks stupid on you. A pissant mama's boy like you shouldn't wear something that's intended for a man."

"Look, I got better things to do tonight than stand here jawing with you guys. So whyn't you just go off to wherever it is you're going and do whatever it is you're doing and leave me to my rounds. Will you just go an' do that? Please?"

Terry and Albert laughed. Will kind of shook his head. "I told you," Will said. "The mama's boy don't get it. He don't get it at all."

"Don't get what?" Bobby asked. He was probably laying himself wide open for some more ridicule, but this time Will was right. He surely did not get *it*, whatever *it* was.

The three of them stood up from where they'd been crouching beside the back stoop of the bank building and pressed close around Bobby.

"Why, mama's boy, we're fixing to ride out of here tonight, you see. And we thought we ought to have a little stake to help us along the way."

"So what we're doing here, Bobby boy, we're robbing us a bank before we go."

"No, you can't do that. I won't let you. I'll—"

He didn't have time to make any more threats. The three of them jumped him and held him and beat on him, and it was worse this time than ever it'd been back when they were kids.

Lordy, but it was a whole lot worse now than it'd been back then.

"You don't have to do this."

"Thank you, Marshal Sam sir, but I figure I do have to."

"They won't get away, Bobby. I've sent telegraph messages to every sheriff, town marshal and railroad detective in Arizona and New Mexico and half of Texas too. They won't get away, and you aren't responsible for those boys choosing to do what they done."

"Marshal Sam, I might not be responsible for their choices, but I'm sure God responsible for them getting away with it. I could have stopped them."

"How? You could've arrested them? Or shot them maybe? All three of them? Three boys you knew and grew up with and never suspected would do anything like this?" The town marshal shook his head. "No, Bobby, no one holds you responsible for this but you yourself." He picked up the badge Bobby had laid on his desk and held it up between them. "I'm going to put this in my top desk drawer here, Bobby. I never lock this drawer. I'd like for you to go home for a few days, hell take a couple weeks. Go home and let some of those bruises heal. Then when you feel up to it, you come back and fetch your badge out of the drawer. It will be waiting there for you."

"That's nice of you, Marshal Sam, thanks." Bobby turned to leave, then paused and turned back again. "Could I ask for a favor, sir?"

"Of course you can, son."

It always hurt Bobby just a little whenever he heard some man call him that, the reason being that for any of the men around town who were of a certain age it could have been the natural truth . . . and Bobby himself not know it or for that matter maybe the man not know it either. It wasn't something he had ever asked about nor anything his mama had ever volunteered.

"You own a couple horses, sir. Could I borrow one of them? I'd like to kind of, you know, get off by myself for a spell and do some thinking."

"You can have the use of that little brown horse my daughter sometimes rides. And don't worry. She never uses him much anymore anyhow and will likely be happy to be shut of the responsibility of him. Anyway go ahead and take him. I'll square it with her come dinnertime."

"Thank you, sir. Thank you very much."

Marshal Sam shrugged and, good to his word, dragged the desk drawer open and laid the badge right there while Bobby watched. "It will be here whenever you want it back."

Bobby nodded and hurried away. He wasn't quite sure what he would tell his mama about this. Nothing, probably. That would likely be for the best.

Bobby stopped, raised the bandanna to his mouth and scrubbed at his lips. They were dry and hurt something awful yet there was this pasty, gumlike stuff that kept accumulating on them, and he hated the feel of it so that he was forever trying to scrub his mouth clean.

The heat lay heavy on him, and he hoped to heck he was going the right way for he was near about out of water.

The brown horse seemed to feel the heat as bad as Bobby did. It moved lethargically, slow of foot and careful of its energy.

Bobby lifted his hat and got the benefit of a false but nonetheless pleasant sense of coolness when the fresh air reached his scalp. He fanned himself a couple times and then set the hat back onto his head, needful of the shade it provided.

A man could set a couple eggs inside his hat when he rode off in the morning, Bobby suspected, and by time for nooning he should have roasted eggs to enjoy with his lunch, it was that hot.

He squinted and tilted his head to one side so as to redirect the trickle of sweat that was stinging the corner of his eye. He could see the mountain ahead of him five miles or so.

He just hoped it was the right mountain.

The other boys called it Red Mountain although he wasn't sure why. It looked the same as all the others so far as he could see. Still, that was what they called it, and back when they'd been thirteen, fourteen years old or so they'd talked about it a lot.

Bobby had never been there himself. He'd never been invited to go along on the so-called hunting trips to Red Mountain. But he'd heard the others talk plenty, Will and Albert and Terry among them.

There was a time when boys reached that age and wanted to get off by themselves. They gave hunting or fishing or such as an excuse to go, but really they wanted to get off where there weren't any grown folks around so they could roll up some cigarettes and smoke them without being made fun of or nip at Mason jars that they'd stocked with odds and ends of whiskey that they swiped from their papas, a little of this and some of that mixing all together in any sort of container that could be stoppered and carried along.

Bobby had heard all the stories about Red Mountain. He'd just never been there before now.

It was a good place for a body to get away to, though. Nobody hardly ever went there. There were no minerals. No graze for cattle or sheep, not even enough to run goats on, or so they said.

Which probably explained too why the hunting parties never managed to bring back any game, nor the fishermen any fish.

Red Mountain lay north and slightly west of town at a distance of twenty-four miles. Or so they said.

Bobby stood in his stirrups—in Marshal Sam's stirrups, that is—and turned in the saddle to peer back the way he'd come.

He took out the compass he'd bought this morning from Mr. Finkel and consulted it. He was riding on a line that put the mountain in front of him at one little diamond pointer thingy to the left of north while behind him he could still make out the stark, tiny little pinprick of white church steeple at a single diamond marker to the right of south.

The dry, barren, craggy lump in front of him pretty much had to be Red Mountain, he thought. He hoped. He prayed.

Yeah, this was it. Had to be. There was a trail, sort of. Maybe it had been made by wild creatures, deer and bighorn desert sheep and those sort of animals. Not that he could tell. Bobby couldn't tell one footprint from another.

All right, that was an exaggeration. He could tell a boot print from a horseshoe print from a bird track. But that was about as good as it got.

He eyed the steep and gravel-strewn path that snaked up into the rocks and decided a horse would likely slip and stumble and snort its way along and could even fall and hurt itself on a path like this one.

In a way that was encouraging because the boys always talked about how poor the path was and how no grownups could ever sneak up on them for their progress would be heard a half mile before anyone got near to the camping spot.

It wouldn't hardly do for him to let Marshal Sam's brown horse fall and break a leg—to say nothing of having to walk all the way home again after—so Bobby followed along beside the base of the mountain until he found a telltale dark gray stain on the rocks. Right below that, just as he'd hoped, was where the creek up above finally came down off the mountain.

There at the bottom, just before it disappeared into the sand, was a little seep no bigger than a washtub. It had four or five inches of tepid but reasonably fresh water in it. Bobby drank until his belly ached—which it already did anyway from the beating he'd taken and the movement of horseback riding all day—and filled his canteen. Then he let the brown horse drink, pulled the saddle and bridle and stashed them under some brush. He hobbled the horse and with a thrill of trepidation turned loose of it. If the dang horse didn't respect hobbles and wanted to start on a beeline for home . . .

Better not to think about that right now, he decided.

He picked up his canteen and a gunnysack that held the canned goods and other necessities he'd brought along, took one final nervous look at the horse and then started resolutely up the path onto Red Mountain.

Now he knew why they called it Red Mountain. There wasn't anything else that could possibly have fit.

The path topped out on a tall, narrow spine as sharp practically as a primitive knife blade. Red Mountain ran north to south, and the west side of it was sheer, a nearly straight drop of more than a hundred feet, maybe several hundred, before the wall was broken up with ledges and protrusions.

The thing was, it was coming evening and the low-slanting sun from off in the direction of Arizona turned that whole sheer wall a soft and lustrous shade of red.

Red Mountain indeed. It fit. The view from up here and the colors down under his feet were breathtaking. Spectacular.

Bobby stood there, poised with half the world laid out below him, and let the rising evening breeze cool and calm him.

He stood there for several long moments, and from deep inside him he sent a formless, wordless, pleading prayer up soaring into the sky.

And then he took his eyes off the magnificent far vistas to look down toward his own shoe tips, clamped his lips tight closed and made his way slowly ahead along the path he'd heard about so often.

The smoke smelled of pine resins, and Bobby's mouth watered at the aroma of bacon frying in an iron spider.

The smell reminded him that he'd been so preoccupied today that he hadn't stopped for lunch, hadn't even thought to munch some of the dry biscuit and cheese he'd brought along. He was ravenously hungry now, and his stomach rumbled and rolled at the thought of bacon and whatever else might be cooking in the pot he could see steaming at the edge of the fire.

He kind of hoped it was something that he liked.

But then he was so hungry right now that he was pretty

sure he would like it whatever it was. Well, if it was anything short of beets, he would like it. Beets always made him want to throw up.

He stopped and very carefully wiped the palm of his right hand along his pant leg to make sure his grip was dry and secure. Then he drew the pistol from his holster and stepped out from behind the rocks where the path let out onto a clearing where at least a couple generations of boys from town had come as part of their passage from childhood to maturity.

It surprised him to note that his hand remained steady, and he wasn't shivering or shaking this time. Not even when he cocked the revolver and held it where they were sure to see.

"Boys," he said, "I'm placing you under arrest on a charge of bank robbery."

They looked startled. But only for a moment. "Jeez. It's just you, Bobby." Will Bayles grinned. "For a minute there I thought we was in trouble."

"Are you hungry, mama's boy? Want something to eat before we send you running for home?"

"You better put that gun down, Bobby. You don't wanta make us mad."

"Let me know when you clowns are done running your mouths," Bobby said. He held the gunnysack tight against his side so he could reach down with his left hand, the one he'd been carrying it in, to grab the bottom and let go of the top so the contents of the bag tumbled noisily onto the ground.

A few cans of food were included as were the crackers and cheese. Most of the bulk though consisted of heavy spancels that he'd gotten from the locker back at the marshal's office.

One by one he picked up the sets of irons and tossed them across the fire to the trio of boys who were squatting in the light there.

"You can do the honors, Albert. There's six pairs. We'll chain you together in a circle, wrist to wrist and ankle to ankle, all three of you in a nice little bunch."

"And if we don't want to be chained and taken back, mama's boy? What are you gonna do then? You gonna cry until we get all sad about being mean to you and give in?"

"Do whatever you think is best, Terry. The thing is, this time it isn't me you're picking on. I guess I still wouldn't do anything rash if that's all it was. But this time you've robbed pretty much every man, woman or child in the county. I took an oath to protect them from the likes of you. Now I'm doing it. And now you are under arrest."

"You won't shoot us, Bobby. Don't forget, we know you. There's no way you'd shoot us."

"But me, Bobby, that's different," Will said. "I would damn sure shoot you." He grinned. "And there's three of us, mind. Just the one of you. You couldn't shoot all three of us even if you wanted to. One of us would get you sure."

Bobby looked Will Bayles square in the eyes. "I admit it, Will. Amongst you you can get me. I probably won't have time to shoot more than two of you before you put me down. That means that one of you will walk free with all the bank's money and not even have to share it with anybody." Bobby's expression softened into a smile that amazed even him because he quite honestly meant it. He wasn't putting on an act. He just . . . meant it. "The question is, Will, which one of the three of you will be left alive, eh?"

He waited a moment, then said, "Put the irons on, boys, or have at me, but whatever you want to do, you make up your minds soon because I'm getting hungry from smelling your damn bacon. Much longer and I'll make the decision for you. Pick up a manacle or a gun, whichever you please." His voice hardened. "Now *do* it!"

• • •

Bobby felt awful. Chewed up, spit out and barely warmed over afterward. His eyes burned from lack of sleep. His muscles ached from all the unaccustomed abuse. He felt light-headed and woozy and was barely able to walk.

All in all, though, he didn't think he had ever felt better in his whole life.

He dropped the cell keys onto Marshal Sam's desk and pushed his hat back off his forehead so he could rub both eyes with the heels of his hands.

"How'd you figure them to be there, son?" Marshal Sam asked.

Bobby shrugged. "A guess. The mountain is in just about a directly opposite direction from Mexico, and that's where everybody thought they'd run to. I thought it was worth taking a chance."

"You know of course that as night marshal you had no authority to be out there arresting anyone. You, uh, did know that, didn't you?"

Bobby managed a smile. "Marshal Sam sir, if you'll recall, I wasn't night marshal at the time. Just a citizen of this county making a citizen's arrest. I believe I recall reading somewhere that such a thing is legal."

"It's legal," the marshal acknowledged.

"There's one thing I'd like to do now. Then I want to go get about forty-eight hours of sleep if you don't mind."

"What's that, son?"

Bobby smiled at the man and stepped forward. He leaned down and pulled the marshal's desk drawer open.

The badge was lying there.

It looked pretty nice, he thought as he reached out to take it up again.

LAW WEST OF LONETREE

by Deborah Morgan

Deborah Morgan has allowed herself to be lured into other aspects of the publishing field in recent years when I believe she should have been concentrating on her own writing. Finally, however, she is beginning to pay more attention to her career, and lucky for us. She seems poised to fulfill the promise of her much anthologized story "Mrs. Crawford's Odyssey." She is at work on her first novel, and took enough time off from that to craft this story of an unusual woman's relationship with an even more unusual range detective.

They were having breakfast when he died.

He'd finished reading his copy of the *Missouri Democrat* and, in keeping with his strict morning ritual, was announcing the day's schedule to his wife.

She was still reading her own copy of the same newspaper, never looking up yet hearing everything he laid out. Her mind was strung that way, like piano wires, and played complicated chords that resonated and created harmony from the many different notes of life.

"Rovie?"

She looked up. In the six years they'd been married, she'd never before heard his pet name for her outside their bedroom. She saw the surprise in his eyes just before he fell forward.

Alarmed by the clatter of china, the maid came running just as the man's wife reached the end of the long dining room table. She sent the maid for the doctor, then lifted her husband's head and mopped his face with a napkin. The monogrammed linen was the same white shade as his skin.

The doctor pronounced the man dead, after which the new widow stepped bareheaded into the July heat, walked the ten blocks to the telegraph office, and sent the following wire:

JAKE GREENWOOD, MANAGER
TRIPLE B RANCH
CHEYENNE, W. T.

BENJAMIN BAIN BRICE DEAD STOP DOUBLE GUARDS STOP
HIRE RANGE DETECTIVE

I REMAIN
MRS. BENJAMIN B. (MONROVIA) BRICE

That done, the young widow returned home (stopping briefly to employ the services of an undertaker), climbed the three flights of stairs to her private chambers in the most elaborate Victorian mansion on Cattlemen's Row in St. Louis, and cried.

PART ONE
Cheyenne, Wyoming Territory

Monrovia Brice wore black well. She was no stranger to it, the occasion having presented itself many times in her thirty years.

She stepped from her private Pullman into the searing heat of the plains and wondered how she would manage in the dark wardrobe. Opening a black parasol edged with jets, she strolled past the milling people to the end of the platform. Soon she found the dry heat a welcome change from the humidity on the great Mississippi, which had left her swooning like a frail Southern belle (a condition she despised).

One of her personal train attendants, a short graying black man named Nathan, busied himself arranging for her transportation to town.

She'd worked tirelessly since her husband's death one week prior, making the necessary arrangements and committing to memory everything she could about operations at the Triple B.

She had put aside her savvy business sense when she married Benjamin Brice, and had slipped easily into the role of society wife. He'd established healthy bank accounts for her, both in St. Louis and abroad, which caused frequent flutters on Wall Street as she shopped in Europe, made regular trips to New York City for the opera, and honed her already impressive firearms skills on retinued African safaris.

She had never understood Ben's aversion to this wild country. He'd made a quick and large fortune in the cattle industry, yet had always treated the ranch trips as required evils. When he returned to the comforts of home (with no small amount of relief), he set about spending his fortune in the best shops, restaurants, and theaters that the Gateway City had to offer.

But, oh, how she'd longed to see the West! Pleading time and again with him to take her along had been fruitless. He had insisted that it was no place for a lady.

Now, although in mourning, she could scarce contain her excitement. Over the past few days, she'd found the vast stretches of land warm and inviting. She had wondered at the endless expanse of sky, virtually untouched by the architecture of man. All of this had lifted the fetters of her prior existence and she smiled in spite of herself. She'd found home.

Gritty dust pelted her skin and she welcomed it with upturned face. Surveying the town, she discovered that Cheyenne was more developed than she'd expected. This fact reassured her. It was close enough when she needed something, but far enough away from the ranch so that she could enjoy the freedom from social obligations.

With her baggage secure in the buckboard, Monrovia climbed up next to the driver and told Nathan goodbye. She didn't look back, even to see if he waved.

Her driver delivered her to the Sterling Hotel and she procured his services for the next day's journey to the ranch. She kept two small valises and left the rest of her belongings in his care.

She checked in and ordered a simple supper of ham, eggs, and coffee sent up to her suite. After settling in, she waited for the meal to be brought. As she waited, she again studied Jake Greenwood's response:

MRS BENJAMIN B BRICE
ST LOUIS MISSOURI

SORRY TO HEAR THE SHOCKING NEWS STOP NO REASON TO BE CONCERNED ABOUT RUSTLERS STOP I WILL RUN

RANCH AS ALWAYS WHICH IS HOW MR BRICE WANTED IT

MANAGER TRIPLE B
JAKE GREENWOOD

She tossed aside the slip of paper and paced the rooms until supper was delivered. The ranch manager's assurances went against everything Ben had advised her to do if anything should happen to him.

Initially, she had planned to go directly to the ranch and meet Jake Greenwood, reason with him. But the more she turned this over in her mind, the more she realized that he had no cause to listen to her. Why should he? Ben had pretty much let Greenwood run the ranch without questioning his methods. A woman—even if she was the new owner—wasn't going to change that. Was she questioning Ben's judgment by taking an entirely different approach? He'd told her to protect her interests. Yet she knew that a woman must approach the situation differently.

She changed her plans. After supper, armed with directions from the hotel clerk, Monrovia Brice was walking through the streets of Cheyenne.

For all its attempts to match the gentlemen's clubs of London, the Cheyenne Club's exterior was anything but opulent, especially next to the elaborate mansions that flanked it on Seventeenth Street and made her feel, momentarily, as if she were back in St. Louis.

The moment she stepped inside, however, she discovered where they'd spent their money. The dark-paneled walls displayed works of art from many globally famous painters, French chandeliers shed electric light on sculptures of Italian marble, and Oriental rugs lent exotic texture to lacquered oak floors. These men of the Wyoming Stock Growers' Association had taste.

She walked gingerly down the immense corridor, dodging the tuxedoed and tipsy cattlemen, stepping over billiard balls that rolled across her path. She'd heard from Ben that most of the members were civilized Easterners and Europeans. They weren't acting like it tonight. The boisterous group seemed determined to partake of nearly every luxury imaginable before moving on to their ranches for fall roundup.

She peered through one doorway and then the next until she finally arrived, surprisingly intact, at a relatively quiet chamber.

She stepped inside the dining room. The men grew quiet as they realized that a female had breached the walls of their inner sanctum.

In this silence, a man of medium height and build sucked the contents from an oyster shell, then tossed it into a large copper pot at his feet. The shell landed with a click.

He glared at Monrovia while wiping the juices from his hands and white mustaches with a steaming towel. Then he called the steward over. "I don't know how this young lady sashayed past your staff, Graves," he said with a Southern drawl, "but I'm sure you will explain to her the error of her ways."

"Yes, Mr. Wainwright." The steward's deep voice echoed as if he were alone in a cathedral. He was a large yet muscular man some years shy of forty and blue-black as a gun barrel. He touched her elbow lightly with a white-gloved hand.

She stiffened. "Gentlemen, I am Monrovia Brice—owner of the Triple B."

Murmurs swept the room.

The man introduced himself as Castle Wainwright,

owner of the Diamond Bar Ranch. He stood and bowed elaborately, his balding crown gleaming pink under white curls. "We were greatly saddened to hear of Benjamin's death. On behalf of the Association and every man here tonight, I offer our deepest condolences."

Monrovia nodded slightly. "I fear that the passing of my husband may present the appearance of opportunity to cattle rustlers, and I would like to speak with you about hiring a range detective."

The man reached for another oyster. "Last I heard, Jake Greenwood was still manager of the Triple B. Shouldn't you be speaking with him about this?"

"But, I'm looking for a certain—"

"Mrs. Brice, if there is need to hire a detective, Greenwood will see to it." He paused, then added, "You *have* spoken with Greenwood, haven't you?"

"No, Mr. Wainwright, but I—"

"You've never been to your ranch, have you?"

"No, but—"

"Graves," Wainwright said loudly, "see the lady to the door."

Monrovia stood her ground for a moment, then finally allowed the steward to escort her from the room.

When they were on the veranda, he said, "Madam, women are not welcome unless invited."

"They made that clear." Monrovia started down the stairs. "Perhaps there is someone in town who knows where I can find Mr. Law."

"Archie Law?" The steward's face showed expression for the first time.

"You know him?"

"Know of him. He's black, madam."

"Yes! I'm sure he's the one."

"*Black,* madam. You should not inquire after a black man."

"It's all right, I assure you. He was a friend of my husband's. I have proof." She pulled a worn piece of paper from her bag and handed it to the steward.

Graves studied the document.

"You should not travel there alone. Allow me to send someone for him."

She smiled. "I don't want to be any trouble. If you'll just give me directions, I'll have a messenger from the hotel locate him for me."

He looked doubtful.

"On my word, Mr. Graves, I am going directly to the hotel from here."

Monrovia repeated the steward's directions as she walked. She stopped by the hotel and retrieved her smallest valise— she had planned to anyway, but it made her feel better to know that she hadn't *really* lied to the steward.

Making her way to the far end of town, Monrovia walked confidently through the jumble of tents and shanties that made up the isolated Negro community. Her trips to Africa had assuaged any unreasonable fear of the color of a person's skin and she met the stares of those around her full on. They quickly dropped their gazes.

She located Law's cabin, with its Union flag tacked to the door, and was glad to see light illuminating a small side window. Before she knocked, a dog barked inside and several in the area answered him.

"Shut up, Luther," came a man's voice from within.

The door opened a crack. When he saw the well-dressed white woman standing there, the owner of the voice jerked back. "One of us is in the wrong place, lady, and it ain't me." He started to shut the door.

"Archie Law?"

He paused. She had his attention.

"I'm Monrovia Brice."

"Brice. Ben's woman?" Something flared quickly in his eyes, but vanished before she could decipher it. "That don't mean you should be here."

"Please, Mr. Law, Ben left specific instructions that I contact you."

A gaunt blue-tick hound bolted out past the man and took off toward a thicket of trees. At length, Archie Law stepped aside.

The one-room shack was scrubbed clean and white-washed and a lantern glowed on a small kitchen table centered in the room. On the north wall an antelope horn rack held three long-barreled firearms. Under that was a small bed, neatly made. Above a washstand was a shelf which held scissors, razor and shaving mug, and a steel comb, all placed in a perfect row.

The room smelled of roasting coffee beans. Monrovia inhaled deeply.

She sat at the table in one of two straight-backed chairs. The man removed a small pistol from his waistband, laid it on the table, and sat opposite her.

He was tall, rangy, and on the lean side of fifty, with black hair silvering at the temples. His mottled brown skin looked faded and old, but in his eyes Monrovia saw everything Ben had told her about Archie Law: strength, patience, brutality.

"Ben said you enjoy a good drink." She reached into her small valise and brought out a bottle of cognac and placed it on the table.

"I never turned down a good drink yet. I'm beholden."

Monrovia then produced two glasses from the valise and filled each from the bottle. She handed one to Archie, clinked hers against it, and threw her drink back in one shot.

Archie set his full glass on the table with a thud. "Haven't you handed me enough surprises for one day?"

"I've spent my share of time in Paris, Mr. Law. They're more lenient with their pleasures."

He drank the cognac. "Mighty fine liquor, Miz Brice, but you didn't come all the way from St. Louie to drink with an old black man. What's on your mind?"

"Do you know Jake Greenwood?"

"Head of the ranch. Never talked to him, though. It's no secret he's allergic to dark skin."

"I wired him when Ben died, told him to double the guards and hire a range detective. This is his answer." She handed him the telegram, then poured him another shot. "I've heard of entire ranches going under for lack of taking the rustler problem seriously, and I don't intend to let that happen to the Triple B."

"You want me to work out there, is that it?"

"Ben said you were the only man he would trust for the job."

Luther whimpered at the door and Archie got up to let him in. "You can forget it. Greenwood would just as soon shoot me as look at me."

"We can tell him it was Ben's decision."

"Won't do no good. There's not a black man'll go near the Triple B."

"I wish I understood why Ben didn't rectify that. Everyone knows he wasn't a bigoted man."

Archie eyed her evenly. "Ben never was here long enough to make changes."

She knew he was right. A long moment of silence passed between them. "Ben said you could do things most men didn't know humans were capable of. If you're that good,

Greenwood will never know you're on the place. Besides, he'll have no need to. You won't be near ranch headquarters. Just patrol the edges, take care of any problems. You'll be dealing with me, not him."

"If I decide to work for you—and that ain't saying I will, but if I do—it might work better if you let Greenwood know you hired me on, show him straight off that you're the new boss."

"If I should decide not to tell him, would that put you in danger?"

"I'd be in danger anyway. Don't let that concern you."

She paused. "Take the job, Mr. Law. I'll pay you handsomely."

"I ain't worried none about the money."

She reached once more into the valise and retrieved a small wooden box.

"Ben's grandfather left New York for Texas when Ben was just a boy. This is the only thing Ben had that belonged to him."

Archie opened the box and removed a small nickel-plated badge. It had evidently been polished recently. He held it close to the lantern in order to make out the worn engraving: "SPECIAL OFFICER."

"This tin star won't work for law up here."

"I thought it might help remind you that Ben had faith in you. So do I. Would you wear it while you work for me? For Ben and me?"

The hound raised its head at the sound of someone singing. Archie looked up. "That'll be Johnny Firewalker. Sounds like he got a head start on us for drinkin'."

The door swung open and a half-breed with long black braids under a floppy hat stumbled over the dog.

"Luther, you damn mutt, get the hell out of the way." He kicked the hound. Luther yelped.

Archie picked up the gun from the table and fired. The half-breed fell, grabbing at his left thigh.

"You shot me, you damned nigger reprobate son of a bitch!" Firewalker sat up, clutching his leg. "What the hell did you do that for?"

"You kicked Luther." Archie knelt and inspected the bullet wound. "Johnny, it done gone straight through. I'll buy you a new pair of pants."

The black man went to the washstand, snatched the towel off the rack, and began tearing it into strips. Firewalker went on cursing.

"You're in the company of a lady, Johnny."

The half-breed stared at the woman. His expression shifted from indignation to remorse. "Bad enough I kicked Archie's dog, but to do it in front of a lady? Damn!"

Monrovia hid a smile. She poured a shot of cognac and handed it to the wounded man.

Archie finished bandaging the leg, then threw the bloody rags into the washbasin to soak. He returned to his seat opposite Monrovia. "Thought you'd be gone by now."

"You haven't given me an answer."

"You just watched me shoot a man. Don't that bother you?"

The patient held out his glass and Monrovia refilled it. "I like dogs," she said.

PART TWO
The Triple B Ranch

Jake Greenwood lit his pipe and walked the length of the large porch. With pale eyes, he surveyed what lay before him with all the pride of a cattle baron.

He loved the West. Its sculpting winds and parching sun

had served him well, chiseling further his already sharp features and burnishing the leather of his skin.

Being ranch manager of Wyoming Territory's largest cattle empire carried with it a certain amount of respect, and he appreciated his station. Although the rich young ranch owner who'd provided it was dead, Greenwood wasn't concerned. The ranch still had to be run, and no one could run it better than he. This fact assured him that he would always have a place working with cattle.

There wasn't a better ranch anywhere, by his estimation. It had several ribbons of water—including the Laramie River and the smaller Lodgepole and Lonetree creeks—and he was confident that there would never be a threat of thirst to man or beast. Abundant grasses assured plenty of grazing for the animals, and the creek borders weren't too scrubby with the tangled brush that cattle invariably got hung up in.

Best of all, the owner had always furnished everything Greenwood asked for without question—just like it should be.

He'd been with the Triple B for almost twenty-five years, having worked first for old man Sanderson before he'd died and his widow had sold the works to Benjamin Brice. Now there was a woman who knew what to do when a man had gone to his reward.

Sitting on the porch's edge, he leaned against a corner post and thought about the telegram he'd received from Brice's widow. He reckoned her to be a panicky sort and he credited that to youth. He assumed she was young, anyway, because her husband was.

Had been. The ranch manager reminded himself that Brice was dead. The young man never did seem to take to the place, only visiting the ranch once or twice a year. In many ways, he had never existed in Greenwood's world.

In the absence of the owner, Greenwood had always figured he owed it to the land, the cattle, and the cowboys who worked for him to present himself as proprietor. It created a stability that was needed for the hands, and the necessary illusion of power and authority that he believed gave him an edge.

Yes, he alone had made the Triple B the dynasty it was. And the last thing he needed was some female trying to tell him how to run it. A skittish filly who'd never even bothered to come check the place out, at that. He fancied himself someone who knew how to handle women, and expected that corralling this one would be no different from any other. He'd spent a lot of time on his response to the young widow, saying in brief but clear terms that he had everything under control.

He knocked the plug from the pipe and let the bowl cool. Placing it in his shirt pocket, he started toward the corrals.

Dust rose thick as new chaps, only to be blown away by the unending winds of the plains. In his early days of cowpunching, he was often surprised to wake up and find any earth left. Now he knew that the wind brought in as much dirt as it took with it, and his world would remain constant and balanced as long as those winds never ceased.

Roundup would begin soon. Although it was a lot of hard work—gathering strays, culling those that belonged on other ranches, branding and castrating, doctoring and hoping that screw worms didn't attack and infect the raw flesh—it had its rewards, too.

His cowboys, although weary after each exhausting day, looked forward to the camaraderie with the extra hands hired for roundup. They gathered after the hearty suppers and played music that created memories to stoke the comforting fires of the mind throughout the winter.

The tone was set according to what the day's work dictated. If it had been a relatively smooth day, "The Yellow

Rose of Texas" would jump to lively fiddle music. A day
that delivered hell-on-hooves would call for something like
"The Cowboy's Lament" or "Cowboy Jack"—Greenwood's favorite—accompanied by the mournful cries of the
harmonica.

The men told stories, too, ones they'd saved up for
months that were too good to waste on the bone crews of
everyday ranch life.

It'd be different this time without Mr. Brice under foot.
Greenwood reckoned the man had been in it for the money.
To each his own. Men like that wouldn't stick, though, if
blizzards or drought or disease or some other act of God
yanked all the coins from their purses.

At the corrals, his cowhands were busy busting broncs,
oiling harnesses, preparing salves, gathering branding irons,
and doing a thousand other chores for the roundup.

Clattering distracted him and he turned to see a buckboard pulled by a matched team of grays approaching the
gallery. Seated next to the driver was a slim young woman
with sharp, striking features. When the driver pulled rein,
the woman quickly climbed from the rig.

Greenwood frowned. He didn't care if she *was* a woman.
Out here, you waited for an invitation to step down.

She surveyed the ranch headquarters, her sharp gaze darting from one building to another, checking the bunkhouse
and tack room, the storage buildings, the main ranch house
and another smaller house, the cookshack with its long
plank tables lined up out front.

Smiling, she looked toward the remuda with its varied
breeds of horses and past that to several groups of cattle that
grazed the land all the way to the horizon.

"It's magnificent! How soon may I see the rest of it?"

Greenwood crossed his arms over his chest. "Miss, we're
not in the habit of giving guided tours."

The woman laughed. "Forgive me, I've forgotten my manners. I'm looking for Jake Greenwood."

"You found him."

"Mr. Greenwood, I'm Monrovia Brice." She extended her hand.

After a moment, he remembered to remove his hat. "That can't be possible," he stammered.

She lowered her hand. "I assure you, Mr. Greenwood, I have the wherewithal to remember my own name."

"Sorry, ma'am, you took me by surprise. If we'd known you were coming out for a visit, we would've fixed things up proper for you."

"I'm sure things are in order." She told the driver to put her belongings on the porch of the main house.

"You don't mean to stay *here,* do you?"

"I certainly can't stay at the Cheyenne Club."

"But—"

"You would've been preparing for Ben's arrival anyway, so I'm sure that whatever was done for him will be suitable for me."

He put his hat back on. He'd never been so caught off guard and he didn't like what it was doing to him. Damned woman.

"My condolences on the passing of Mr. Brice, ma'am." He took off his hat again. "Quite a shock for a fella so young to pass on. Anyhow, I figured you knew I'd handle the ranch just like I always have. No need for concern."

"Mr. Greenwood, I'd be here if Charlie Goodnight himself were in charge."

Greenwood replaced his hat and chewed on this new piece of information for several seconds before turning toward the corrals. "Overfield. Topeka. Get over here."

Two cowboys trotted across the gallery, slapping dust from their clothes with their sweaty hats.

"Put this stuff in the house." The manager waved a hand, indicating the baggage.

One of the cowboys, short and wiry and ten years older than his companion, grunted when he heaved a trunk up to his shoulder. "Women sure do pack a lot of stuff for a holiday. Not like a man. No sir. A man, he don't need hardly nothin'—"

"Topeka," the other cowboy snapped. "If you'd put all that energy into your back instead of your mouth, you'd get the job done a hell of a lot faster. Sorry, ma'am." His sour expression didn't go with the sentiment.

"Don't apologize, Mr. Overfield. If I'm going to be a part of ranch life, I'd better get used to the savory language."

Greenwood's jaw clenched. "I would reserve making any decisions about staying in the West if I were you. Ranch life isn't suitable for someone used to modern conveniences. Your husband came to realize that early on."

"My husband was a good man and a good provider—for all of us. Unlike him, however, I prefer to get involved." She started up the steps.

He ran ahead of her. "Before you go inside, I should tell Iris to spruce things up a bit for you. She's the housekeep. Does any cooking that needs done for the housefolk, too."

Leaving Mrs. Brice on the porch, he stepped inside the main house and stood in the entryway, thinking. What in the hell was he going to do now? He'd have to be quick on his feet, or be skirt-whipped for sure.

Shouts came from the gallery and the buckboard's driver slapped harness to the grays. Greenwood watched out the window as the rig headed east, presumably back toward Cheyenne. He wondered if the woman really intended to stay on, or if she'd given the driver instructions to return after a period of time.

When the two cowboys vaulted down the staircase, he

said, "Take Mrs. Brice down to the corrals. Tell her I'll be there in a couple of minutes."

When they left, he went to the kitchen.

Iris, a young woman with dull blond hair pulled into a tight bun at the nape of her neck, was making a peach cobbler.

He filled her in on the new houseguest. "While I'm showing her around, you get my gear and put it in the other house. No need her knowin' I been staying here. I suppose you'd better do what she says till we know what's going on."

She peered out the kitchen window, apparently sizing up the woman standing at the corrals. "Reckon she'll make you toe the line, Jake?"

"Watch your mouth, Iris."

"She's probably thirsty. It's a long ride out from Cheyenne." Iris rummaged through one of the cabinets, found a silver tray and draped it with a starched doily, then set a pitcher of lemonade and a tall glass on it. She walked out the kitchen door. Greenwood followed.

He introduced the women. The widow offered her hand. Iris took it and bowed slightly. "I'm not sure if we have the things you like to eat, but I'll have supper ready for you at six, if that's okay."

Mrs. Brice drank some lemonade. "Actually, Iris, I was thinking it would be nice to eat out here with the cowboys. It would give me a chance to meet everyone. Does that sound good to you?"

Iris glanced at Greenwood.

He said, "Tell Lynch to set her a place."

Lynch, the slipshod range cook, wore a dirty undershirt stretched over a potbelly hammocked in a grimy apron. Greenwood smirked. It was obvious from the woman's reaction that she wished she'd taken Iris up on the offer to prepare supper.

But good, simple meal and the dry wit of the ranch hands seemed to agree with the woman from back East. She might prove more difficult to discourage than he'd hoped.

After supper, the cowboys shuffled wearily toward the bunkhouse while Greenwood walked Mrs. Brice to the main house. He was irritated at having to stay in the smaller house while she was here, and even more irritated that he'd be sleeping alone. Iris had told him that it wouldn't look right if she wasn't in the main house tending to the needs of the new occupant. He'd grudgingly agreed.

As they stepped inside, the widow said, "Mr. Greenwood, don't you think it's time we discussed the cattle-rustling situation?"

He removed his hat and started toward the elaborate hall tree. He stopped, realizing that the movement seemed too comfortable, and hung the hat on the doorknob instead. Next thing he knew, he'd be walking in without knocking. He sighed heavily. "Like I told you in my telegram, there *is* no situation. Your husband put faith in me to run this place and I expect you to do the same."

"I haven't said that I doubt your abilities as ranch manager. But don't you agree that Ben's death might make rustlers believe we have our guard down? We shouldn't sit back and allow them to take property right from under our noses."

"You're overreacting, Mrs. Brice. Now, I'm sorry that Ben passed on, but you need to try and understand. He wasn't even here most of the time. I hate to be the one to say it, but his death won't matter one way or another to the rustlers. If anybody wanted to rustle Triple B stock, they'd be doing it whether he was dead or alive."

"How do you know they haven't been?"

"Because it's my job to know, damn it!" He slammed the door. His hat fell to the floor and he scooped it up. That took the head off his steam. "I mean no disrespect. It's just that I ain't used to anyone questioning how I do my job."

"If there is nothing to worry about, then all I will have lost is a little money. It won't be the first time, and it probably won't be the last."

"You've got a lot to learn about ranching, and I'll be happy to fill you in when there's time, but for now you need to leave things to me. You've had a lot of changes come about in the last week."

"I assure you, I've prepared myself. I studied Ben's ranch ledgers before I left St. Louis."

"Good. Then you know what we need in the way of operating funds. You see to that, and I'll see that the place stays afloat. I'll even have some of the boys ride the lines, see if there's any sign of rustlers. Deal?"

"You'll have the money to operate, same as always," she said flatly. She stared at him for a long time and he wished he knew what was going on inside her head. At length, Iris walked in and offered to show Mrs. Brice to her rooms. She told Greenwood good night and followed the housekeeper up the stairs.

PART THREE
Somewhere on Lonetree Creek

He'd been here before.

The last time, he'd tracked two men through Nevada and the Colorado territory, serving a keen brand of justice on them for raping and killing a marshal's daughter. None of the whitefolk there had cared that Archie Law was black, any more than they cared how he exacted restitution . . . They cared only that he did.

He stretched out on his belly and propped himself up on his elbows behind a jagged granite outcropping at the crest of the creek's bank. In the valley to the south, roiling dust clouds steadily grew larger.

His knowledge of tracking and deduction had paid off. Earlier in the day, he'd surveyed the valley, mapping with the skill of a visionary the route by which the rustlers would come.

He reached for the Creedmore that lay beside him. The rifle had been exposed to the sun for more than two hours, and the forged steel of the rolling block singed his palm. He did not permit himself to flinch, but rather allowed the metal to sear his flesh as a reminder to remain focused.

He brought the rifle farther up, minding the sun so as not to give a reflection.

Six bottlenose .44s were stationed in a neat row beside him, glittering like gold against the flannel cloth upon which they rested. He picked up one of the long cartridges, hefting its solid weight. Carefully, he slid it into the chamber and eased the block mechanism shut.

Snugging the walnut stock into the hollow of his shoulder, he fixed the glinting barrel into a pronged vee of granite. He adjusted the folding sight to six hundred yards and zeroed in on the lead rider.

The wind was from the east and he heard, faintly, the man's voice prodding the cattle onward. With his keen eyes, Law made out enough physical details to confirm what he'd learned before leaving Cheyenne. The man in his sights was one who had been building a sizable herd from Triple B stock.

Using nature to calculate the shot, Law studied the effect of the wind upon the shimmering water, judged its velocity by the ripples that skimmed the bright blue surface of the creek. He measured with a glance the swaying branches and rustling leaves of the trees and bushes, calculating how much he would need to adjust his aim.

His target moved steadily alongside the cattle, and Law waited several minutes for the herd to come into full view. Taking in everything before him with quick, darting glances, he again checked the ripples, then the leaves, then his target. Thumb on the hammer, he eased it toward him. The *click, click* registered, echoed against his eardrums.

All this was completed in a matter of seconds. He wrapped a long finger around the trigger and squeezed.

The rustler's jaw dropped slightly when the bullet broke through his chest wall with a thud. Law watched the burning cheroot tumble from the man's lips. The body slumped, then slid away. Dust to dust.

One.

Instantly, Law reloaded and pivoted, swinging the barrel to the right. He drew a bead on the second rustler. Fluid movements, quicker now, yet as precise as the first kill.

From past and frequent experience, Law knew that the first man was on the ground before the report was heard in the valley. The second rider saw his partner fall, and sat stupefied for what seemed like hours before whipping around to search for the source. Law squeezed the trigger just as the man turned.

Two.

He watched closely. Both men lay on the ground, unmoving. Their horses and the frightened herd had turned and scattered back toward the south.

He walked to the camp he'd made earlier under a stand of pines a short distance beyond the western rim of the creek. His buckskin's ears shot forward and it pawed the ground impatiently. Law mounted. The old Union saddle creaked as he leaned forward and urged the horse into a trot toward the valley.

After making sure that both men were dead, Law reached into one of his vest pockets and pulled out two Union uniform buttons, each stamped "U.S." The brightly polished brass winked in the glaring sun.

He placed a button in each man's shirt pocket, then rode back toward camp.

While the coffee boiled, he chewed on some hard tack and thought about the coming days. What would be his tally this time? Five? Fifteen? It didn't matter. He would do the job he'd hired on to do, for as many days as it took. And as many lives.

Come morning, he would break camp and stake out the ranch's western border near the easiest pass through the mountains.

PART FOUR
Line Shack on the Triple B

Greenwood leaned against the makeshift corral and rubbed the small of his back.

Having Brice's widow on the place over the past week had pushed him to do more physical labor than he'd done in years. He tried to tell himself that being on the farthest stretches of the ranch beat having run-ins with the woman, but he wasn't so sure. At least she didn't know how to find her way out here.

He shuffled toward the well for a dipper of water.

Hearing hooves thundering over the ridge, he shielded his eyes from the intense afternoon sun to get a better look. A few of his cowboys crested the western hill. Just what in hell did they think they were doing? There was no way they could've finished the work he'd sent them to do a couple of hours ago.

That's when he saw someone draped and tied over the saddle of one of the horses.

The bunch came to a dusty halt at the corral.

"What the hell happened?"

"It's Shaw."

"I can see that, damn it. Is he dead?" Greenwood loosened the lariat strings and lowered the man to the ground.

The others dismounted.

"Yessir." A cowboy they called Pink, a heavy boy with a round face that only had to be shaved twice a week, spoke rapidly. "Found him over by Medicine Bow Pass. Must've been one hell of a slug to rip a hole through him that big."

"Did you check around for any sign of what happened?"

"Sure did." He paused. "Not a thing, Boss. It's like that bullet dropped right ought of the sky."

Greenwood slapped his hat against his thigh. "Damn it to hell!"

A Triple B hand named Lancaster had been riding fence to the north and galloped up to the group. He dismounted and pushed his way through the knot of cowhands gathered around the body.

"What's going on?"

"Somebody shot Shaw. He's dead."

Lancaster inspected the wound. "Looks like a match to the ones I heard about in Laramie last night. A couple of

Diamond Bar hands were shot the same way—ambushed, it appears, with a large-caliber gun."

"Any idea who done it?"

"They said the killer's leaving a mighty unusual sign." Lancaster pushed aside Shaw's vest, reached past the pocket flap on his shirt, and brought out a shiny disc.

"Yep, here's your calling card."

The ranch manager grabbed the brass button, rubbed his thumb over the letters.

"Get him buried, boys."

Greenwood saddled up and rode hard toward headquarters.

PART FIVE
Four Jacks and a Queen

Monrovia was enjoying the relative peace and quiet on the ranch. Greenwood had taken a crew and gone to the western borders of the ranch a few days earlier and she was enjoying the break. Although she had expected it to take him a while to get used to her, she hadn't been prepared for his belligerence.

It was mid-afternoon, and she'd needed some fresh air before continuing work on the account ledgers. She sat on the front porch and watched as the wind rushed along the prairie. It dipped and skimmed over the long grasses, creating an illusion of unseen creatures slithering through the blades. She shivered in spite of the heat.

Her gaze was so fixed upon this phantasm that she didn't notice the carriage approaching from the east until it was almost upon her.

Its great wheels ground to a halt and the driver climbed down and opened the carriage door. Four men stepped carefully from inside. When she recognized Castle Wainwright,

Monrovia bristled. Instinct told her that a visit from the Cheyenne Club couldn't be good.

Wainwright said to the driver, "Don't get too comfortable. This won't take long."

He turned to Monrovia. "We require a moment of your time, Madam."

"Certainly. Won't you join me inside for some refreshment?"

She saw the men to the library, went to the kitchen to tell Iris they had guests, then returned and took her place behind the massive mahogany desk.

Wainwright introduced the brothers Hale, identical twins with white hair and gray eyes, in identical blue worsted suits and black bowlers. Their ages added up would put them in the triple digits.

Malcolm Hale said, "Our spread joins yours on the south, miss. It's called, appropriately enough, the Double H." He giggled and Wainwright hushed him up.

The fourth man was introduced as Jarvis Pickard. He was the only one of the four who looked at home in the West. His tan Stetson was creased and slightly worn and his Western boots were run down at the heels. He had a ranch above Wainwright's own Diamond Bar to the north.

Wainwright's hand fluttered. "Enough with the pleasantries. We have a problem. I'm sure you are aware of the recent killings, Mrs. Brice."

She wondered if he was spokesman by self-appointment. "Killings? No, I'm not. Who's been killed?"

"Two of my best hands, for starters."

"That's right, miss," said Malcolm Hale, seizing a cup of tea from the tray Iris brought in. "Two of his best."

His twin brother, Lyle, bobbed his head energetically.

Wainwright proceeded. "Frankly, I'd forgotten about

your visit to the Cheyenne Club, but Jarvis here reminded me of your intent to hire a detective. It appears you went ahead with it. Is that true?"

She leaned back and crossed her arms. So they wanted to cut to it. "Where were your employees killed, Mr. Wainwright?"

"That doesn't matter, madam. What matters is—"

"It does matter. If they weren't on my property, then I have no interest in the episode. If they were, then I'd say many questions have already been answered."

"Mrs. Brice." Wainwright leaned forward. "We're always hiring cowhands that drift from one place to another."

The others murmured their agreement.

The spokesman continued. "Most of us haven't yet seen the need to invest money stringing up that infernal barbed wire. All our ranch managers know to work together, which is why you should've taken my advice last week and let Greenwood handle things."

"You wasted no time having me escorted from the premises of the Cheyenne Club, yet you assume you can come out here and tell me how to run my ranch?"

His eyes were shrewd. "Who did you hire?"

"What good will it do you to know that?"

"The word around Cheyenne is that it's some stinking black Buffalo Soldier who still thinks he's fighting a war. If that's true, then you've brought a lot more down on us than you realize."

"I can't say that I noticed the color of his skin. Black or white, I judge people by their ability to do a job."

"Hire a black man or two, then, to cowboy on the ranch. I have a few of them myself. They're hard workers. Just don't entertain the notion that they can be trusted any further than that.

"Those cowboys your man murdered," he went on, "were some of the best shootists in the territory. He's nothing more than a cold-blooded killer. A sniper, obviously, or he would never have survived a run-in with my men. "We don't need someone like that lurking around out here."

"Like what, Mr. Wainwright?"

"Mrs. Brice." Jarvis Pickard crossed his legs and hung his Stetson on his knee. "You're not used to how things are run out here. If we don't rope this situation, the government will bring in the army and then I'll allow you'll learn what real trouble is. If that happens, not a durned one of us will have any rights left."

"My right is to defend and protect what's mine. And that's what I will continue to do."

Once again, Wainwright took the reins. "Lady, don't make me take matters into my own hands. The Wyoming Stock Growers' Association will not back your play. Call off your killer. Or you'll force us to do it for you."

She eyed him evenly, spoke with a steady voice. "Threats don't affect me, Mr. Wainwright."

He stood, leaned over the desk, and pointed a finger in her face.

"If you think you can get away with hiring one of them to take the upper hand on the range, murdering whites and God knows what else, then you've got a lot to learn! I'll be damned to hell if I'm going to sit back and allow it!"

"You have no choice."

"You listen to me. He's killed four or five men this week that we know of. There's more at stake here than a few head of cattle. I'm putting an end to it."

Monrovia stood, towering over him. He backed away.

"Law can take care of himself," she said. "And so can I."

"We'll see to it that he is stopped." He turned to leave. The others stood and followed suit.

She called after them. "If you send gunmen out here to try and kill Law, they'll not leave here alive."

Monrovia sat down. She heard the front door slam. A moment later, it opened and she heard someone coming back through the house. She braced herself for another encounter with Wainwright.

But the man who burst into the library was Jake Greenwood.

He kicked the door shut behind him.

PART SIX
Branding on the Prairie

"That's the tallest drink of muddy water I ever saw." Topeka stoked the fire pit, then took a few steps toward the black stranger approaching on a feisty buckskin pony.

Overfield untied the calf he'd just branded. It stumbled to its feet and took off, bawling for its mother. As the stranger approached, Overfield muttered to Topeka, "That son of a bitch is black as a branding iron. What the hell does he think he's doing on Triple B range?"

"Why don't you ask him?"

Overfield did.

The black man ignored the question. The star pinned to his dark blue tunic flashed when it caught the sun.

Overfield scowled. He eyed the uniform, the Army saddle, the pair of Colt's in regulation U.S. holsters. Didn't this stupid black bastard know that the war was over?

The black man said, "Roundup start already?"

"That's none of your damned business, nigger. Now get off this land. We don't hire your kind."

"Already got a job." The black man tapped the star with his thumb.

"That don't got nothin' to do with us, so git!"

The black man motioned toward a blanket smoldering behind Overfield. Several places on the large piece of fabric were burned with the Triple B brand—three B's butted together at the ends so that their spines formed a triangle.

"Mighty pretty embroiderin' you fellas are doing there."

Topeka and Overfield glanced at each other, but said nothing. The black man continued.

"Hair branding is a handy way to mark these calves until Mrs. Brice goes back East, ain't it? Then, when the hair grows out, you can re-brand with a different mark and sell off the beeves as your own."

"You think you're damn smart, huh, nigger?"

"Smart enough to know that what you're doing boils down to rustlin', plain and simple."

Overfield straightened his stance. "How the hell do you know the Brice woman is in these parts?"

"Didn't your mammy learn you no math, cowboy?"

Overfield went for his sidearm.

He was fast.

The black man was faster.

"Seven," he said.

Topeka started to claw at his hip.

The black man aimed. "You wanna be number eight?"

Topeka lowered his hand. "Hell, no, mister. I'm just doin' what Mr. Greenwood told me."

"You're rustling for Greenwood?"

Topeka's neck itched, but he was afraid to reach up and scratch it. "Yessir," he said then. "Didn't start out to, but he's drawed me in enough that I didn't have no choice. It was either that or have him kill me. Ever since that widder woman showed up here a tellin' him what to do, Mr. Greenwood's a little quicker on the crazy trigger."

"Why didn't you just move on, find another ranch?"

"It ain't that easy for a cowboy my age." He looked closely at the black man. "You ought to know how that is," he added.

The black man stared at him for so long that it got the best of the cowboy's nerves.

"Go ahead and finish it, damn it!" he spat. "A yeller belly like me don't deserve to live." He bowed his head, slid off his hat, and held it over his heart.

The wood fire crackled in the silence.

The black man spoke. "Go tell Greenwood I'm waiting for him."

Topeka trembled uncontrollably as the man rode away.

PART SEVEN
The Library

"You hired a detective behind my back, didn't you?"

Monrovia wasn't ready for another confrontation. "Mr. Greenwood, I really don't have time for this right now."

"Make time."

She folded her hands on the mahogany desk. "It's been days since you said you would send someone out to check on the rustling. Do you finally have a report for me?"

"That shows how much you know about this ranch. Hell, the borders can't even be rode in a week!" He threw the button on the desk. "Here's your damned report. One of my men just came back dead."

She stared at it. "Where did you get this?"

"It's a signal, ain't it? You're paying so much for each button. If that's it, then you've made one hell of a mistake. You're paying for the murder of Triple B hands."

She felt a stab of regret. "You mean to say that you found this on one of our own ranch hands?"

"That's right. One of the best hands I had. Shaw's been murdered, and it's on your head, lady."

She thought. She'd trusted her late husband, taken to heart his warnings, his instruction. That meant that she must also trust the man Ben had told her to hire.

When she spoke, her voice was steady. "Apparently, your man wasn't as faithful as he should have been."

"So you *do* know who killed him!"

"It's my money, Mr. Greenwood. And it's my ranch." She picked up the button. "I hired someone before I left Cheyenne, and it's a good thing I did. Our own men are stealing right from under us, and you obviously didn't know it."

"Who is it? Who did you hire?"

Monrovia paused. She hadn't realized he would be this upset. She gripped the arms of her chair. "I hired Archie Law."

Greenwood's face turned red, the veins in his neck bulged. His lips curled back from his teeth. For the first time, she was actually frightened.

Topeka burst into the room, followed by Iris.

Monrovia jumped.

"I'm sorry, ma'am. He blowed right past me."

"We got big trouble, Boss." Topeka was out of breath and his voice was shaking. He didn't seem aware that Monrovia was in the room. "He killed Overfield quicker'n you can blink. Caught us hair-brandin' calves over by the river. I had to tell him you was behind it all."

"Shut up, you damned old fool!"

"He's waitin' for you, Boss. Told me to tell you he's out there waitin'."

"I said shut up!" Greenwood drew his sidearm and fired.

Topeka fell. His legs twitched violently. The rowels of

his spurs gouged white curls out of the hardwood floor. Slowly, he grew still.

Iris shrieked. Greenwood wheeled and struck her with the pistol. She crashed against a bookcase, then crumpled to the floor.

He turned the pistol on Monrovia.

She was standing now. She felt hollow and weak.

"Sit."

She sat.

The young cowboy they called Pink came through the door, gun in hand. "What's the shooting about?"

"Tie her up, Pink. Then go up by the Laramie. Find the black bastard what killed Shaw and Overfield. Tell him that if he doesn't get here by midnight, he'll have her blood on his hands, too." He steadied his aim.

Pink didn't move. "How am I gonna find him without he kills me first?"

"Tie your bandana to your rifle, fool. You *won't* find him. He'll find you."

PART EIGHT
Roundup

Her hands had gone numb from the ropes bound tightly around her wrists. They'd been waiting several hours, and she wondered whether Pink would be able to find Archie. What if he didn't? Would Jake Greenwood really kill her? He'd killed Topeka without hesitation.

When Iris regained consciousness, she took shelter inside her servitude. She brewed a fresh pot of coffee and brought a cup to Greenwood without ever looking at Monrovia.

Monrovia wished she had eaten. She'd been so caught up in comparing Greenwood's ledgers to those she'd brought from Ben's safes in St. Louis, that when Iris brought a luncheon tray to the library, she hadn't allowed herself the luxury. The tray was still on a small cart behind her. Her stomach rumbled.

Greenwood peered out the window. Pink had returned thirty minutes prior, and had assured those in the house that he'd delivered the message. Greenwood instructed all the ranch hands to watch for Law.

"What if he's just telling you that?" Monrovia asked. "What if he didn't find Archie?"

"He knows better'n to cross me like that. You see, there's one thing I have on this ranch that you don't. Loyalty. The cowboys are loyal to me, just like Iris, here." He pulled the housekeeper to him. "Ain't that right, Iris?"

"Iris, don't allow him to rule your life."

Greenwood glared at her. "Don't make me kill you before Law gets here."

"What makes you think you can outshoot him?"

Greenwood returned to the window. "I've never crossed paths with a nigger yet and let him live. Why should I now?"

"Because you've never met me."

Greenwood wheeled toward the new voice. Archie Law had two pistols pointed toward him.

"How the hell—?"

"You all right, Miz Brice?"

"Yes, Archie."

Law looked at Iris. "Step away from him, miss."

Iris started to move. Greenwood grabbed her.

Law said, "Ain't it a caution how a man who hates women will hide behind one's skirts at the first sign of trouble."

Greenwood slung Iris aside and went for his belly gun.

Law fired both his pistols. The first slug went into Greenwood's shoulder. The second dug a canal alongside his temple.

Greenwood clapped a hand to his skull. "You don't even know how to kill a man. Be done with it!" He swiveled his head right and left. "Iris? Iris! Help me! I can't see! You black bastard, you blinded me!"

"Jake, I'm here." Iris untied her apron and wound it around Greenwood's head.

Law holstered his weapons. "I expect color won't matter so much to you now, will it?"

The following year, blizzards struck with a force and vengeance never before seen upon the plains. Men and horses froze to death, cattle perished by the thousands.

The entrepreneurs known as cattle barons—those great men of power and vision and wealth—cursed the land that had once made them rich. They abandoned their property and returned east. Many said that challenging the West was a manifestation of insanity.

Wyoming Territory became a state in 1890, and the frontier was officially closed.

Castle Wainwright, having had the most cattle (though it was speculated that over half were stolen from his fellow cattlemen), suffered huge losses. He is said to have died in the arms of a Chinese whore in a brothel on the outskirts of Omaha.

Nerve damage caused by the bullet wound to Jake Greenwood's temple rendered him permanently blind. Iris cared for him on a small farm in her native Kentucky until his death.

It is not known what became of the stock detective named Law.

Monrovia Brice sold all her holdings in Missouri and

funneled money into the Triple B until she staunched the deathflow of the savage winters.

She actively ran the ranch until her death in 1933, and is buried under a tall pine on the upper banks of the Lonetree.

THE TAILOR OF YUMA

by Marthayn Pelegrimas

Under a pseudonym, Marthayn Pelegrimas has recently turned to mystery writing. Under her own name, however, she has consistently turned out odd, quirky, thought-provoking stories in a variety of genres, like "We Love You, Baby Sue" (horror) and "I'm a Dirty Girl" (noir), which has been optioned for a film. Here she turned her talents to the western field for the first time with, well, quirky results.

"Why did they have to go and bury you so goddamn deep?" Maude cursed at the corpse of Tanner Moody, still resting three feet underground. Dropping the shovel, she straightened up, rubbed her aching back and turned her anger to the lone buzzard circling lazily above. "Git outta here, you ugly son of a bitch! You can't have him till I get what I come for!"

There was no shade this hour of the day, in this desolate spot. Jake had never told her why Moody ended up being buried in the middle of nowhere. Come to think of it, she hadn't cared enough to ask.

Maude unfastened the buckle of her worn belt, took a

deep breath and wiped sweat from her forehead on the sleeve of her dirty shirt. Three canteens hung from the saddle, one for the horse and two for her. She walked over to a cactus where the animal was tied, and after refreshing the paint, collapsed near his feet. The sun was unforgiving and if she hadn't been so tired, she would have sent more curses flying upward.

Jake Fletcher was a simple man. He had always been that way and chances were very good he would remain that way forever. There weren't many things he wanted out of life. Certainly nothing fancy. He'd settle for a cool, dry place of his own somewhere in town, maybe even a small business. Maude and he might even get married. But before any of his plain dreams could come true, he had to get out of prison.

The guard banged on the bars. "Three days to go, Jake. My boy leaves for Prescott on Saturday, how those britches comin'?"

Jake Fletcher was a master tailor. His great-grandfather, it was rumored, had suited two heads of state and one king. Grandpa Benjamin, next down the line, worked his own shop. And while his stitches were the finest on the eastern coast, his extravagant spending left only debts to his son—Jakes's father.

Jake looked up at the guard. "They'll be ready tomorrow."

"Be sure to make them good and strong. They gotta see him through the trip as well as a good piece of time before he gets hisself situated."

"I know, Bill, you told me."

"Did I tell you he's going up there to work for the foreman? The boss of the whole outfit?"

"Yeah, you told me." Jake pushed his thick glasses back

up the bridge of his nose. "Railroad—Atlantic and Pacific, comin' together. You told me all of it."

The guard looked down at the small man, grunted his disgust and said, "You're just jealous, bein' as how you're a drunk, locked up in here with no plans for a future. Can't say as how I blame you for bein' so ornery."

Jake saw no need to respond.

"I'll expect them britches by tomorrow then?"

Jake nodded.

The guard turned on his heels and marched down the dingy corridor. Several prisoners reached through the bars to snatch at his sleeve. Jake smiled. "Thanks for all the thread. I don't know what I would have done without you." He bit off a loose end and threw the pants on the floor.

"Finally! Lord Almighty, there he is!" Maude ran to lead her horse closer to the deep hole. "Jake better be right, that's all I gotta say," she muttered to herself. Racing around to the side where a long stretch of rope was tied to the saddle horn, she unlooped it, tossing the free end down into the open grave. She intended to lower herself slowly on top of the coffin, but her excitement instead pushed her over the side in an anxious leap. The force of her ample weight caused the pine to immediately give way beneath her feet. The crack startled her horse, causing it to rear back slightly.

Dropping to her knees, she picked through the splinters and dirt, clawing her way through the coffin lid until she was face to face with Tanner Moody: one-time faro dealer, ex-miner, retired prison guard.

"Poor ole Tanner Moody." Maude dusted off the lapel of his blue serge jacket. The pin holding the prison guard badge to the fabric had started to corrode and she struggled to free it. After a few frustrating moments, she decided to just yank it from the suit. But each yank only brought Tanner Moody with it, making him look like he was trying to sit up. Maude finally pulled a small knife from her belt and cut the tarnished badge from Moody's death suit.

After shinnying up the rope, and out of the deep hole, Maude brushed the dirt from the front of her chaps. "Looks like Jake wasn't full of cow manure after all." She held the badge in her gloved hands and read the letters engraved on the front. "Guard Territorial Prison, Yuma. Official enough," she said, placing the metal object carefully in her saddlebag. Glancing back at the grave, she silently read the wooden marker and calculated that Tanner Moody had been forty-two when he'd died in the spring of 1888. Then she wondered, only for a few minutes, if she should spend the extra time covering the grave back up.

"Naw. You can have him now!" she shouted up to the buzzard who had been joined by two others. "I got what I came for." Then she mounted up and rode back to town.

He'd been working on the shirt for weeks. The jacket had been easy to come by. Especially once he'd thought the plan out from beginning to end. Yuma was always hot, but in the summer, when the rains came, what water didn't seep into the powdery earth steamed on the buildings in billowy clouds. Even the Colorado River being so near didn't offer any relief. All Jake had to do was wait for the right time of year.

When the warden wasn't around, it was common practice for his men to shuck their jackets, roll up their shirt sleeves and make rounds as quickly as possible. So when he saw the neglected jacket, thrown in a corner like a rattler's old skin, Jake snatched it up. Besides, Jake had to do it by himself. He couldn't afford to bribe Luther Mills, the pack rat in cell block fifteen. And it wasn't just the money to consider, he couldn't trust anyone with his plan . . . except Maude.

He had met Maude Winston five years earlier. At the time he had only been a petty thief. No more than a scavenger. He'd followed some of the great ones, though. The James Gang, the Youngers, and his favorite, Butch Cassidy. Those train jobs had left not only chaos in their wake but loose change as well as fistfuls of paper money. And Jake was there to pick up all the strays. He'd made a good living at it, often wondering why he didn't meet others like him, until one day he figured it out. He was unique—one of a kind.

It was at the site of one of his early jobs that Jake caught sight of the beautiful Maude. Time may have put a few pounds to her frame, and maybe the dry air did make her look a might older than her actual years, but Jake saw her the way she was back then.

He had been following the gang for days, studying their methods and when the time was right, hid himself in a thicket, waiting for the inevitable explosion. After the money had been removed from the train, he watched them ride off. Before the authorities arrived, Jake scrambled to snatch up his cut. And that was when he was startled by the beautiful stranger.

She was dressed in a violet skirt with ivory trim that matched her blouse. He remembered how her yellow hair glistened, looking like a halo, even though it had become unpinned and messed with bits of grass. She had her arms folded over her bosom and glared down at him.

"What you lookin' at?" he demanded.

"A bigger fool than me, if that's possible," she said.

"Were you on the train? I didn't see you get off," he asked, crawling toward a gold piece.

"I got left behind just like that coin you're holdin'."

That made him stop. Why on earth would anyone leave behind such a treasure? he wondered but did not voice his question out loud.

"All you men are worthless. Know that?" she shouted.

"Quiet. Either help or go away and let me do my job."

"Some job," she sniffed. "You ain't nothin' more than a leech. A dog lookin' around for some scraps . . . no, a pig, that's what you are. Rootin' around there in the dirt."

Jake stood up. Peeking between several tree branches, he watched the railroad inspector questioning a conductor and engineer. "When you leave, could you go without makin' too much of a commotion? I just need a few more minutes here."

Maude wasn't going anywhere. "Then what?"

Jake stood tall, gathering all the dignity he had left. "Then I track and wait for the next job."

"How long you been doin' this kind of thing?"

"Comin' on seven years now."

She looked amused. "And in all that time you ain't never been caught?"

"Never."

Her expression changed while she mulled over his success rate. "I admire a man who don't have no boss to answer to. And I do find myself low on funds right now, especially since one of them bastards," she pointed in the direction the train robbers had fled, "just left me high and dry."

"The ugly redheaded one? With the gray hat?" Jake thought he had looked mean as well as dishonest.

"How'd you know?" she asked, surprised.

"You have to be able to figure people in this line of work."

"Didn't even leave me my clothes. All's I got is what I'm wearin'."

Jake decided then and there, without one moment of hesitation, that it was time to take on a partner. "Come with me;

I stashed my gear at a hotel in the next town. You can have a bath and then we'll buy you a few things."

When Maude Winston agreed to go with Jake, he considered himself the luckiest man alive.

They'd never had a place of their own. Moved around too much. But ever since Jake had gotten thrown in prison for stealing the governor's wife's garnet hatpin, right out of her hair, Maude had planted herself on the second floor of Mrs. Prescott's boarding house. The best thing she could say about the place was that it was clean. She hadn't tried being nice to any of the boarders, didn't think she'd be there long enough to make friends . . . but she'd been very wrong about that.

The first time the circuit judge was due to hear cases, he'd gotten in some sort of accident with his horse, postponing everything for a month. The next time the judge was due, there had been an outbreak of spotted fever at the prison and everyone, including the guards, was quarantined for eight weeks.

After the last delay, when Judge Silverton was called to preside over a murder trial in Snowflake, she'd convinced Jake that his escape plan would work. And so he began piecing together a complete prison guard uniform.

Laying back on the soft bed, Maude turned Tanner Moody's badge over and over in her hand. The star in the middle was scratched up pretty bad. She wondered if it had happened during years of wear or the few short months he'd spent in the ground. What a stroke of luck it had been, him retiring and then dying so suddenly just a few days after the party the warden had given for him over at the hotel. She laughed remembering how she'd even dressed for the event and partaken of some of the cake and finger sandwiches. Jake would have loved it. But she couldn't risk telling him, not when they were alone, and especially not in a letter. There was too much at stake.

"Only a few days more, and then you and me'll ride outta here, maybe even take the stage. This means we're respectable," she rubbed some of the graveyard dirt off with her thumb, "for a while."

Sitting up, she took the heavy badge over to the bureau. Lifting the large pitcher painted with yellow roses, she poured a few handfuls of warm water into the matching yellow bowl. Carefully she placed the badge into the water and swished it around.

Inspecting it again, closer by the window, she still wasn't satisfied. "We can do better than that," she said to herself. "Have to make everything real pretty for Jake. Special like."

Drying her hands, she rummaged through the top drawer, feeling for her silk scarf. Then with methodical attention, Maude set about polishing the badge that would insure Jake Fletcher's freedom.

"Gary buttons." Jake told the guard who sat in front of him. "If you want that dress for your daughter to be extra special, I'll need eight gray buttons, like the ones on your shirt."

The guards had come to rely on Jake and his expertise with a needle. These were the times Jake knew he could make an honest living as a tailor . . . once he escaped from prison.

Maude hadn't taken to his plan at first. She wanted him to sit tight until the judge arrived. It wasn't as if he'd stolen anything really important—like a horse. It was only a fancy bauble. Neither of them figured such a tiny thing would amount to doing much time. But all their calculating never took into account getting involved with the governor.

And he wasn't as young as he used to be—who was?

After Billy Dunbar, his first cellmate, had shown the guards how Jake had fashioned Billy Jr. a shirt out of an old sheet, the line started forming. One guard, Big Fat Ben, kept needing his pants let out. Didn't have the money to buy a new pair after each holiday. His wife being such a good cook and all. Then the warden asked a special favor, wanted his wife to have monogrammed gloves to match a silk bag he'd bought her in San Francisco. And after each job, Jake was left with fabric scraps, odd pieces of thread, buttons and hooks. Needles and scissors were locked up each night, but that only slowed down his progress with the escape uniform; it certainly did nothing to stop him.

"Miss Winston? Are you all right?"

"Nosy old bitty," Maude hissed to herself. "I'm fine, Mrs. Prescott," Maude shouted through the door.

"When you didn't come down for supper I got worried. It's not like you to miss a meal."

After carefully putting the badge in her top bureau drawer, Maude tiptoed toward the sound of her landlady's voice and jerked the heavy oak door open.

Mrs. Prescott stood, bent over level with the keyhole. Surprised, she straightened up. "Miss Winston . . . you . . . ah . . . frightened me."

"Shame on me, Mrs. Prescott. How inconsiderate I am to expect some privacy."

"I will remind you, young lady, that this is my home and I have every right—"

Maude slammed the door in the old woman's face.

"Not for much longer, you don't." She threw her large frame across the bed.

Jake mentally took inventory as he lay on his cot. Pants. That had been the first article of clothing he had managed to get.

An old guard had asked him to repair a ripped seam along the right leg. Then the same guard suddenly dropped dead that night in the yard. "Bad heart" was the report. So Jake folded the pants neatly and tucked them inside his pillowcase.

Shoes. The guards' shoes and prisoners' shoes were pretty much the same. Black leather, government issued. He could get away with his own.

The jacket had practically been thrown at his feet during a near riot one afternoon last month. Bull from El Paso was coming back into his cell when his new cellmate, a confused man by the name of Truxton, grabbed him from behind. No one was sure what was going on inside the fella's head but while the cellblock cheered on the brawl, a guard struggled out of his jacket and slammed Bull against the wall. A second guard came racing down the corridor aiming his rifle at the two. The guards wrestled the men down to solitary while Jake managed to reach through the bars and snatch the jacket. He'd successfully kept it hidden for weeks. Even when the guard came back looking for it.

The shirt was last, and once he got his hand on the right buttons, all that he had to do was wait for Maude to smuggle the badge into him. He hadn't seen her in a week. God willing, she'd found the grave of Tanner Moody.

Wednesdays had become the only days she looked forward to. But this Wednesday was extra special. First Maude inspected her reflection in the mirror. Her hat had gotten flattened on their last move and she tried propping up one of the bent posies that adorned the straw brim. She wanted to look pretty for Jake. Next she inspected the badge. It had taken some work, but she'd managed to shine the golden star in the middle, making it look good as new. She admired her work one last time before slipping the badge down the front of her blouse. The cool metal felt good between her bosoms.

Wednesday. He'd made it. Everything was in place; now if Maude came through, Jake Fletcher would soon be a free man. Then they'd ride west and keep going until they saw the ocean. The sandy plains of Yuma now seemed as abrasive to him as those thorny fences ranchers used to divide and protect their land. He longed for blues and green. The Arizona he knew was brown, hot and dry. Further west maybe he could breathe, become his own man instead of living off the exploits of others.

He tried napping to make the time go faster but kept waking up. Ticking off his inventory again and again as each minute crawled by.

The guard inspected Maude's bag. She smiled, like she did each week when the horse's ass poked through her things with his fat, ugly fingers. She smiled broadly knowing it would be the last time she would have to endure his haughty demeanor.

"Escort Miss Winston to cell block three."

The second guard led her down a corridor she had become all too familiar with. She kept her eyes focused on the backs of his shoes as she tried containing her excitement.

When the third and then the final and fourth iron door had been unlocked and relocked, she found herself standing in front of Jake's cell door.

"Opening number eighty-one." Never turning his back to Maude or Jake, the guard waited for assistance. When there were two of them, one lifted the large iron key ring hooked on his belt and unlocked Jake's cell while the other held his rifle pointed at Maude.

"Sit here," the first guard commanded, pointing to Jake's cot.

Maude obliged.

After the door had been secured, leaving Maude and Jake locked inside together, they hugged.

"Have you got it?" he whispered into her ear, then kissed her cheek.

"It was right where you said it'd be."

"Good." He took her face in his hands and looked at her with such pride. "You done good, old girl."

"Why would you ever doubt me?"

They sat down and made idle talk, waiting for what would seem a normal amount of visiting time. But each knew they were only stalling.

"You'd better get goin'," Jake said after about thirty minutes.

Maude stood, ready to rush into the act they had planned.

Jake stood and then fell against her. "Guard," she shouted, "I got a sick man here! Hurry up, I need help!"

While the guard ran the short distance, Maude held Jake to her bosom, allowing him time to retrieve the badge.

Along the way, the first guard had summoned the second, and now both of them stood at the door. "What's the problem here?"

"I think he's gonna need a doctor."

The procedure that followed getting Maude into the cell was now reversed. While one guard unlocked the cell, the other held a gun on the couple inside.

"Put him down on the bed," the larger one ordered the smaller. "And you," he turned to Maude, "come on out of there."

Maude did as she was told and stood with the rifle aimed at her until the cell was locked.

"John, escort the lady outside while I report this to the Warden."

Maude put her hand through the bars, reaching out toward Jake. "Take care honey." As she walked away she complimented herself on that melodramatic touch.

The doc sent for Jake later that afternoon and no one even thought twice about it when the convict insisted on bringing along a pillowcase stuffed with clothing. Everyone knew the doc's twentieth wedding anniversary was next week and Jake was working on a special present for the missus.

After Doc Williams checked the sash that Jake had stitched with lace trim, he smiled. "Have a lie down, your color looks fine. Maybe it's just the weather, or something you ate. Relax, you earned it."

When the doc left the room, Jake stashed the guard's uniform he had made for himself behind a large apothecary chest in the corner.

By lights out, Jake was back in his cell. He knew as long as the guards could see him breathing and he answered their shouts every few hours, they'd leave him alone. He also knew the guards rotated shifts at twelve-thirty. He would have to make it back to the infirmary before then.

"I'm sick! I need to see the doc!" Jake shouted when the time was right.

"Help me, I'm sick too!" A prisoner mocked.

"Me too!"

"I can't see! God help me, I'm blind!" a voice screamed.

The cell block erupted with one disease after another.

"Shut up! Every last one of you!" the guard shouted as he ran into the middle of the narrow hall.

Jake pushed his face against the bars. "Here! Down here! I saw the doc before. He said I could come back if I was feelin' poorly. Go ask him."

"Take me!" the prisoners tried to outshout each other. "Me! No me!"

It was near the end of the guard's shift and he was tired. Besides, he remembered seeing Jake being taken to the doc's office earlier. "Okay, he said, unlocking the door, "come here. Move it!" Outweighing the little tailor by at least fifty pounds, the guard knew he had nothing to fear from the man. Pushing him toward the end of the hall, he kept one hand on the long club swinging at his side.

When they reached the office, there was no one inside.

"I'll have to stay here until someone comes to tend you." The guard looked angry.

"Time for you to go home, huh?" Jake asked, clutching his stomach and wincing.

"Yep."

A young doctor entered the room before any more small talk had to be made. "What's the problem here?" he asked the guard.

"Doc tended him earlier." He nodded toward Jake. "Should be some record of it somewhere. My shift's up; I'm heading home."

"Fine," the doctor said after scrutinizing Jake. "I'm sure we'll be fine."

The guard didn't waste one more second. As Jake watched the large man exit the room, he thought how glad he was that this was the new doctor, and how he wouldn't feel too bad hitting him on the head with the heavy medical book on the table.

The doctor went down easy. Never having hit anyone before, Jake was surprised how easy. Quickly he gathered the bundle of clothing from its hiding place and started tearing off his own. Pulling the tailored pants on, then the shirt and finally the jacket, Jake reached inside the front pocket and was relieved to find the guard's badge still there. Fastening it to his lapel, he stepped over the unconscious man and opened the office door, walking into the corridor full of dozens of uniformed guards. Half were coming on duty and the other half were going home. He blended in easily. Considering the high turnaround, unfamiliar faces were more common than the old-timers.

Keeping his head down, Jake made it to the front gate, even said good night to the armed guard. It was a cool evening, the moon was full and Jake was more giddy than if he'd downed three whiskeys. But he walked straight and purposefully.

Maude would be waiting just down the road for him, should have the horse hitched up. He was thinking about how they'd celebrate their first night back together when the moonlight struck Jake's badge and it lit up like a beacon.

"What's that on your chest?" the man beside him asked.

"My badge, that's all," Jake mumbled.

"Ain't never seen a badge like that," the man persisted.

"Regular, just like yours."

"No sir, mine don't have that shiny piece in the middle. Cal, come take a look at this."

Before Jake could move, he found himself surrounded by three curious guards.

"The only time I seen one like that was when Tanner Moody retired. The warden had it made up special. Gold-plated the star."

"Poor Tanner Moody," one of the guards said sadly, "died real soon after that."

Desperate to run, Jake turned but the men caught him

under his arms and lifted him up, dragging him back inside the prison.

Maude looked up at the moon. "Hurry, Jake, I'm waitin' for you, sweetheart."

THE CAST-IRON STAR

by Robert J. Randisi

Robert Randisi's most recent western novels are Leg-end (a collaborative western written with Loren Estleman, Elmer Kelton, Ed Gorman, Judy Alter, James Reasoner and Jane Candia Coleman) and The Ghost with Blue Eyes. *Here is a story about a young man's legacy and where it leads him.*

1

The kid looked like he hadn't shaved a day in his life, yet he wanted to be sheriff.

He said his name was Starkweather. He got off the noon stage, looked around, then turned to catch his bag when the driver dropped it down to him. Without saying thank you, he mounted the boardwalk and started for the hotel, which he'd spotted from the window of the stage on the way in.

"Help ya?" the desk clerk asked.

"I need a room."

"How many nights?"

"I don't know," Starkweather said. "Let's start with one."

"Okay."

Starkweather signed the register and accepted his key. He went upstairs, dropped off his bag, then came back down and presented himself at the desk again.

"Help ya with somethin' else?" the man asked.

"Which way to City Hall?"

"Out the door, turn left, three blocks. Brand-new building."

"Much obliged."

"Uh . . ."

"Yeah?"

"You mind if I ask why you want City Hall?" the clerk asked. "Most folks ask for a saloon, or restaurant, when they first get into White Rock."

"I'm applying for the sheriff's job."

The clerk started to laugh, but something in the kid's eyes stopped him. As soft as the kid's face looked, there was nothing soft about his eyes.

"Something funny?" Starkweather asked.

"Huh? Uh, no, it's just that—well, the mayor's been wantin' an older man . . . you know . . . with more experience."

"Has he had any luck getting one?"

"Uh, no, not up to now."

"Has anybody volunteered for the job?"

"Not that I know of."

"Maybe that'll make a difference," Starkweather said. "Thanks for the directions."

The clerk watched the young man leave the hotel. He wondered how all fired anxious he'd be for the job if he knew about the Jacob Gang.

"Mr. Mayor?"

Mayor Harold J. Galvin looked up at his secretary as she

stuck her head in the door. It wasn't a very pretty head, but then Mrs. Galvin had personally chosen her for the job.

"Yes, Mary?"

"There's a, uh, young man here to see you."

"About what?"

"About the, uh, sheriff's job."

"Well, show him in, Mary," Galvin said, "It's not like we've had a lot of luck finding somebody who even wanted to interview for the job."

"But sir . . ."

"What is it, Mary?"

She lowered her voice and said, "He's very young."

"Send him in, Mary," Galvin said. "If the boy wants the job he should at least be heard out."

"Yes, sir," she said, and thankfully withdrew her head. He'd asked her to address him that way because the only thing worse than looking at Mary Conklin's head was looking at her whole body, too.

Galvin stood, straightened his jacket, tugged his vest down over his significant paunch and waited for his candidate for the sheriff's job to enter his office.

When Starkweather entered the mayor's office, he saw a thick-set man in his fifties in a three-piece suit, with gray hair and mustaches, standing behind his desk.

Mayor Galvin saw a young man of medium height, not overly impressive-looking despite the gun on his hip, who looked all of twenty-two or -three.

"Mr. Mayor?" Starkweather asked.

"That's right, son."

"I understand you have a job opening for a sheriff?"

"Right again, but—"

"I'm here for the job."

Galvin stroked his facial hair a time or two and then said, "Have a seat, son."

"The name is Starkweather," the young man said, but he sat, as invited. The mayor lowered himself into his own chair.

"Do you have any experience, Starkweather?"

"Not as a lawman."

"As what, then?"

"I can track."

"Why do you think that's important for this job?"

"Because you want your sheriff to stop the Jacob Gang," Starkweather said, "and to do that, they have to be tracked."

"So, you know about the Jacob gang?"

"Yes."

Galvin sat back in his chair.

"What makes you think you can find them?"

"Like I said," Starkweather replied, "I can track."

"And when you find them? What makes you think you can handle them?"

"I guess I won't know if I can until I do find them."

"Son—"

"Starkweather."

"Starkweather," Galvin said, "this job calls for an older man, with experience—"

"How many have turned the job down, Mayor?"

"Well, there have been a few—"

"How many are lined up asking for it?"

"Well, none—"

"How much longer do you think the Jacob Gang can go unchecked?"

Galvin frowned.

"You're from back east, aren't you?" he asked.

"What's that got to do with anything?"

"So—Starkweather—"

"Mayor," Starkweather said, "I believe I have the one important qualification for this job."

"And what would that be?"

Starkweather stood up. "I want it."

2

Starkweather walked out of the mayor's office as Sheriff Starkweather, of Chula Vista County, New Mexico.

"What's your full name?" the mayor had asked.

"Just Starkweather."

Mayor Galvin had taken a bent piece of tin from the top drawer of his desk and offered it to Starkweather. It was barely recognizable as a star.

"I'll get my own made," Starkweather said. "That won't command any respect."

"It takes the man to command the respect, Starkweather," Galvin had said.

"Don't worry about that, Mayor."

But the Mayor was worried, and as Sheriff Starkweather left his office Galvin wondered if he had just gotten a young man killed.

Sheriff Starkweather's first official act was to find the town blacksmith and commission him for a job.

"You want me to do what?" Asa Calhoun asked.

"Make me a sheriff's star out of cast-iron."

"Ain't badges usually made of tin?"

"Too flimsy," Starkweather said. "I want something that will go the long haul."

Calhoun studied Starkweather for a few moments.

"Are you sure you got the job?"

"You can check with the mayor if you want," Stark-weather said. "The county will pay you for the work. Can you do it?"

"Well, sure, I can do it," Calhoun said.

"How soon?"

"Well, if I drop everything else," Calhoun said, "proba-bly tomorrow—"

"Good," Starkweather said, "because I want to get under way. The Jacob Gang isn't going to come and find me."

"Are you really going after the gang?"

"That's what I was hired to do."

"How old are you?"

"Old enough."

He left the blacksmith's shop. His next stop was the liv-ery, to buy a horse. After that he'd need a rifle. Everything would be paid for by the county. When he was completely outfitted he'd be on his way. He knew nobody was going to be concerned that the new sheriff was leaving town already, because the real reason he was being hired was to find and stop the Jacob boys, who had been terrorizing Chula Vista County for months.

But it wasn't going to go on much longer.

Mayor Galvin surveyed the assemblage of men in his office. Calhoun, the blacksmith; Worrell, the liveryman; Stanley, the gunsmith; Obermyer, who owned the general store.

"He wants a horse and saddle," the liveryman said.

"And a rifle," the gunsmith said.

"And enough supplies for a week," Obermyer said.

"And," Asa Calhoun added, "a cast-iron badge."

"Give him what he wants," Galvin told them.

"And who's paying?" Worrell asked.

"The county," Galvin said. "Didn't he tell you that?"

"He did," Calhoun said, "but we wanted to check with you."

"Well," Galvin said, "you checked. Just do it."

The merchants grumbled because they knew they wouldn't be getting full value for their merchandise, but turned and filed out. Calhoun remained behind a moment longer.

"Harold," he asked, "do you know what you're doin'? He's just a boy."

"He wants the job, Asa," Galvin said. "Do you?"

"I never claimed to be lawman material—"

"Well, he apparently does," Galvin said, "and all I'm doing is giving him a chance to prove it."

"Or get himself killed."

"Either way," Galvin said, "the job is his. Now you just worry about yours."

Asa Calhoun said, "Yes, Mayor," sarcastically, and left the office.

3

In the morning Sheriff Starkweather picked up his new badge first.

"Is it ready?" he asked Calhoun.

"It's ready," Calhoun said, and handed it over. The star was crude, not smooth, with five very sharp points. "The undertaker does lettering, so I had him do it."

Etched into the star in a curve on top was the word "SHERIFF," and on the bottom "CHULA VISTA COUNTY."

"Good job," Starkweather said.

"It'll hang heavy on your shirt, though."

"That's why I'm wearing a leather vest," Starkweather

said. The vest was black, and when he pinned the heavy star to it, the leather bore the weight well.

"Can I ask you a question?" Calhoun asked.

"Why not?"

"Why a cast-iron star?"

Starkweather hesitated, then said, "I said you could ask, but I didn't say I'd answer," then turned and left.

The dead man lay in the middle of the street for all to see. The man who had killed him was already on his horse, riding away. The boy broke from his mother's grip and ran to see. He had never seen a dead man before, and he was curious. He ignored his mother's cries to come back and ran on until he reached the fallen man. He looked for all the world as if he was asleep, and the boy was disappointed, but then he saw the blood seeping out from beneath the man's shirt. That was when he saw the hole that had been drilled right in the center of the star the man had been wearing on his chest . . .

Starkweather picked up his horse from the livery, one he had picked out himself from a corral in the back. To the consternation of the liveryman the young man knew his horseflesh and had picked out a dun-colored five-year-old who would offer both speed and stamina. The man knew he'd probably get ten cents on the dollar of the value of the animal.

Same went for the saddle.

Next Starkweather went to the gunsmith's shop for his rifle, a Winchester the man had worked on until it was almost like new.

"What about a handgun?" the man asked.

"I'll go with this old Colt," Starkweather said, indicating the gun on his hip.

"I got some new weapons you'd like. Got a spring-loaded—"

"I don't need anything fancy," Starkweather said, cutting the man off. "After all, I'm just going to kill a man."

After Starkweather left, the gunsmith wondered what he'd meant about killing "a man." Wasn't he going after the whole Jacob Gang?

Starkweather rode his horse over to the general store and picked up his supplies. To the relief of the owner the man had not brought a packhorse with him. Apparently, the new sheriff was only going to take what he could carry in a gunnysack tied to his saddle.

When Starkweather was fully outfitted to his satisfaction, he rode over to the City Hall and once again presented himself at the mayor's office.

"Are you ready to go?" Galvin asked.

"I'm ready," Starkweather said, "except for one thing."

"What's that?"

"My pay."

Galvin laughed.

"You haven't even been sheriff a day, yet."

"I'll be on the trail a long time," Starkweather said, "until I find the Jacob Gang. I'll need at least a month's wages in advance."

"A month?"

"If I run out I'll send you a wire for more."

"Now see here—"

"I can't very well stop and turn back when I run out of money," Starkweather said, "can I?"

Galvin fell silent.

"Do you want this gang caught, Mayor?"

"Of course I do," Galvin said, "and keep in mind this isn't the Old West anymore, Starkweather. We're on the verge of a new century. You're to bring Mack Jacob and his gang back alive."

"If I can, Mayor," Starkweather said, "I will. But one way or another, I'll bring them back."

Galvin saw that look in Starkweather's eyes that all of the merchants had already seen, cold, black eyes, as cold as the iron the badge on his vest was made of.

Galvin turned, opened a safe that was behind him, and then handed Starkweather a wad of money.

"A month's wages," he said.

"Much obliged, Mayor."

Starkweather turned and started for the door.

"Sheriff?"

"Yes?" Starkweather turned.

"Don't give me reason to think I wasted the town's money on you."

"Don't worry, Mayor," Starkweather said, "you'll get your money's worth—I guarantee it."

4

His mother told him more times than he could remember, "You think just like your old man," or, "You're just like your father," or, "It's like I'm seeing your father all over again."

Starkweather knew who the members of the Jacob Gang were. He'd read up on all of them and—if the reports were correct—he knew their strengths. He did not know their weaknesses, but he believed if you knew a man's strengths, then you were ready for anything. Of course, a man's strength could also be perceived as a weakness.

The gang had been terrorizing all of Chula Vista County, which meant they weren't going to go far.

By the third week out Starkweather had found his way to a town called Lassiter. There was a big poker game there, and the word had spread they were looking for players. Dean Parker, a member of the Jacob Gang, fancied himself a poker player, and where Parker went, so did another gang member, Paul Cline.

Starkweather rode his horse to the livery and dismounted.

"That's a mighty unusual star, Sheriff," the liveryman said. "A change from the usual tin stars I see."

"Tin bends," Starkweather said, "and breaks." *And gets holes shot through it.*

"You some young to be a lawman, ain'tcha?" the liveryman asked, himself in his late sixties. "How old are you?"

"Old enough."

He left the livery and walked to the town marshal's office. He introduced himself as the sheriff of Chula Vista County.

"What brings you to my town, Sheriff?" the marshal asked, with a look of amusement on his face.

"I have reason to believe there are two members of the Jacob Gang here, Marshal," Starkweather said.

"And if there are?"

"I'm taking them in."

"Alone?"

"Only if you won't help me."

"Son," the man said, "I didn't stay alive this long by going after members of the Jacob Gang. I'd advise you to turn around and ride out."

"And I'd advise you to stay out of my way if you're not going to help."

The marshal, a man in his forties with a paunch that was stretching the leather of his gunbelt, raised his hands and said, "Consider me out of the way . . . Sheriff."

"There's a big poker game in town."

"That's no secret."

"Is it going on now?"

"It is."

"Where?"

"Hansen's Saloon," the marshal said, "just down the block."

"Thanks."

Starkweather headed for the door.

"I'll be along after the shootin', son," the marshal said. "I'll see you get a proper burial."

"You're going to be disappointed, Marshal."

"Just like your father," his mother complained, "always playing with that gun. I don't care how good you get with it, it'll do you no good."

Starkweather entered Hansen's Saloon while the tournament was in full swing. Men were playing poker at five different tables, with the goal of getting down to one table, winner take all.

One player was not going to make it that far.

Starkweather walked to the bar and ordered a beer. From his position there he could see all five tables. He had descriptions of both men, so he recognized the man he wanted, Dean Parker. Before he could move, however, he had to locate the other man, Paul Cline. He waited until his beer was gone, and still Cline did not put in an appearance. Apparently, the man was occupied elsewhere.

"Who's Hansen?" he asked the bartender.

The man had jughandle ears, a large nose and a perpetually sad look on his face. With those features, who could blame him?

"I am, Sheriff. Is there a problem?"

"I'm going to take a man out of your game."

"Who?"

"His name's Parker."

"Only one Parker here," Hansen said, "and he's with the Jacob Gang. You don't want to mess with him, Sheriff."

Since the bartender knew who he had in his game, Starkweather asked, "Where's the other one?"

"Who?"

"Cline," the young sheriff said. "Parker doesn't go anywhere without Paul Cline."

The man stuck his finger into his ear and then into his nose.

"You done your homework, Sheriff," he said, finally. "Cline's upstairs with a whore."

"Don't make a move to help Parker," Starkweather warned.

"I won't, Sheriff," Hansen said. "I run a saloon, and a poker game. I ain't part of no gang."

"What about these others?"

"Nobody's gonna back Parker, Sheriff," Hansen said. "It's you and him. I gotta ask you, though . . ."

"What?"

"Where do you want your body sent?"

Starkweather pushed his empty beer mug over to the bartender and said, "Your beer's warm," then turned and walked toward Dean Parker's table.

5

When Starkweather walked over to the poker table, they were in mid-deal.

"Dean Parker?"

Parker looked up at Starkweather just for a second before looking back at his cards. They were playing draw and the young sheriff could see that Parker had been dealt a pat hand.

"Put it down," he said.

"What?" Parker asked, absently.

"I said, put down the cards."

Parker folded the cards in his hands and then looked up to take a good look at Starkweather.

"Who are you, boy?"

"I'm the sheriff of Chula Vista County, and I've come to take you in," Starkweather said.

Parker laughed. He was a good-looking man in his thirties, wearing a black suit and boiled white shirt, a "gambler's" suit.

"I'm in the middle of a game here, son," he said. "Go away."

"Put the cards down," Starkweather said. "That's one pat hand that's not going to be played."

"Wha—"

The other players all tossed in their cards and said, "I'm out."

"What the hell—" Parker said. He threw the cards down on the table and stood up. Starkweather backed away, but did not back off.

"You young pup!" Parker said. "You cost me that hand."

"I'm going to cost you a lot more if you don't come quietly," Starkweather said. "Drop your gun."

"You know, sonny," Parker sneered, "it takes a lot more than some crude iron badge to make a lawman. You think you can take me in. Well, have at it."

Parker pushed his coat back off his gun and dropped his hands to his sides. This would be Starkweather's first gunfight—or his last. The other men at the table quickly left their chairs and made room for the two men. Others in the saloon moved out of the line of fire.

"I'm Sheriff of Chula Vista County," he said, "and I'm taking you—"

He didn't get to finish because the gambler went for his gun. Starkweather drew and fired by reflex, all the hours of practice paying off in that split second. The bullet struck Parker in the center of his chest, before he could get his gun out. He coughed once, sank to his knees, crossed his hands over his chest and looked up at Starkweather.

"How old are you?" he asked, and then blood flowed from his mouth and he fell onto his face.

"Old enough."

Starkweather holstered his gun and tried not to look like someone who had just killed his first man.

"Did you all see it?" he asked.

"He drew first, Sheriff," one of the players said.

"You got no problem with that, Sheriff," another said.

"Tell that to the marshal when he comes in," Starkweather said, holstering his gun. He turned to the bartender. "What room is the other one in?"

"Top of the stairs," the bartender said, "but he's sure to have heard the shot, Sheriff. I'd try the alley."

"That's a good suggestion," Starkweather said. "Thanks."

He went out the batwing doors, turned right and entered the alley just as a half-dressed man with his holster slung over his shoulder dropped to the ground.

"Hold it!" Starkweather shouted.

The man froze, and his holster dropped from his shoulder to the ground.

"Turn around," the young sheriff ordered.

The man obeyed. He was wild-eyed, hair mussed, trousers only on one leg, and shirt open.

"Paul Cline?"

"W-what happened to Dean?" the man asked.

"He's dead," Starkweather said.

"You killed him?"

"That's right."

Paul Cline cast a longing look at the gunbelt on the ground.

"Don't think about it, Cline," Starkweather said. "Parker's hand was a lot closer to his gun than yours is, and he didn't make it."

"W-what do you want?"

"The Jacob Gang," Starkweather said, "or more specifically, Harry Jacob."

"Harry? He'd kill you."

"Maybe," Starkweather said, "but right now it's you and me, Cline. What do you want to do?"

Cline thought a moment, then said, "Whatever you say, Sheriff."

"That's a good answer," Starkweather said. "Here's what I want. I want you to go to Harry Jacob and tell him a man wearing a cast-iron badge killed Dean Parker, and let you go."

"You're lettin' me go?"

"I am, but only to deliver this message."

"Oh, I'll deliver it, all right, Sheriff," Cline said, "and when I do Harry will come for you."

"Exactly," Starkweather said.

"What?"

"Just listen carefully," Starkweather said, "and deliver this message word for word. Understand?"

"I understand."

And Starkweather told him what to say . . .

6

"And don't forget," the man told the boy, *"ain't no tin star ever gonna stop a bullet, you wait and see . . ."*

". . . so he says to give you this message word for word," Paul Cline reported to Harry Jacob hours later.

Jacob and the other two members of the gang sat around a table in the small shack they were using as a hideout and listened to Cline's tale.

"This snotty-nosed kid with a funny badge—" Cline was saying.

"Scared the shit out of you, didn't he, this snotty-nosed sheriff?" Able Dillon said, with a laugh.

Cline glared at him.

"Outdrew Dean Parker slick as snot, I hear," the fifth member of the gang, Carter Birch, said.

"Shut up, both of you," Jacob said. "Finish up, Paul. What'd the kid have to say?"

"That I should tell you that 'a sheriff with a cast-iron badge and an old Colt was gonna take you in and make you pay for your sins.' "

"Sins?" Jacob asked.

"What?"

"He said sins, not crimes?"

"Nope, he said sins."

Harry Jacob rubbed his jaw. Couldn't be, he thought. No way.

"You know this kid, Harry?" Birch asked.

"Maybe."

Jacob looked around at his remaining three men. Parker had been his best one. The rest of these were the best of a bad lot when he first put the gang together. At fifty-five most of Harry Jacob's contemporaries were dead or in prison. With a new century approaching he had formed his new gang out of men twenty years younger than him. Now a man maybe ten years younger than them was going to bust it up?

"What else did he have to say?"

"He said he'd be waiting for you in a place called Moonrise," Cline said, "and a saloon called—"

"The Bullet Hole."

"How'd you know that?"

"What the hell is Moonrise, Harry?" Dillon asked.

"A ghost town," Jacob said, "a long dead ghost town."

"And the Bullet Hole?" Birch asked.

"A place I used to drink," the outlaw leader said, "also long dead and gone."

"How could this kid know about these places?" Birch asked.

"Because I told him about them."

"You ain't goin', are you, Harry?" Birch asked.

"He's gotta go," Cline said.

"Why?" Dillon asked.

"Because this lawman ain't about to stop comin', that's why," Cline said.

"You mean this snotty-nosed lawman scared you?" Birch asked.

Cline hesitated, then said, "You didn't see his eyes."

"What're they like?" Dillon asked.

"They're black, and cold, almost like dead eyes," Cline said. He looked into Harry Jacob's face, then into the old man's black, dead eyes, and what he had been about to say died in his throat.

"You goin', Harry?" Able Dillon asked.

"I'm goin'."

"We'll go with you, then," Birch said.

"Naw," Jacob said, "this is somethin' I got to do alone, boy."

"But, Harry—"

"You don't think some snotty-nosed lawman with an iron badge and an old Colt can outdraw me, do ya?"

"Well, no, but—"

Jacob pushed his chair back and stood up.

"I'll be leavin' at first light," he said, and left the shack.

"Whataya suppose that's all about?" Dillon asked.

"Whataya, stupid?" Birch asked. "That lawman's his kid."

"Yer crazy!" Dillon said. "Harry ain't got a kid."

"You didn't see his eyes," Cline said. "It's his kid, awright."

"Well, kid or not," Dillon said, "he killed Parker, he killed one of us and I, for one, don't aim to let him get away with it."

"Whataya plan to do?" Birch asked.

"If Harry's leavin' at first light," Dillon said, "we're leavin' right after him."

"We are?" Cline asked.

Packer looked over at Birch, who said, "Yeah, we are."

7

The stories of your childhood stay with you, especially when they're all you have left to remember a father by. Stories of a town called Moonrise, a saloon called the Bullet Hole, and days when both had a lot to offer . . .

When Starkweather rode into the ghost town that was once Moonrise he felt a chill. After all these years was he finally going to meet his father face to face? The man who, when he abandoned a mother and a son, left little behind but tears, stories, one broken heart and one hardened one?

Starkweather clung to the stories, and to the old Colt. He depended on both to get him what he wanted—revenge on a father he hardly knew. He knew *of* him, though. Even years ago his mother had explained what a *desperado* his father was, and how no lawman could bring him in. That was when Starkweather decided what he wanted to be when he grew up. Not only a lawman, but the lawman who brought in Harry Jacob. He practiced with the old Colt his father had left behind until he thought his hand would fall off, and then practiced some more. And he knew what kind of badge he'd wear when the time came, the kind not so easily punctured by a bullet.

These were the only things left behind by his father as his legacy—except for his mother dying of a broken body, broken spirit and broken heart. It was over her grave that he swore to bring his father to justice—or die trying.

Starkweather left his horse in the abandoned livery. He removed his saddle, and managed to find a handful of hay to feed the animal. He left him in a stall, and left the barn door open, because there was a possibility he would not return. In that event the horse should have the option of walking off and taking care of itself.

He carried his rifle and canteen with him to the Bullet Hole, the saloon his father used to tell him about when he was a small boy in St. Louis. St. Louis was, apparently, as far east as Harry Jacob had ever gotten. Starkweather had not seen the man since he was four years old, the day Jacob drilled the sheriff right through his tin badge and then rode off, never to be seen or heard from again.

The Bullet Hole had been a lively place, if his recollection of his father's stories was accurate. Now the batwing doors hung from a hinge each and dust covered everything. He had to right a table and two chairs so he'd have someplace to sit, and then it took a while to find some that had all four legs. Eventually, though, he was able to seat himself at a table in a place where his back was to the wall and he could see the whole room. He set his rifle and canteen on the table, tried to still the pounding of his heart, and settled down to wait . . .

First he heard the footsteps on the boardwalk, and then the creaking of the boards as the footsteps came closer. Finally, the figure appeared in the doorway and he was surprised. His childhood memories were of a big man, with big hands and a booming voice. This man was hardly bigger than he himself was, and he was old. His face was craggy, weathered, and his hair as it stuck out from his hat was gray. Starkweather could only see the resemblance between them in their size, but the old man had lost weight and was now slighter than the son.

"Hello, boy," Jacob said, and at least that was the same, that booming voice.

"Come on in."

Jacob chuckled.

"Will I get as far as the table before you throw down on me?"

"Come and sit," Starkweather said. "We can talk before there's any gunplay."

The old man walked across the floor and sat opposite the boy he had not seen in over twenty years.

"You favor me."

"You're not going to make any points like that."

Jacob chuckled again.

"I hear you took Dean Parker pretty easy," the old man

said. "Kinda makes me proud, even though Dean was my best man."

"He wasn't good enough."

"You growed up tough."

"I had to."

"How's your Ma?"

"Died when I was seven," Starkweather said.

"She get sick?"

"She got worn out. Hard work with no man around makes that happen."

"How'd you grow up so tough, then, with no Ma and Pa?"

"You just answered your own question."

Jacob looked at the badge on Starkweather's chest, "I see you learned somethin' from me," he said. "That ain't no tin star on your chest."

Starkweather didn't reply.

"What name you go by?"

"Starkweather."

"That all? No first name?"

"Sheriff."

Jacob chuckled again. It was a sound Starkweather did not remember, and did not like.

"Been a lawman long?"

"A few days."

Jacob raised his bushy gray eyebrows.

"Did you take the job just to come after me?"

"That's right."

"Lots of lawmen have come after me over the years."

"I know."

"And you still came?"

"I swore I would."

Jacob spread his hands and said, "And here you are. What now?"

"Now," Starkweather said, "you're under arrest."

Jacob sat back in his chair and stared at the young man with the cast-iron badge.

"You thinkin' I won't kill you because you're my kid?"

"I'm not your kid."

"You're my blood—"

"I'll kill you if I have to," Starkweather said, cutting the man off. "I expect you'll do the same."

"You got that right, boy."

There was a tense moment between them when either one of them could have gone for his gun, but they were interrupted.

"Just sit real still, Sheriff," a voice said. "You got three guns on you."

Starkweather moved nothing but his eyes. Two men appeared from a back way, and one through the front door, all holding guns. He tried to figure his chances of drawing and killing the old man before they killed him.

"I'd be thinkin' the same thing in your position, boy," Harry Jacob said, "but put it out of your head. It ain't gonna happen."

8

"I thought I told you boys to stay behind."

"We didn't think you meant it," Birch said.

"Well, I did."

"Packer said we should come," Cline said in a weaselly tone.

"Your idea, Packer?" Jacob asked.

"We can talk about this later, Harry," Dillon said. "Sheriff, drop your gun and your rifle to the floor."

Jacob looked across the table at Starkweather, who was reading something in the old man's eyes.

"You plannin' on shootin' my kid in cold blood, Dillon?"

"See?" Birch said to the other two. "I tol' you it was his kid."

"It don't matter," Dillon said. "He's a lawman, ain't he?"

"Answer my question, Dillon," Jacob said.

"Harry—"

"You gonna shoot my boy in cold blood? Huh?"

Starkweather knew something was coming but when it came it surprised him.

"I told you hombres to stay behind," Jacob said. "Ya shoulda listened."

When the old man drew, Starkweather did as well. He was fast enough to figure that, but he was almost too fast. He was about to fire at Jacob when he realized the old man was not pointing his gun at him, but was turning to fire at his own men.

Like Starkweather, all three men were surprised, but they did not react as quickly. Jacob squeezed off a shot that put Dillon right down. He was turning his gun on Birch when Starkweather shot a shocked Paul Cline. Birch squeezed off a shot, but it was a death throe, fired into the floor as Jacob's two shots took his life.

Before the sound faded, both men were facing each other with their guns dribbling smoke.

"What the hell—" Starkweather said.

"You don't think I could have the likes of them killin' my own flesh and blood, do ya?" The look in the old man's eyes was one of absolute glee, tinged with more than a little madness.

"And now what?" Starkweather asked.

"That's up to you, boy," Jacob said. "Still gonna take me in?"

"I am."

"Well, I ain't goin'," Jacob said, "so you're gonna have to put me down to stop me."

"I will."

Jacob holstered his gun.

"Have at it, then," the old man said. "Put your gun back in the leather, or shoot me in cold blood."

Starkweather looked over at the three dead men. The whole Jacob Gang was gone, and the old man had undoubtedly saved his life, but he owed this to himself and to the memory of his mother.

He holstered the weapon, and seconds later both men drew and fired . . .

Mayor Galvin watched from his window as Sheriff Starkweather rode in on a buckboard with bodies stacked like cordwood in the back. Son of a gun, the kid had done it.

He was seated behind his desk when Starkweather entered.

"You got 'em?" Galvin asked.

"I got them."

"All of 'em?"

"Yes."

"The old man, himself? Harry Jacob?"

"They're all dead," Starkweather said. "They're all in back of the buckboard."

"Well, get 'em over to the undertaker's, and I'll have a photographer—" He stopped abruptly as the cast-iron badge struck his desk, bounced once and then lay still.

"That's a job for your sheriff," Starkweather said.

"You're the sheriff."

"Not anymore."

"But—"

Starkweather turned and walked out. Galvin picked up

the cast-iron badge and looked at it. Right in the center was a small dent, but other than that it was perfectly usable for the next man—and whoever that was, the job would be a lot easier, now.

Starkweather mounted his horse and rode out of town, leaving the buckboard full of men behind for others to deal with. He was heading back to St. Louis to go to his mother's grave and tell her she could now rest easier.

The left side of his chest was still sore as hell from where the bullet had hit him. He wasn't sorry he'd killed the old man. Heck, that was what he'd set out to do, and he'd decided long ago that nothing the old man said or did would deter him, or make him feel guilty after it was all over. Besides which, that old man had drawn and fired first.

The only thing he didn't know for sure was if the old man had shot for the star out of reflex, or if he'd done it on purpose, knowing that the bullet would not drill through it, as it would have done a tin star.

CREDITS